I0721372

ONLY ONE LOVE
(ONLY ONE SERIES BOOK 7)

Wilson

I was the bad boy on and off the ice.
I loved it — owned it.
Hockey. Women. Money.
Until she came into the picture.
Now, all I want to do is be better.
I want to prove to myself I don't have to be the guy everyone thinks I am.
She knocked down the walls I spent my whole life building.

Franny

My last name opened the doors, but proving I was worth the title of TV producer took all of my time.
He walked in with a chip on his shoulder.
I was happy to point out all his flaws.
Falling for him was inevitable.
When scandal hits, no one expected me to stand by his side.
Not even him.
But I've learned that you get only one love.

BOOKS BY NATASHA MADISON

The Only One Series

Only One Kiss

Only One Chance

Only One Night

Only One Touch

Only One Regret

Only One Mistake

Only One Love

Only One Forever

Southern Series

Southern Chance

Southern Comfort

Southern Storm

Southern Sunrise

Southern Heart

Southern Heat

Southern Secrets

Southern Sunshine

This Is

This is Crazy

This Is Wild

This Is Love

This Is Forever

Hollywood Royalty

Hollywood Playboy

Hollywood Princess

Hollywood Prince

Something So Series

Something Series

Something So Right

Something So Perfect

Something So Irresistible

Something So Unscripted

Something So BOX SET

Tempt Series

Tempt The Boss

Tempt The Playboy

Tempt The Ex

Tempt The Hookup

Heaven & Hell Series

Hell And Back

Pieces Of Heaven

Love Series

Perfect Love Story

Unexpected Love Story

Broken Love Story

Faux Pas

Mixed Up Love

Until Brandon

SOMETHING SO, THIS IS, AND ONLY ONE FAMILY TREE!

SOMETHING SO SERIES

Something So Right
Parker & Cooper Stone
Matthew Grant (Something So
Perfect)
Allison Grant (Something So
Irresistible)
Zara Stone (This Is Crazy)
Zoe Stone (This Is Wild)
Justin Stone (This Is Forever)
Something So Perfect
Matthew Grant & Karrie Cooley
Cooper Grant (Only One Regret)
Frances Grant (Only One Love)
Vivienne Grant
Chase Grant
Something So Irresistible
Allison Grant & Max Horton
Michael Horton (Only One Mistake)
Alexandria Horton
Something So Unscripted
Denise Horton & Zack Morrow
Jack Morrow
Joshua Morrow
Elizabeth Morrow

THIS IS SERIES

This Is Crazy
Zara Stone & Evan Richards
Zoey Richards
This Is Wild
Zoe Stone & Viktor Petrov
Matthew Petrov
Zara Petrov
This Is Love
Vivienne Paradis & Mark Dimitris
Karrie Dimitris
Stefano Dimitris
Angelica Dimitris

This Is Forever
Caroline Woods & Justin Stone
Dylan Stone (Formally Woods)
Christopher Stone
Gabriella Stone
Abigail Stone

ONLY ONE SERIES

Only One Kiss
Candace Richards & Ralph Weber
Ariella Weber
Brookes Weber
Only One Chance
Layla Paterson & Miller Adams
Clarke Adams
Onlye One Night
Evelyn & Manning Stevenson
Jaxon Stevenson
Victoria Stevenson
Only One Touch
Becca & Nico Harrison
Phoenix Harrison
Dallas Harrison
Only One Regret
Erika Markinson & Cooper Grant
Emma Grant
Mia Grant
Parker Grant
Matthew Grant
Only One Mistake
Jillian & Michael Horton
Jamieson Horton

Cover Design: Jay Aheer

Photo by Wander Photography

Editing done by Jenny Sims Editing4Indies

Proofing Julie Deaton by Deaton Author Services

Proofing by Judy's proofreading

Interior Design by Christina Smith

ONLY ONE

Love

THE ONLY ONE SERIES

ONE

FRANCES

THE PHONE RINGS as soon as I sit down in the car. "Hello." With a huff, I answer it after just one ring as I put my bag on the passenger seat.

"How are you already done with your workout?" my sister mumbles, and I can hear the rustling of covers coming from her end of the line.

"I couldn't sleep," I answer, "so I figured I'd start the day early."

"It's the ass crack of dawn." Her voice sounds far away, so I know she's under the covers.

I laugh, pulling out of my driveway. "You know what they say." I have to roll my lips, knowing how much she hates this saying. "The early bird catches the worm."

"No one says that," she groans. "Let me take that back. No one under sixty says that."

I shake my head, laughing. "I'm an old soul."

"I've seen your soul. There is not much there, and

what is there isn't old."

"Aw, that's the nicest thing you've ever said to me," I joke.

"But seriously," she says, and I can hear her moving. "It's six o'clock."

"I have that big meeting today," I remind her. "And I want to make sure I'm ready."

"You were born ready." She tries to give me a pep talk.

"You weren't there yesterday," I tell her. "Do you know how many times one of the men said 'yes, dear'?" It's my turn to groan. "Like, I'm not your fucking dear."

"Did you answer them like that?" She laughs while she asks, and I can hear a cupboard door slam. "Because if you didn't, maybe you should."

"No, God no." I pull into the line at Starbucks and order my drink. "Can you imagine what they would have said?"

"Yeah, they would have said don't fuck with that one. She comes from New York." We both laugh.

"It's been two days." It's still surreal that I have this job. When they came to me a month ago, I thought it was a joke. I was creating content for an online sports show, and even that was a fluke. I started creating the content for my high school and really enjoyed it, so I decided to pursue journalism. After I completed the internship at my grandfather's media company, I knew the only reason I got a job was because of who I was. "They just have to get to know me. I figure we can have this meeting today, and they can see what I'm going to do."

"Or they expect you to bow down to them." I cringe at the thought. When Andrew Keeland came calling, I knew I had to take that leap. He loved what I did, and then he offered me my whole show, producing my own show. It was a dream come true, and I got it because of my skill and not who I was. So, I took the job without telling anyone or asking anyone's advice. Jumped in with both feet without testing the water or even looking at it. Little did I know what I was walking into. You see, apparently, it's a man's world.

"Well, I'm not doing that," I say as I pull up to the office building. "They are going to have to pull me out kicking and screaming if they expect me to just cave."

"That's my girl." I can hear her clapping her hands. I put the car in park and look out to see the sun starting to come up. "Now go get your fishing rod and get that fish."

I laugh. "No one ever says that." I grab my bag and my phone, changing it from Bluetooth to speaker, then turn back to grab my coffee. "Now, wish me luck."

"I'll get a shovel, just in case," she jokes, and I laugh, putting the phone in my purse as I walk into the office building. I'm the only one here, and my nude pumps click on the tile floor as I make my way toward my office.

I take a deep breath when the elevator doors open, and the sun streams in from the windows. The big brown desk right in front of the doors sits empty since Tanya doesn't start until eight o'clock.

Turning to walk toward my office, which I moved into two days ago, I have all these flutters in my stomach. Looking around, I see I'm the first one in. I smile at myself, knowing that people will notice, and it means I have one check mark in my column. A column I'm the only one participating in.

Walking into my office, I toss my bag in one of the empty chairs that face the desk. Reaching over, I put my coffee cup on the desk while I slip off my black blazer. I must have changed my outfit five times this morning before finally settling for cream pants with a sheer white silk, short-sleeved shirt.

Sitting in my chair, I log in to the computer and take a minute to look at the empty walls. I make a mental note to come in on Saturday and start making this office my own. I work my way through emails, and as always, I watch the highlights of the games from the night before. It's just preseason games right now, but it's good to see the boys back at it.

"Good morning." My assistant, Ava, sticks her head into my office with a smile. "You are here bright and early." She hands me a cup of coffee she picked up for me.

"That is so kind," I say, smiling at her.

"My pleasure. Should I get my notes, and we can talk about the meeting today?" I found this out yesterday on my first day here, when Ava told me that my new board meeting would be today. I would be the only lady there, so they wanted to know if I had any needs. *Assholes.*

"That would be great." With a nod, she walks out of the office, grabbing her notepad and coming back in. "Let's throw some ideas around," I tell her, but in my head, I already know what I want to pitch. It was something that came to me last night while I was taking a shower.

When I tell her my idea, her eyes light up. "That sounds really good." She smiles, and when she walks out of my office, I get up, the nerves in my stomach starting.

"Ms. Grant." I hear Ava call my name and look over at her. "It's time."

Getting up, I grab my iPad and we head over to the conference room. I walk with my head high and my blond hair pinned in a ponytail, straight into a room with a table full of men who all look in their forties and fifties. "Gentlemen." Pulling out the only available chair, I sit down with my papers in front of me. Water bottles are lined up in the middle of the table.

"You got here bright and early," Jeffrey says, looking at me with a smirk. From what Ava told me, he's the oldest one here. He has his head stuck in nineteen ninety and thinks we should just recycle shows. "Nervous?"

I smile at him instead of doing what I want to do, which is glare. "Not even a bit." I grab my pen with my hand instead of flipping him the bird, which is something else I want to do. "Shall we get started?" I look around the table at the six men, all of them dressed in button-down dress shirts. "Why don't we go around the table, and we can hear everyone's idea?"

One of the guys chuckles, and I know they are testing me. It's like a pissing contest. "Unless you guys don't have any ideas, and then I can just jump in." The guys all look at me with condescending looks.

"I have an idea," Spencer says, and I look over at him.

He's the youngest of the whole bunch, and from what Ava said, he got here about a year before me. "What about the series of has-beens?" He looks around the table. "Big back in the day and nowhere to be found."

"She has a whole family of that," one of them mumbles, and my blood starts to boil. It's one thing for me to insult my family, but it's another for someone else to do it.

"I like it," I tell him honestly. "We could also do players that were drafted first but didn't live up to the hype," I say, leaning back. "Of course that would be like no one in my whole family since they were pretty much drafted first and then hit the top of the leaderboard with points." I look around the table, and some of the men avoid my eyes. "But what do I know? So we will put that one on the board." I then look around. "Anyone else have anything that they want to bring forward?"

"What do you have in mind?" Earl asks, his stuffy white mustache hiding his whole top lip. "Since they brought you in to brighten up the network."

I ignore the last part of his sentence. "I was thinking we could do a weekly show on bad boys of hockey," I start the pitch "Past, present, and future. Everyone always looks at the bad boys when they are on the ice, but no one knows how they got the title." I smile. "I mean we, the press, give them the title of bad boys, but who are they really?"

"I like that." Spencer tilts his head to the side. "I like that idea better than my own." He smiles at me, and I nod.

"We could perhaps make a list of people and reach out to them." I flip over my notes. "I do have a couple in my family I can ask." I look over at Earl. "Figure they can brighten up the screen."

"It's not a horrible idea," one of the men says.

"Good," I say, pushing back from the table. "Since no one else has any ideas, besides Spencer." I look over at Spencer and smile at him. "I'm going to call it and confirm this will be our weekly segment." I look around the table, waiting for someone to come back with a snide comment. "I'll set up an email and send it to all of you with the details on how I want it, as well as any names I come up with." I gather my things off the table. "Gentlemen, this was a great first meeting." Turning, I walk toward the door, stopping when I pull it open. "And for future meetings …" My voice comes out tense. "Why don't we stop wasting everyone's time and actually come prepared?" I don't give them a chance to say anything to me because I walk out. My whole neck burns, but I force myself not to show just how mad I am.

"Oh, *oh*," Ava says when she sees me walking back. "That didn't take long."

"Oh, *oh* is right. If they thought they could come in and be all broody, they obviously didn't do their homework." I shake my head, laughing, not adding in that my whole family is filled with broody men, starting with my father. "In other news"—I fold my arms over my chest—"we got the bad-boy segment."

TWO

WILSON

I WALK DOWN the red carpet toward Martin's office, mixing my protein shake. I just got off the ice from practice, and fuck, it felt good to be back with the guys. I took two weeks off after the end of the season, and then I started training again. I am getting older, and my body was telling me that I wasn't a spring chicken anymore, so I wanted to be as prepared as I could this year.

"You're looking fit," Michael says when I walk past him in the hallway. He was traded here last year after he had a fight with his coach. It was plastered all over the media, but he never said a word about it to anyone.

"You're looking like you are getting the dad bod," I joke, and he laughs, shaking his head.

"Dad bod, my ass." He lifts his shirt to show me his abs.

"Gross." I shake my head and walk away from him.

Smiling at a couple of the guys, I knock on the closed

door before Martin yells to come in.

Opening the door, I step in, stopping when I see Nico, the owner of the team, seated with him. "Oh, shit," I say, and they laugh when I walk into the office and close the door. "It's like I'm in trouble or something. Going to the principal's office."

"Nah." Martin shakes his head. He's been the coach for the past three years, and I have nothing bad to say about him. He pushes me and never ever throws my shit in my face after the fact. He has plenty to say after I fuck up, and usually, it's never good. At times, I'm a horse's ass and a jack-off, but after he rants, it's done. Unlike the last coach who used to throw shit in my face all year long.

"We just wanted to have a little chat," Nico says, and I sit down in the empty chair in front of them. "Maybe go over the season a bit." He looks over at Martin. "What you expect from us and what we expect from you." Nico puts his hands together on the table, folding them. He took over the team not too long ago. His father gave it to him, but truth be told, it was a horrible, horrible team. I've been a Dallas player my whole career. I was drafted to them sixteenth overall in the first round, and three years ago, I signed a contract extension for six years worth thirty-one million dollars.

I get ready for our talk. "Okay, let's do it," I agree, taking a gulp of my protein shake.

"I'm going to start by saying you are a key player on our team," Nico says. "The guys love having you as one of them." I tilt my head to the side. "A little less when you fuck up, but nonetheless, you've shown them you have their back time and time again."

"That's a good way of putting it." I laugh at both of them. Before Nico took over for the team and actually wanted us to succeed, we were at the bottom of the standing every fucking year. It was brutal. It started one game with frustration. We were losing our tenth straight game, and I just fucking swung at the first person I saw. It didn't help that it was after the whistle, but it put some juice in the boys. We are a team. Did it always help? Fuck, no. At least for that game. We still ended the season at the bottom of the list. But when I would see my teammates just defeated, I would drop the gloves.

So, as long as it was helping them, I became known as the asshole on the ice. "I'm sure they thought otherwise when I got a two-game suspension last year." Five years ago, I got my first ever game suspension. It was in the preseason for a late hit on the play. I felt horrible after it happened, but that's when the media really started putting me in the bad-boy category. It didn't matter that I had four points in the game. It mattered that I fucked up and made an illegal hit. No one knows I reached out to the guy and apologized or that we are very close friends. They just see what was on paper.

"Well, we are hoping that history doesn't repeat itself," Martin says. "The team needs you on the ice, not sitting on your ass watching."

"I agree," Nico confirms. "Watching you sit out fourteen games five years ago was not fun."

"That was bullshit, and you know it," I point out.

"The media is the one who pushed for that one. The league had to come out and call me a repeat offender." I pfft and shake my head. "It was such bullshit that after the third appeal, they put me back on the ice." Just the thought makes my stomach burn again. Was I innocent? No. But that hit didn't merit a twenty-game suspension. Thankfully it got overturned after fourteen games and I was allowed back.

"We can go on and on about this." Nico holds up his hand. "But let's cut to the chase." I look at him, waiting for the other shoe to drop. "This is a new year, and we want your word you will be on your best behavior." I chuckle. "I'm not kidding, Brad." Nico uses my first name. "I want to show all those people out there that you are more than just a bad boy on the ice. I want them to eat their words."

I nod now. "Fine," I huff. "I can give you my word that I will do my best." I shrug. "I can't do more than that." Nico leans back in the chair and just looks at me. "Fine, I'll really try this time."

"Good," Martin says. "We need the support on the ice." I nod. "Lots of young kids this year. We need someone to help mentor them."

I laugh. "Trust me, the last thing they need is to learn from me." I look down and wonder how much longer the team will keep me if I fuck up again. "Listen, in my defense, I never wanted to be that boy on the ice."

"It's that pretty-boy face of yours," Nico jokes. "Those blue eyes and scruff drive the women wild." I groan and roll my eyes. "It looks like we are on the same page." He claps his hands together. "And let's show the press why we extended your contract, yeah?" Nico stands. "Now get the fuck out of here and get ready for the game next week."

"Will do, boss." I salute him and walk out of the meeting, my shoulders heavy from that talk. Walking into the dressing room, I see some of the rookies hanging around talking. "Later," I say to them, grabbing my keys and heading out.

Sitting in my Land Rover, I make my way over to my house. My mind replays the conversation. By the time I get home, I have so much pent-up energy I walk straight to my home gym. I bought this house as soon as I turned twenty-one. It was a crazy purchase, and I knew it was too big for me, but I just wanted something that was mine.

Climbing on the bike, I turn on the television to the sports network. They are doing a replay of baseball. I watch the replays while I go as fast as my legs can, peeling the T-shirt off me and tossing it in the laundry basket in the corner. I put my hands forward as I start to run out of steam when the phone rings. Picking it up, I see it's my mother, and I groan. "Hello," I answer it while I stop pedaling. I get up to grab a bottle of water from the fridge in the corner.

"Hello, son," she says, and I can tell she wants something.

"What's up, Mom?" I take another pull of water, my stomach almost throwing it up when I hear her next sentence.

"Why does something have to be up?" she shrieks. "Can't a mother just call her son?" I close my eyes, knowing this phone call has nothing to do with her caring how I am doing. My mother had me when she was twenty-two. I was the result of her sleeping with her boss at the law firm where she was working. An affair with a married man who did not want his name or family tarnished. So what did he do? He paid my mother off. Every month, he would send her a check to cover her rent and everything that had to do with me. It was the only reason I went to a private school and she could afford to put me in the top hockey league. I was good at the game, but those lessons put me where I am today because of all the money he kept sending to her. Of course, that stopped when I turned eighteen—not because of my age but because he had a heart attack at work.

"I've been fixing up around the condo," she explains. I bought her a condo when I signed my first contract. You would think after eighteen years, she would have put money aside, but that would be too obvious. "And the air conditioner unit gave out." And there it is.

"How much?" I ask, knowing I'll fix it for her.

"They said I should put in a new unit, but you know I don't have the money for that."

"Of course you don't," I mumble.

"Don't you pull that shit on me, Bradley." I roll my eyes now. "You were the one left with a trust fund, not the one who raised you," she hisses. "That sorry son-of-a-bitch excuse of a man could have at least taken care of me since I gave him his only son." And there it is—the bitterness that lives inside her.

"Send me the number, and I'll call the guy," I say, rushing to get off the phone with her.

"Thank you. How are you doing?"

I shake my head, walking out of the room toward my bedroom. "I'm fine, Mom."

"Are you in any more trouble?" she asks as I turn on the shower.

"Not yet. But the season just started."

"Well, try to stay out of trouble," she scolds. "With all the extra money you might have from not paying back to the league, you can send your mother a check."

"Sorry, Mom, someone is at the door." I use any excuse to get off the phone with her. "Send me the information, and I'll get it settled right away."

"Thank you. And if you need anything, let me know." I almost laugh out loud at that last line.

I hang up the phone, shaking my head. "Best behavior," I remind myself. I look at myself in the mirror. "You can do it." If only I believed those words myself.

THREE

FRANCES

AVA STICKS HER head into my office. "If you don't need anything else?" She smiles. "I'm going to head out."

Looking up at the clock in the corner of the computer, I see it's just after six. "I'm so sorry for keeping you later than five. How about if you work later than five, you can take off the hours on a Friday?" I smile at her as her eyes light up.

"I think working for you is going to be really good." She grins. "Also nice email."

I roll my lips, thinking back to the email I sent to everyone, including the owner. It wasn't a bad email, just a recap of what was discussed in the meeting and the other idea brought forward. I'm not going to do this he said/she said bullshit with any of them. It'll all be documented from the beginning. "I just informed everyone on what I was going to do on my end."

Ava chuckles. "You sure did." Turning, she walks to her desk to grab her purse. I open the email again to reread it, and if I could, I would give me a high five.

Picking up my phone, I pull up the number and press the blue phone button. It rings twice, and then he picks up. "Well, well, well," he says, and a smile just fills my face. "Why are you calling me and not FaceTiming me?"

"Well, first, I didn't know if you would pick up." I hear the ringing of the phone and look down to see that he is trying to FaceTime me. I click connect and watch the little wheel go around in a circle while it connects. His face fills the screen, and my heart clenches in my chest when I realize how much I miss home. "Hi, Uncle Max."

"There she is," he says with a smile on his face. "Miss Producer."

I roll my eyes. "Or just Franny."

"How're you doing?" he asks, and I have to swallow the lump in my throat. I will never admit to anyone that I'm out of my comfort zone or I regret this decision.

"Amazing," I lie. "Had my first board meeting today."

He whistles. "I see you're kicking ass and taking names already." And I can see that he's at home in Long Island. Last year, when my cousin, Michael, moved to Dallas, it didn't take him long to follow. It also helped that Michael had his first child, and the thought of not living by their grandchild was just too much for both him and my aunt Allison.

"I don't know about that." I try to keep my voice calm and not let him see how I really feel. "But my segment got approved."

"Is that a good thing?" He's not sure if he should be happy or not.

I smile now. "It's a great thing."

"What are you not telling me?" His eyes narrow to slits. "Do I have to come over there?"

I laugh nervously. "Not yet, but …"

He shrieks, "Aha!" He points at me. "I knew there was more to this phone call."

I gasp. "Hey, can't I just call to say I love you?"

He shakes his head, laughing. "You can, but you didn't."

I hold up both my hands now. "Okay, fine, I didn't," I admit. "I'm calling to ask if you would like to be part of my show."

"For you, anything." He agrees before I even tell him what it's about.

"Well, why don't I give you my whole pitch, and then you can tell me if you're in or not?" I say, my heart speeding up. I rub my hands on my pants as I look into the phone. "It's going to be a weekly segment on the bad boys of hockey." The minute I say the words, he groans.

"Why, why, why do I always get lumped into the bad boys of hockey?" he moans and throws his head back, his hands going to his face to rub it.

"It's because you're sexy," my aunt Allison says. "And you were a bad boy once upon a time." She comes into view, smiling at me and kissing my uncle on the cheek. "Hi, honey."

"Hi, Auntie." Seeing her just makes me even more

homesick. "Did you hear about my show?"

"I did," she confirms excitedly. "When do you need him by?"

"Why?" my uncle cuts in now. "I've paid my dues." We both laugh now. "I won a Stanley Cup. I've created the Max Horton Children's Foundation." He shakes his head. "Like I'm a good guy."

"No," I say, not smiling now. "You're the best guy."

He rolls his eyes now. "Okay, that was a lie." He points at me. "And you did it with a straight face."

"I can tell no lies." I hold up my hand in a Scout's honor gesture. "I would be honored to have you as my guest. And if it makes you feel any better, I'm also going to be hitting up Uncle Viktor."

"Fine," he huffs. "You better have your father on that freaking list."

I smile sadly. "It's kind of hard to do when he's not talking to me." My heart hurts in my chest, and the lump rises to my throat. I shrug my shoulders and try not to let the tears come as I blink away the stinging in my eyes. It's safe to say he did not support my decision to take the job in Dallas. Which has been really hard because, in all my life, he's always supported me. "It's fine," I say, shaking my head and wiping away the tears trying to escape from my right eye with my thumb.

"Oh, honey," Allison says softly. "He's going to talk to you."

"Yeah, well." I'm angry now. "Maybe I don't want to talk to him," I say, folding my arms over my chest, and it comes to me that I sound like a kid throwing a tantrum.

"He's just mad that you didn't tell him about the job until you signed the papers." Max tries to plead his case.

"And why do you think I did that?" I retort, angry that it's getting to me. Angry that it still bothers me.

"I'm sure you have your reasons," Max says softly, and if we were in front of each other, he would no doubt lean over and hug me.

"Ugh," I groan. "I didn't do that to upset him or whatever is spinning in that big fat head of his." My voice goes loud, and I look up to make sure no one can hear me. Looking out, I see that no one is in the office. Not one person. "I did it because I didn't want him going all, well, him," I say, using my hands now. "If I would have told him about it, he would have went over my head." I look at the phone. "He would have been all like a caveman or I don't know, the *Godfather*. Put a horse in the bed or something like that."

"Oh my God." Max laughs. "You really know your dad."

"I just …" I take a deep breath to calm myself. "I wanted to get this job because I merited this job, not because my last name was Grant and my grandfather owned the media company. Or that my father called a friend."

Max throws his head back and laughs. "One, your father doesn't have friends."

I roll my eyes. "He knows someone everywhere," I huff. "I just for once wanted to get a job because I deserved it. I didn't want anyone to think I got it because of who I know or what my last name is."

"Honey," Max says. "You got that job because you do deserve it. Your father, regardless of how he is handling this, loves you with everything he has." I don't say, yeah right. Instead, I just listen to him. "The only thing he wants is for you to be okay."

"Well, how is he going to know I'm okay when he doesn't speak to me?" I shake my head. "It's fine. It'll be fine. It's whatever." I shrug.

"We are coming down for the home opener on Saturday, and we are having a family lunch on Sunday," Max says, and my heart sinks.

"No one told me anything." My voice goes low. "Maybe I'm not invited." I swallow the hurt.

"Of course you're invited," Allison replies, and I can see her eyes fill with tears. "There isn't any way that you wouldn't be invited." She looks at Max. "I'm going to …" Her teeth clench together as she threatens I don't even know what.

Max holds up his hand at Allison to get her to stop mumbling and then turns back to me. "Saturday, you will come to the game. He can't ignore you if you're right in front of him."

"We'll see." I don't commit, but I know in my heart I'm going to go if my whole family will be there.

"There is no we'll see," he says. "If you want me on your show, you'll be at the game and at lunch."

"That's blackmail," I point out to him, laughing. "And that is how you got the bad-boy title."

He groans when Allison laughs. "Okay, see you Saturday. Keep your chin up, yeah?" I nod my head.

"Love you."

"Love you, too." I disconnect the phone for just a second before I dial my sister.

She picks up after two rings, and I can see she's at the brownstone in the city. "Are you coming to the game on Saturday?" I ask, and she just looks at me.

"What game? Where?" she asks, and the hurt goes away just a bit.

"The home opener in Dallas," I fill her in. "And the family lunch on Sunday."

"Only our family plans an event in Dallas for a home opener to a team that is not in our city." She laughs. "Are we going to Montreal for Dylan's home opener?"

"Well, Dad is coming, and I need some sort of backup," I tell her. "So pack your bags."

"I had the whole weekend planned out already," she groans. "And nowhere on that itinerary was it *fly to Dallas*."

"What happened to being spontaneous?" She glares at me.

"That word gives me hives." She scratches her arms and moves up to her neck. "Like literally hives."

"You can stay with me." She rolls her eyes. "I'll even get the creamer for your coffee you like."

She throws her head back and rolls it from side to side. "Ugh, fine." She stares at me. "But you owe me, and when you and Dad make up, I don't want to hear from either of you for a full month."

I laugh. "Like you can go two days without calling me."

"Goodbye," she says, hanging up, and I get up to leave. I turn the computer off, grabbing my phone that suddenly feels like it's a million pounds in my hand.

"Just text him," I tell myself. "Just do it and get it over with."

I pull up his name and see that the last time he texted me was the day before I gave him the news I was moving. My finger moves over the last text that he wrote, *Love you.*

My fingers type before I can change my mind. I press send and watch as the message goes blue and says delivered.

Me: Are we on speaking terms yet?

FOUR

WILSON

THE ALARM RINGS, and I slowly open my eyes. My hand reaches out of the covers to stop the buzzing. I press the button next to the light to open the electric shades. I roll on my back and groan as I stretch and feel the pull in my legs. "Fuck, I'm getting old," I say to myself, looking out my bedroom window as the sun lights up the room.

My phone beeps beside my bed, and I don't move, enjoying the calmness before the storm. Tonight is the season opener, and everyone is on pins and needles, including me. The beginning of the year is like the first day back at school. Everything is like a fresh start.

It's also the first time in five years that I'm actually not suspended for the first game, so that in and of itself should get some sort of medal. The phone beeps again, and I see that I have a bunch of texts that have come through.

One is from my agent, Richard, who wishes me a

good game. The others are from numbers not stored in my phone, so I don't even bother reading them. Then I get to one from Tiffany, my recent ex.

Tiffany: Do you want to meet up after the game? ☺

It takes me two seconds to answer that one.

Me: Fuck No.

I put her on "do not disturb" and head to the bathroom. Turning the water on in the sink, I wet my face and run my hands through my dark brown hair. As I look at myself in the mirror, my eyes go from green to blue in a blink of an eye. It got me the name green-eyed monster one year. I shake my head and laugh, wondering if I should bother shaving.

Making my way into my walk-in closet, I grab a pair of boxers from one of the drawers. Slipping them on, I look over at my wall of suits. Should I go blue or black? My phone buzzes, reminding me that my ride will be here in thirty minutes.

I grab the blue suit I haven't worn before, slipping the tailored pants on with a white button-down shirt. Once I have on my brown Tom Ford belt and matching shoes, I walk over to the mirror and look at myself before deciding on a blue tie with small white dots. Sliding on the jacket completes the outfit, and I grab my aviator sunglasses, then walk to the front door and out to my waiting ride.

"Good evening." The driver opens the back door of the Tesla car, and I just shake my head.

"No way am I riding in the back." With a laugh, he closes the back door and then opens the front one.

"Thanks, Frank," I tell him. "Thought I would forget." I shake my head. The last time I saw Frank was when I attended Michael's wedding and didn't want to drive to the venue and back. So, he drove me and picked me up at 5:00 a.m. when I woke up. I definitely did not plan on drinking so much I passed out.

He gets into the driver's side now. "I have water for you in the back." He points at the water in the cupholder in the back.

"Thanks, buddy," I say, leaning into the back and grabbing it. "Are we on time?"

"We are," he confirms. "We'll be meeting everyone on the street right behind the arena." I nod at him and go through Instagram while he drives me to the arena. Because it's the season opener, we are all arriving one after another and walking the red carpet. The fans have been lining up since this morning to get a shot at seeing a couple of us as well as getting to take some pictures with us.

We pull up along all the other Teslas, and Patricia, the team's public relations manager, comes over and knocks on the window. "Hi," she says, bending to hand me four Sharpies. "This is for you to sign if you want to." She smiles. "Lots of fans out there are waiting for you." She turns and walks to the car that just pulled up behind us.

Frank starts to get texts telling him when it's time to go. I look out the window, my finger tapping one of my legs as he makes his way over to the arena. The street is closed off, and a police barricade is in place to only allow our cars to pass. Fans are lined up on both sides of the carpet, and the press is there snapping pictures. "You are second to last," he says, and I nod, my heart starting to pump just a touch faster as he moves up one more spot.

I can hear the fans screaming when Michael Horton gets out of the car in front of me, and he holds up his hand. "You can get out," Frank says, and I open the door, stepping out and hearing the roar of the fans outside.

It's utter chaos as I wave to the fans across the street and then walk toward the carpet. "This is nuts," I say once I get close to Michael, and he laughs.

"I think it's going to be even worse once we get down the carpet," he replies, and I walk over to one side and start signing stuff.

Fans have team pictures and shirts for the players to sign. Someone even had my rookie card. I smile at him when I sign it. "This is old." I smirk as they snap a picture of me signing it. The fan noise just gets louder when Cooper and Manning arrive together. Little does everyone know that he's retiring after this year, and from the looks of it, Cooper is going to step up to the plate and take the C from him.

It takes an hour before we walk into the arena. "Are your ears buzzing?" I look over at Cooper, who walks in with me, and he laughs.

"Did you see that one girl yelling your name?" Cooper claps his hands. "I swear I thought she was going to flash her tits just to get your attention." My mouth opens as I look back at the door, and Manning comes in. No press is allowed past the doors, and it's a good thing because his wife, Evelyn, is there with their kids as they snap a picture with him. I watch him with his family for longer than is normal.

Turning, I walk into the dressing room. "There he is, Mr. GQ," Raphel, one of the rookies, says, and I just shake my head.

"That's Miller's title." I point at Miller, who flips me the bird while he gets dressed into his workout gear. "I'm Mr. Bad Boy."

"So how many girls you bringing tonight?" Jake, the other rookie sitting beside him, asks, his eyes wide as he thinks about it. "Last year, someone said you brought triplets."

I laugh, shrugging off my jacket. "I did," I say. I don't add that I ditched them as soon as we left the party because there was only so much squealing a man can take. "But tonight." I hang my jacket and take off my tie. "I'm going to be flying solo." They both look at me with their mouths open. It's rare I attend functions alone, but for the past six months, something has changed, and I don't know what it is. "It's better to go in solo and then sweep up all the girls once you're there." I wink at them, and they both laugh. Little do they know that as soon as the party is over, I'm going home by myself so I can fucking rest. The preseason game we had three days ago was brutal, and even though I didn't fight anyone, it was physical, and I'm still fucking dragging my ass from it. But I'm going to hide that shit deep inside. No one gets to know that but me.

I mix my protein shake and walk to the gym. Everyone has different exercises that they go with. I get on the bike and pedal while I watch the news recap of today. The number of fans is always surreal, but today was something extra. When I finish with the bike, I go lift weights before changing into my uniform.

The nerves in my stomach start now, and then the smile when I slip the jersey on. I have not done many things that I can be proud of, but being a hockey player is one of them. I grab my stick as we skate on the ice for pre-warm-up. The only fans in the building lined up by the glass are family members. I stand in front of Cooper and Michael as they both shake their hands at their kids. One of the little girls looks over at me and waves, and I hold up my gloved hand and wave back at her. "Don't smile at her like that," Cooper says, pushing my shoulder. "She already kept the puck you gave her last year."

"What can I say?" I skate in front of him, ready to get the puck passed from the other side of the ice. "Girl's got taste." I grab the puck and toss it softly over the glass. The little girl shrieks and grabs it. "That's a 'good luck' puck," I tell her, and she turns and says something to Erika, who just rolls her eyes at me.

"Behave," she says, and I just smirk at her. She was my agent for a little while, and then we decided to go our separate ways. In other words, she fired me and handed me off to someone else at the firm who sucks balls and doesn't do anything for me. But it's what I have to live with.

"Me." I point at myself. "I'm an angel."

I skate away, and when the horn sounds, we all skate off the ice. Normally, we would wait for the Zamboni to pass and then get back on the ice, but everyone is being introduced tonight. We stand in the hallway by number. One by one, we skate out, and I bounce on my skates with nervous energy. Only six of us left—Michael, Cooper, Miller, Ralph, Manning, and me.

"New year, boys," Manning says, and we look over at him. "Last year." It's a huge step to walk away from the game when it's all you've known your whole life.

I can't even imagine making that decision, but as the days go on, it's on my mind more and more. "Wilson," the guy says, "you're up next."

"Here we go." I move to the white X that shows us where to stand. I can see the lights coming in from the ice.

"How about you don't give me any white hairs this season?" Manning suggests, and I just shrug.

"I wouldn't have to give you guys white hair if you weren't pussies and made me fight all your battles." I smirk at them, knowing that they would drop their gloves for me in a heartbeat. "Now, let's put some points on the board, yeah?" When I hear the announcer say my name, I walk down the tunnel toward the ice. The music is blaring, and the minute I slide my skates onto the ice, the whole place erupts.

"Let's do this," I tell myself as I line up with the rest of the guys, shutting out the noise.

FIVE

FRANCES

"I CHANGED MY mind," I say to my sister, Vivienne, when we park the car in the underground garage at the arena. "I don't think this is a good idea."

All she does is laugh at me, turning off the car and getting out while ignoring what I just said. My heart is in my throat as I reach for the handle of the door and open it. The minute I close the door, we hear the roar of the fans. Arriving after the festivities was Vivi's idea so we aren't sitting around awkwardly. "I guess the guys are getting on the ice," Vivi says, laughing as I walk side by side with her toward the family entrance.

"I think I'm going to throw up." I look over at Vivi, who just side-eyes me.

"Well, you look like you're dressed for war." She points at my outfit, and I stop walking.

"You said this was good!" I shriek, looking down at my outfit. My black jeans mold to my legs, and I paired them with a gray sweater. Instead of opting for heels like she did, I wore my white sneakers with black stripes. "What's wrong with my outfit?"

"I think maybe it's the leather jacket." She points at the leather jacket I threw on at the last minute. "Sort of a *Sons of Anarchy* vibe."

I snort, pushing her. "You're just jealous"—I start to walk again—"that your feet hurt and mine don't."

"Ugh," she moans. "I'm wearing five-inch heels, and we're the same height." She shakes her head. "It's not fair. You got legs for days, and I got none of that."

I laugh, pulling open the door, and the security guard stops us. "Passes." He holds his hand out. I look down at my purse, my long blond hair falling around my face. I opted to leave my hair loose instead of tying it up.

"Here is mine," Vivi says, handing the man the square plastic pass that we were all given. And by all given, my father gave Vivi mine last night when they got here.

"You're good," the man tells her. I slip my pass out and hand it to him. He looks down at it and nods his head, allowing us to walk into the arena. The floor literally vibrates under us as we walk over the carpeted hallway toward the family lodge.

"Okay, how do I look?" I ask her nervously. Not only do I have to vomit but I also think I'm going to shit myself. Why the fuck am I so nervous? *Oh, 'cause your father isn't talking to you*, I remind myself.

"You look like you always look," she says, and I roll my eyes, irritated with her. Unlike our height, we have the same hair and eye color. Except mine turn green sometimes in the sun, whereas hers stay crystal blue the whole time.

"Seriously," I say. The door to the lodge opens, and I stop breathing. I'm literally holding my breath, expecting it to be my father, but it's my uncle Max.

"Whoa," he says, looking at us in surprise. He's wearing jeans and a Dallas jersey, which looks so weird on him. Since he played for New York, that is the only jersey I'll ever see him in. This one no doubt has his name on it because of Michael. "There you are," he says, looking at my sister and then at me. Vivi steps up to him, kissing his cheek, and then I walk to him, and he gives me a hug. "Relax," he whispers in my ear. "It's going to be fine." Just him saying that brings back the stinging to my eyes.

"I smell food," Vivi says and walks into the lodge, leaving me with my uncle Max.

"I have never ever felt this unsure in my life." I look up at him. "And I moved cities for a job that I'm probably unqualified for."

"Hey," he scolds, his voice tight. "None of that bullshit. You got the job because you were qualified." I smile tightly. The past week has not been an easy road. The condescending emails are nonstop, and even though I ignore them, hoping they'll go away, it hasn't been easy. I'm giving them a month to get to know me, and then I'm going to just basically explode and let the chips fall where they may. "Now get in there. Your mother has been looking for you."

"Only my mother?" I joke with him and smile.

"Your father, too, but he's Mr. Tough Guy and has been ignoring it. Yet every time the door opens, his eyes fly to it. He thinks he's slick." He leans in. "He's not. Come on, I'll be your wingman." I laugh, nodding at him and walking into the lodge.

It's jam-packed. "Look at who the cat dragged in," Alex, my cousin and Michael's sister, says. "And looking like she just got off a runway." She comes over and hugs me.

"You're one to talk." I look her up and down, and she would make a potato sack look sexy.

I take two steps in when I see Cooper and Erika's little girl come running for me. "Auntie Fran!" Felicia jumps, and I catch her in my arms. She wraps her arms around my neck. "Did you bring my lipstick?"

I kiss her neck. "Um, of course I did, silly." I put her down and open my black Chanel bag to take out the clear lip gloss. "I got one for your sister, too."

"Mia!" Felicia yells, making everyone turn around, and all eyes land on us. "Auntie Fran brought lipstick." I look around and spot my mother and father standing together. I smile at them and then look back down when Mia comes over. I thought I was ready to see him, but I'm not.

"Here." I look over at Erika and smile when she hands me a glass of whiskey. Erika is Cooper's wife, the two of them were best friends for the longest time and finally woke up and figured out they loved each other. "Thought you might need this." She's also one of my closest friends and, besides my sister, the only one I confided in about the job in Dallas before everyone else.

"Thank you," I say, taking a little sip of the amber liquid. The burning starts as soon as it touches my tongue and works its way down to my stomach. "I guess I should go over and say hello." I blink away the stinging.

"Want me to come with you?" she asks. "Or I can get the baby, and you can hold him as a shield."

"I think I'd prefer talking to that Matthew instead of the other one." I mention my nephew, who is named after my father. When my brother said his name, we all groaned. There are so many double names in this family, and it's hard to keep up.

"Well, he said fuck this shit yesterday," Erika says, and my eyes go big. "When I said it was time for bed."

"That's always fun." I laugh at her. "Okay, here I go." I take a deep breath and make my way to my parents. It's like the parting of the sea when I start walking toward them. Everyone is chatting away, but I can feel eyes on us, and I hate it. Usually, it's light and upbeat, but you can cut the tension with a knife right now. My mother is beside my father and whatever she is saying to him is between clenched teeth. My father just looks at her like he always does. There is no mistake as to how he feels about her. From the stories he's always telling us, he took one look at her, and he was toast.

"Hey," I say awkwardly when I get close enough. My mother looks up at me, and I do the only thing I can. I avoid looking at my father just like I did when I was seventeen and crashed his three-day-old car when I drove it into the garage and then into the wall. I bend to give my mother a hug, and I can hear her sniffling.

"You look beautiful," she whispers in my ear. I'm trying really hard to keep it together in front of her. I want to say that the only relationship affected is the one with my father, but that is a lie. My mother and I have been dancing around the subject since the big fight at their house. She still calls me every day, but it feels like a massive elephant is in the room, and no one is mentioning it.

She lets go of me, and I swallow down the lump and finally look over at my father. "Hey, Dad." I lean in for a side hug, making my neck burn with nerves. This is the most awkward hug in the history of all hugs.

"Hi." He puts one of his hands on my shoulder and pats it.

"Matthew fucking Grant," my mother says. I look over at her because her tone is not one I've ever heard before, and trust me, I've heard them all. I was the wild child who used to make sure I could see just how much I could get away with. "So help me God, if you don't make this better." She shakes her head, then looks at me. "The two of you are the same person." She looks at me and then my father. "It's been a month. It's long enough.

"You, too." She points at me, and I look at her, shocked.

"Me?" I point at myself. "I'm not the one avoiding the other one." I take a sip of my whiskey. "It's fine." I avoid looking back at my father because the hurt that we can't joke hits me right away. "Maybe one day he'll forgive me for following my dreams," I mumble and then turn when I hear my aunt Allison calling my name. I walk away from them, ignoring the fact I want to curl into a ball and cry.

I hug my aunt, and then I turn to see my grandparents walking in. I'm about to walk over to them when I turn and see my father standing in front of me. He's wearing a suit, just like he always is. His hands are in his pants pockets.

"Maybe we should talk."

"Maybe?" I ask. When he looks at me, I can see the hurt in his eyes. I hope he can see the hurt in mine.

"Fine," he huffs. "We need to talk."

My heart hammers in my chest. I don't care how old you get, when your father says we need to talk, you get nervous. "I think that would be good."

"You think?" He comes back with a joke, and I smile and look down.

"Fine," I huff. "It would be good to talk to you."

"Tomorrow, then," he says. "Come by the house before lunch."

When I take a second and pretend I'm thinking about it, he laughs, and tears hit me like I just ran face-first into it. "I'll be there," I say softly and wipe away the tear threatening to fall. He leans in, taking my neck in his arms and kissing my head.

"Good," he replies and turns to walk away to greet

his parents.

"See, that wasn't so bad," Vivi says, and I just sniffle. "Although I did think he was going to go in for a chokehold." I throw my head back and let out the biggest laugh I have in the past month. Maybe things will be okay after all.

SIX

WILSON

"TWENTY MINUTES, BOYS," I huff. "We cannot lose on opening night." I'm taping my stick between the second and third period. "Especially with an after-party." I shake my head. "Not tonight." I make sure that the tape is on good before I sit back down.

"He's right," Manning agrees, sitting at his spot on the bench. "We are down by one goal, so we still have time to turn this game around."

No one says anything as we line up to get back on the ice. "Manning!" Coach yells. "Your line is up."

I look down the line at Miller, who skates onto the ice, followed by Cooper, Michael, and me. "Let's do this, boys." I crouch down and put my stick on the ice. The puck drops, and Cooper wins the face-off, sending it back to Manning, who lets the puck sit on his blade while we skate up. Manning sees me open, and it looks like he's going to pass it to me, but I nod toward Michael, who is waiting at the line with no one in front of him. He slides it to Michael, and he takes it into the zone while I skate to the other side. Michael sends it over to me, and one of the other team members gives me a body check. He falls to his knees next to me, and I knock his head down, skating around him. He gets up and starts tapping the back of my legs with his stick while I watch Cooper and Michael pass the puck back and forth to each other, then slide it back to Manning.

"Pussy." The guy tries to goad me, but instead, I'm watching the play. The guy messing with me is so distracted that he doesn't see Michael skate up right behind him and shoot the puck right over the goalie's pad. When the place goes crazy and the horns blow, I look back at the guy.

"Who's the pussy now?" I ask. He lifts his hand in the air, holding his stick in both hands. It comes so fast I don't have a chance to protect myself before he cross-checks me across the face. My head flies back, and I hear ringing in my ears. I slip and fall on my ass, the guy falling on top of me, trying to hit me in the face. I get up on my skates, throwing my gloves to the side. One of the referees grabs me by the shoulders, telling me to calm down, while another referee is holding the other guy back. "You better hold him back," I say. "Because I'm going to make his face look like a pussy."

They put us both in the penalty box, and I grab the towel on the bench, wiping my nose that got the brunt of that hit. "You got two minutes for unsportsmanlike conduct." I shake my head, not even bothering to argue with them. The announcer then declares the other guy is getting a five-minute major and one game misconduct. Manning comes over, bringing me my stick and gloves. "You good?"

"Yeah," I say, grabbing them from him. "Nothing I haven't felt before."

"Well, after the game, how about I give you a sticker for being a good boy?" he jokes. I give him the bird before he skates away.

I spend two minutes in the box, and when there are ten seconds to go, I stand and wait for the countdown. As I watch the play in our zone, the team passes it to the defenseman, who passes it along the boards to the right side. I slide out of the box at the same time that Manning clears the puck, and it goes over the defenseman's skate, landing right on my blade. I skate into the zone and see that Michael has hustled over to help me. Moving the puck to the back of the stick, the goalie slides to my side and sticks out his stick, and as soon as he does that, I slide it right behind him. The red light behind the goal goes off, and I see the fans get to their feet. I jump up with my back toward the glass. Michael joins me, followed by Cooper.

When Manning and Miller make it to us, Manning hits my helmet with his gloves. "You get two stickers." He jokes with me as we skate to the bench to high-five everyone. The rest of the game is uneventful, and Cooper buries an empty-net goal, so we win the game by two.

I get first star of the game, so I skate around the rink, tossing pucks to the crowd. When I skate off, a reporter waits to ask me questions, but all I want to do is take a shower. My face throbs from the hit, and my neck is hurting from being shoved back. When I walk into the locker room, I head straight for my spot, taking my jersey off and tossing it in the bin.

When I come out of the shower, the only one left is one of the rookies slipping on his pants. "Are you going to the after-party?" he asks, and I nod my head. "I'll wait for you."

Fuck, I think as I get dressed. I'd hoped I could skip it. But I walk over to the pub across the street, and we can hear the music coming from the restaurant. My phone rings in my pocket right before I'm about to walk in. "I'll meet you in there," I say when I see that my agent, Richard, is on the phone. I step to the side, away from the door, pressing the green button.

"You don't get paid extra for calling me after a game," I joke with him when I answer, and I can hear him laughing.

"What a fucking game," he points out. "You were on fire." I look around, seeing the front door of the bar open. Two women come out, and my eyes go straight to the blonde who stands beside another woman as they look down at the phone in her hand. They are having a conversation with someone on the phone. My eyes stay on the blonde as she throws her head back and laughs at whatever is being said. "Hello," I hear Richard say, and I look away to focus on my call.

"Sorry," I reply. "What did you say?"

"I was calling because we got a request from an up-

and-coming show." I groan loudly. "I know what you're thinking, but hear me out." I roll my eyes.

"If you know what I'm thinking …" I put the hand that isn't holding the phone on my hip. "Why are you even bothering me with this bullshit?"

"Because I'm thinking it would be a great opportunity for the world to see you as someone besides an asshole," he says without skipping a beat. "It's called the *Bad Boys of Hockey*."

"Are you fucking kidding me?" I ask, getting heated.

"It's not what you think. Listen, they sent me a list of the other players doing the show, and it's kind of like a bad-boy redemption." I don't say a word now. "Max Horton has signed on as well as Viktor Petrov." He starts naming a few. "I think you should do it."

"I'll think about it." I look back and see that the women have gone back inside.

"Good," he says. "I'll call you tomorrow, and we can talk more about it."

"You better not call me until after three." Disconnecting the phone, I put it in the inside pocket of my suit jacket.

When I walk over and pull open the door, the hot air hits me right away. I take a couple of steps toward the stand that says "hostess" as I look around the dimly lit room. The place has been shut down for our after-party, so no one is standing there.

The round tables in the room are filled with players and their family members. A buffet has been set up along the right side of the room, and a bar runs the length of the back wall.

"There he is." I look over to the left and see Nico walking toward me with a big smile on his face. He holds out his hand for me to shake. "The game-winning goal."

I shake his hand, and he slaps me on the shoulder with his other hand. "Not the game-winning goal," I correct. "That was Michael." I look around and see him standing with his wife.

"Nah." Nico shakes his head. "That was the closer. Yours was the game-winning one."

I laugh, looking to see that people are literally everywhere. My eyes find the blonde who was outside. She sits with Erika, Cooper's wife, as they laugh at something. She gets up and looks around the table, asking them something, before turning and making her way to the bar.

"I'm going to get something to drink," I tell him. "Do you want anything?" He shakes his head.

Making my way to the bar, I'm stopped a couple of times to talk about the game tonight. I try not to be rude to any of them. When I get close to the bar, I see her leaned over it, looking around for someone to take her order. I spot the bartender at the other end of the bar. Slipping in beside her, I hold up my hand, and the bartender sees me right away. He finishes serving the round of shots before turning and making his way over to me.

"I'll take a bottle of water," I say and then turn to look at the blonde. Fuck, she's even better looking up close. "And I think the lady wants to order something."

"Thank you." She nods at me and looks at the bartender. "I'll take a whiskey on ice."

With a nod, he turns to fill our order. "Have we met before?" The words come out before I can take them back, and I swear even I want to groan at how cheesy they sound.

She turns to face me and puts one of her elbows on the bar. I take in her outfit, the running shoes making it known that she gives zero shits about dressing up. Usually, the girls who hang around the rookies and stuff are always dressed to the nines. Fuck, even a couple of my dates have shown up with platform stilettos. "We sure have." Her answer shocks me.

I turn to face her, mimicking her stance. "I think if we met, I would remember." I smirk at her. The bartender comes back, placing my water bottle in front of me and setting her whiskey on one of the napkins that he lays down.

She picks up the whiskey and takes a long pull from it. I wait for her to hiss from the burning, but instead, she takes a step closer to me. Her smell has a familiarity to it. Looking at her, all I can think of is this woman is confident. Even the way she stands here, she commands the room, and fuck if it doesn't make her even sexier. I try to place her, looking into her blue eyes. She's fucking beautiful.

"I'm Cooper Grant's sister," she says, and my stomach sinks. "We met at my cousin Michael's wedding." I don't remember half of the night, having drunk too much with the rookies to pretend I was still young. She leans in just a touch closer, looking around to make sure that no one can hear her. I don't know what I'm expecting her to say, but it's definitely not the words that come next. "We fucked twice, and when I went back for a third, you …" She looks down at my cock, my eyes going big in shock. "Well, had performance issues." She takes another sip of her whiskey. "Have a great night." With a smirk, she walks away, leaving me with my mouth hanging open.

SEVEN

FRANCES

I ROLL MY lips, trying not to laugh as I walk away from Wilson. Bet he wasn't expecting to hear how we knew each other. I make my way over to Vivienne, who is laughing with Erika about something. "I'm going to head out." I down the rest of my whiskey and put the empty glass on the table. She starts to stand. "You don't have to come. Stay and mingle."

"I'm exhausted, and my feet literally feel like ogres." She points down at the black heels she thought were a good idea. I kiss everyone goodbye, the whole time feeling eyes on me, and when I look back at the bar, he's standing there looking at me. His mouth is no longer hanging, and his hands are tucked in his pockets. If I thought he was hot at the wedding, I was wrong. Also, his musky scent had my body on alert.

"Okay, you two." I hear Cooper from beside me. "Let's go."

I look over at him, confused. "You're leaving?" He nods his head as his hand slips into Erika's. The four of us walk across the street, and as soon as Vivienne gets into the car, she slides her shoes off.

"I can't even try to get them back on." She holds one of the shoes up, and I put my head back and laugh. She drives home, neither of us saying anything, and when we get to my house, she parks in the garage. When I took the job in Dallas, it was the first time I felt like I had to do things on my own. This house was the first thing I bought on my own. I had my aunt Zoe help find me a place, and I was lucky it came furnished since the owners were moving out of the country. The only things I replaced were the mattresses in all the rooms.

We walk up the three steps to the mudroom. "Night," she mumbles, going toward the stairs to the bedrooms. "See you in the morning."

Walking to the kitchen, I grab a water bottle from the fridge and head upstairs to my bedroom. It's the only place I've truly decorated, and it's what sold me on the house, to be honest. The floor-to-ceiling windows lead out to a covered patio set. When I visited, I could picture myself sitting out there looking at the stars. But in the two weeks I've lived here, I have yet to even step foot outside. Walking into the room, I shrug off my jacket and walk right past my bed toward the walk-in closet. I kick off my shoes, then grab my shorts and tank top.

Slipping under the covers, I lean over to turn off all the lights, then pull the covers up to my chin. I look out the big windows, and it takes me less than a minute to fall asleep.

As we meandered down the hotel hallway, our hands brushed against one another's. "This is me." He stopped in front of his door. "Which one is yours?"

"Three floors up," I told him as I stepped closer. I smelled his musky cologne, and it was a good thing that this dress had a built-in bra because my nipples were aching to be touched. "Are you going to invite me in?" I asked as my hand rubbed up the lapel of his jacket.

His hand wrapped around my waist as he pulled me to him, and I felt his cock on my stomach. "You're playing with fire," he hissed.

"It's okay." I wrapped my arms around his neck. "From the feel of it, you have a hose to—" I didn't even have time to finish before he attacked my mouth. His tongue slid with mine, and I didn't even feel my feet touch the floor.

He turned us, and in the blink of an eye, we were behind closed doors. The cold door hit my back, making me arch forward. "I have to taste you," he said as soon as he let go of my mouth. He lifted the long dress, and for once, I was happy I went with the loose bottom instead of the tight mermaid style. "No panties," he hissed right before his tongue came out and licked through my slit. He had his fingers in me, his tongue all over me, and after a minute, I came on his hand. "Your pussy tastes like honey." He continued to lick me long after I came.

My hands going to his hair, fisting it. "My pussy needs to be fucked."

The covers move off me, and my eyes fly open. "Your spare bedroom is haunted," Vivienne says as she slides into bed with me.

I laugh, turning as the sun shines into my face. "What time is it?"

"A little after eight," she mumbles. I wait a couple of seconds, and I know she'll get up. She can never just lounge. If she's up, she's out of bed. "Coffee?"

We have coffee and get dressed, then head over to my parents' place in Dallas. I walk in and can smell the cooking. "Hey!" Vivienne shouts from the front door. "Is everyone decent?" The last time we came early, we were the ones surprised and then scarred for finding our parents on the couch. One should never have to see their parents that way.

"Very funny," my mother says, coming down the stairs. "Your father is in the kitchen."

She comes over and gives us each a hug and a kiss. I walk into the kitchen, still unsure and not really myself.

"Hey," I greet when I walk into the kitchen. My father looks up from his iPad, and he smiles.

"Vivienne," my mother says, "would you like to come with me outside?" Vivienne looks at me, not sure what to do. "They'll be fine." My mother puts her hands on her hips. "Besides, we'll be outside."

"You don't have to go outside," I inform them, leaning against the counter, looking at my father. "There really isn't much to say." I tilt my head to the side. "I got a job offer, and I took it. I don't know what the big deal is. When Cooper got traded from New York, did you go off on him?"

"That is very different," my father starts. "One, it was his job." I glare at him. "I mean, he had no choice." He points at me. "You had a choice."

"And I chose my dream job," I say. "I don't know why you are so upset about it."

"I'm not upset about it," my father explains. "I'm disappointed you didn't talk to me beforehand."

"Disappointed is worse than you being upset." I shake my head. "Did it ever occur to you that I needed to do this for myself?" I ask, and he doesn't say anything. "I needed to prove to myself that I could survive without the safety net."

"There is nothing wrong with having a safety net," my father says. "I'm upset you didn't come to me and talk about it."

"Why do you think that I did that?" I ask him and take a deep breath. "Because you are you, and you would have probably gotten on the phone and done a whole background check of the company before I even left the house."

"There is nothing wrong with that!" he shouts. "I don't want you or anyone who I love to be taken advantage of." He slaps the counter. "Or used as a pawn."

"Wow! So you don't think I got this job because I merited it?" I look down and shake my head. "You think I got this job because they wanted to get to you?"

He doesn't say anything because the front door

opens, and I hear my grandparents announce that they are here. My father and I just stare at each other, and nothing gets resolved. It just makes me angrier with him. My grandfather comes over and takes me in his arms. "How's my independent girl?" he says. "Is your father giving you a hard time?"

"My father is pigheaded," I mumble.

"He gets that from your grandmother," he says, making me laugh. "I'll talk to him."

"No." I shake my head. "Nothing anyone says is going to change his mind."

"Frances Grant," he says, and I look at him. "You don't see this now, but one day, you will. You may be in your twenties, but to your father, you will always be that little girl he needs to protect." I don't say anything to him and just nod my head. When I look over, my father is outside with my mother. She's telling him something, and from the looks of it, she is not happy. The caterers are setting up all the tables around them, trying not to eavesdrop.

I don't get a chance to find out what it is when more people come in. Cooper is next with Erika and the kids. Followed by Michael and Jillian, his son on his hip. I'm sitting at one of the tables with Erika and Jillian.

"Can someone tell me how a family lunch ends up being fifty people?" Alex mumbles when she stumbles in with Jillian's sister, Julia, beside her. The two of them have become close ever since they met and take the two empty seats.

"Just when I think I've met all of the family members,"

Julia says. "More come out."

"It's like *Gremlins*," Vivienne says. "Don't feed us after midnight."

We all laugh. "So how are you enjoying Dallas?" Jillian asks me.

"It's okay from what I've seen." I shrug. "I've been busy at work."

"Forget about work," Julia says. "Have you started dating?"

"Yes," Alex agrees, pointing at me. "That."

"No." I shake my head.

"What?" Erika shrieks. "Why not?"

"Because I suffer from something called big-dick syndrome," I say, making everyone laugh. "The minute they find out I'm independent and can live without them, it's like I take away their man card," I groan. "The men are always trying to prove how powerful they are."

"Or are you too busy trying not to catch feelings?" Vivienne looks at me. "It's easier to bang without getting to know them." My heart starts to speed up when she questions me. I've never thought about it like that.

"What if all I want is to bang?" I look down at my hands, my head spinning from this conversation. "What if I'm too busy trying to build a career, and all I need is to scratch the itch?"

"What if you actually meet someone who can scratch the itch and be there to support you?" Vivienne counters, and my mouth goes dry.

"Well, if there is such a man out there," I huff, "I haven't met him."

"You aren't even trying." Alex laughs. "You go out with fuck boys because you know that is what they are." I don't get a chance to respond because one of the kids falls down, and everyone rushes to see which one it is.

My phone buzzes in my hand, and I pick it up to see it's Richard. For the past week, I've been trying to establish relationships with the sports agents out there. I have called all of them and introduced myself. I've been trying to pitch the show to all of them, in case they have clients who would be a good fit. Of course, I reached out to Richard because he had a client who would be perfect for us in every single way.

Richard: He's in. Send me the details.

I smile and put my phone down. It looks like Mr. Wilson and I will meet again.

EIGHT

WILSON

I PARK THE Land Rover and grasp the handle of the door to get out. My body screams at me as I stand and stretch, arching my back. Reaching back in, I grab the keys, my phone, and my suit jacket.

I'm about to text Richard when a door opens, and a woman comes out with a headset on and a clipboard in her hand. "Mr. Wilson." She smiles at me, and I look over at her. "I'm Catherine." She holds out her hand for me, and I shake it. "I'm here to welcome you and take you over to the makeup chair."

"Great," I huff and then pull up Richard's text chain.

Me: I'm here, and you're not. Do you see something wrong with this?

I walk into the studio, and the only light comes from the fixtures in the ceiling. It looks like it was a commercial lot transformed into a studio. Walking past makeshift rooms, I see tables and chairs but no ceiling. The people walking around are all wearing black with headsets on. I bet they aren't happy to be here on a Sunday either.

Turning down a hallway, Catherine stops at a door and leads me into what is the makeup room. Four chairs are pushed up to a long counter in front of a mirror with black makeup containers scattered on it. Makeup brushes are lined up in front of one of the chairs. "This is Aimee, and she will be taking care of you," Catherine says. "Do you need anything? Water, coffee?"

"I'm fine," I reply curtly as the phone vibrates in my hand. Ignoring Catherine, I look down at it.

Richard: Parking.

My annoyance goes even higher when I read his text. Not only am I here on a Sunday, my day off, but we also got our asses handed to us by Washington last night. It was not a good game for anyone. Every check was harder and harder, and every single battle for the puck seemed to be lost. "Where do you want me?" I look at the makeup girl, and she pulls out the first chair.

Sitting in the chair, I look at her. "I don't want anything that will cake on my skin," I tell her. "Like none of that foundation crap."

She laughs. "Lucky for you, all I have to correct are the circles under your eyes." I let her do her thing, and then I hear a knock on the door and turn to look at Richard coming in.

"Hey," he says with a smile and a cup of coffee in his hand. "There you are."

"Where else would I be? I was told to be here at eleven, and I was here at eleven. You know who wasn't here at that time?" I ask. Aimee looks over at him, and her eyes go big. "You."

"Excuse me," Aimee says, taking the chance to escape the room.

"I got here five minutes ago. I was chatting with the producer and the host of the show," he tells me, sitting down in the chair next to me.

"Did you tell them that my family life is off-limits?" I look over at him, and he nods.

"Made it crystal clear," he says. "They assured me there would be no questions asked."

"Good," I say, nodding my head. "How long do they think it's going to take?"

"I can go and ask that we speed it up," he says, getting up, and he stops when we both hear the clicking of heels coming closer.

I look over at the door, and my mouth drops open when I see her walk into the room. "Gentlemen." She smiles and her voice is smooth. I look her up and down. The last time she was wearing sneakers and a leather jacket, but now she's all business. Her pants are a blush pink and are tight on the hips but then are loose all the way to the bottom, hiding her high heels that we just heard clicking down the hallway. Her white sleeveless top is tucked in and tight, going high to her neck, but it molds to her tits. Her long hair is tied on top of her head in a bun, and my hand moves when I think about how it felt between my hands. My heart speeds up when looking at her, but I can't even try to contain what is happening inside me. My stomach is flipping over that she is here.

I've thought of her every fucking day since the bar, but I told myself to forget it. But with her standing in front of me, this is the universe giving me a sign. Either that or the universe is fucking with me and showing me yet again what I can't have.

"So we meet again," I say, smirking at her. She looks over at me and tries to hide the sly smile on her face.

"We do." She looks up, and I can see she's playing it as a professional. "I just came in to introduce myself to you," she starts, "but since we already know each other …"

"I didn't know you knew Frances," Richard says, and I look at him, then back to her.

"Oh, we met at … what was it?" I point at her, and I can see she is unfazed by me. "Michael's wedding, I think it was."

"It was." She doesn't even try to hide it, and little does she know that since she left me at the bar, I've remembered that night. I remember it all, and she is a little confused about how it ended. "But I'm sure you met many people that night."

"None that I remember," I say. "But I remember you."

I can see that gets to her when she swallows hard. "I guess that's a good thing, then." She puts her hands in her pockets, and I can see the silver Rolex on her wrist with a gold love bracelet. For a split second, my stomach burns with the thought that a man could have given her those gifts. What if she has a man, and I'm here thirsting over her? Just the thought pushes me in uncharted territory.

"And then we met last week at the after-party, right?"

I don't wait for her to answer that question. "You know what they say. Third time's a charm." I smile at her.

"Or three strikes and you're out." She tilts her head to the side, and then I hear someone talking. She reaches behind her and grabs the walkie-talkie from her back. "I'm with him. I'll bring him down," she says and clips it back. "They are ready for you on the set."

"I've got a call to make," Richard says. "I'll meet you in the producer box. " He looks at Frances and smiles at her. "Save me a seat." I get out of my chair, and the image of me throat punching him flashes through my head. Richard walks out of the room, leaving Frances and me alone.

"I thought you said your name was Franny?"

"It's a nickname my friends and family use," she says, not moving as I walk toward her.

"Aren't we friends?" I ask, and for the first time in my whole life, I'm having fun. This conversation with her is everything.

"More along the line of acquaintances." She tries not to smile, but it comes out as a smirk.

"We've seen each other naked." I say the words quietly and look around. "Surely, that puts us in the friends category."

She doesn't have a chance to answer me before more conversation comes across the walkie-talkie. "We should head to the set." She turns, and it's the wrong move, at least for me. The walkie-talkie is clipped in the back pocket of her pants. But her ass fills out those pants, and my cock goes hard because all I can think about is bending her over. "Are you coming?" She stops when she notices that I'm not behind her.

"I'm just taking in the view." I smile, and she rolls her eyes.

"You've seen the view before." She doesn't even try to hide it. "Up close and personal also." She stops walking and leans in. "You even bit it and smacked it."

If my cock wasn't hard before, it's rock hard now. I look down and make sure it's not noticeable. The last thing I need is for people to think I'm jonesing over her. Even if I am, it's no one's business. "Is that so?"

"Tough loss last night." She changes the subject as we start to walk down the hallway, and more people come into view.

"Yeah, it's never fun to lose." I try to keep my cool as we walk toward the set, passing all the empty rooms. Her hand grazes mine, and it's the straw that broke the camel's back. It's the same thing she did that night when we walked toward my room.

I grab her hand and pull her into one of the rooms, catching her off guard. I slam the door shut and cage her in with her back to the door. My hands go up by her head. "I remember that night." I lean in so close to her that I can hear her breath hitch. "It took me a second …" One of my hands comes down, and I rub her cheek with my index finger toward her lips. "The memories, they aren't going away."

"Well, you need to create new ones to erase the old ones." She tries to keep her voice level and pretend she isn't affected by me, but I can see her eyes, and they've turned a light green on the bottom.

"Nah." I lean forward and rub my nose with hers. I'm so close I could just lean in and taste her lips, but the next time I kiss her, she'll be the one begging me for it. "I don't think I can ever get the memory of your pussy out of my head." I can see her holding her breath while my heart hammers in my chest. I look into her eyes so she can see that I remember. "I definitely remember what you taste like."

NINE

FRANCES

"I DON'T THINK I can ever get the memory of your pussy out of my head." I hold my breath, trying to get the hammering in my heart to slow before he sees it coming out of my chest. He looks me in the eye, and I can see that same look he had that night. "I definitely remember what you taste like." All the words come to my head, except nothing comes out of my mouth. Not a single sound escapes me. "I remember what you taste like." He rubs his nose on mine again, and I want to arch my back and lunge for his lips. "I remember that noise you make right before you come." His words hypnotize me. "What I wouldn't do to make you come right now." My hand itches to come up and hold his hips and pull them to me while I hike my leg over his hip.

I'm about to say something to him when the walkie-talkie goes off, and we hear static. "We can't find Wilson," Catherine says, and I just look at him.

"Seems there is a search party looking for you," I say, grabbing the walkie-talkie from my back pocket.

"I have him," I confirm. "He was a runner, but I caught him. He's in the little boys' room." I smirk at that comment. "I'll bring him right over." I clip the walkie-talkie back on my pocket.

"I've never seen you as a liar," he says, stepping away from me, and I want him to come back to me.

"Excuse me?" I ask him, confused.

"You said I was in the little boys' room." He starts to joke. "We both know it's not little. I believe …" He tilts his head to the side and puts his finger on his chin, looking up. "Someone said it's the biggest they ever had."

I roll my eyes. "I was just trying not to make you feel bad." I'm lying, bald-face lying straight to him. He was the biggest I've ever had, but no one but me needed to know this.

"You're lying." He points at me. "I can tell from your eyes. When you try to lie, one eye is a bit darker than the other." I try not to show how shocked I am that he noticed that. The only ones who know this are my mother and sister.

"Whatever," I mumble like a child because there is nothing else I can say.

"I'm so full." He throws my words at me again. "I'm going to feel you for days."

"I was drunk." I try to pass it off as me being drunk, trying not to let him see he's getting to me. "And delusional."

He claps his hands together, and his whole body shakes with his laughter. "Good one." He points at me, and I grab the door handle to open the door. I hold the handle, looking back at him.

"We need to get you on the set." I ignore the way he stands there with his hands in his pockets. His pants fit him perfectly, no doubt custom-made. The white dress shirt he is wearing, the first two buttons are undone, and his sleeves are rolled up so you can see his forearms. The same forearm I held when he finger-fucked me in the shower. I shake my head to get the memories to go away.

"Yes, let's get me to set," he says, his voice smooth as he walks to the open door. "However." He stops in front of me. "This conversation isn't done."

I cock my hip now. "What do you want to do? Sit down and go over it play-by-play?" I ask.

"It's better if it's a reenactment," he says and walks out of the room. This time, I'm the one left with my mouth hanging open. He looks back now. "You coming?" he says, and my eyes go big. "To the set, I mean."

I walk out of the room toward the set. The two cameras face the stage with two chairs on it and a table between with a bottle of water on each end for them. "Bill," I say to the host we hired for the show. He has been a sports reporter for the past twenty years, so he knows the drill. He was my first pick, and he jumped at the chance to do this when I called him. "Brad Wilson," I say. "Mr. Wilson, this is Bill …"

"Hynes," Wilson says, holding his hand out to Bill. "How're you doing?" He smiles at him. "It's been a while."

"I was in retirement when this one called me up." He points at me with his thumb. "Was about to say no, but then she told me about the show, and I couldn't wait." He smiles, putting his hands in his pockets. "Glad to see you on the list."

Wilson laughs at him. "Glad to be on the list."

"Okay." I look at both of them. "This is how it's going to work. Bill will go through a series of questions. Don't jump to answer them if you aren't sure," I tell him. "We can always edit it down, so there is no rush. Take all the time you need."

"I always take my time," he says, and I ignore the pull to look back at him.

"Good to know," I say. "If at any time you need a break or you just want to stretch your legs, just say the word."

"So you're the one in charge, then?" he asks, and I turn to look at him.

"This is my show," I finally say. "I'm the producer, so yes, I'm in charge." He just nods at me. "I'll be sitting right there." I point at the chair behind one of the cameras. "I'll have a headset on, so if you need anything, you just let me know."

"I will," he says, and I look over at Catherine, who comes in and starts putting his mic on.

"How do you think this one is going to go?" Dominic, my director, asks me.

"I mean, it's a toss-up," I say, putting on my headset. "He had a list of do's and don'ts, and we all know Bill gives zero fucks about any lists." I shrug. It was another reason I wanted Bill. He's been in the business for so long, he doesn't care if people blacklist him and never work with him again. He had his own segment during Saturday night hockey in Canada, and they fired him not once but twice. From what he said, he's never going back again, so this got him a chance to get out there and do what he loves best.

"Stand by," David says from the middle of the room. I see Bill in his chair and Wilson in the chair next to him. He's adjusting his shirt, and I take him in. His hair is longer than it was when we were together. His eyes are a light blue, and his lips are full, his scruff a touch longer than at the wedding. "And take one."

Bill looks into the camera. "Thank you all for joining us for the *Bad Boys of Hockey*," he says, and I look over at Wilson, who just rolls his eyes. "My next bad boy, Brad Wilson, plays for the Dallas Oilers. You must hate that nickname."

"I'm not a fan," Wilson says, and the crew chuckles, but I'm too busy watching him. His eyes are a darker color, and I can tell this is his guarded look. When he looks at me, or the couple of times that he did look at me, his eyes danced with lightness.

"What bothers you about the title?" Bill asks.

"Everything," he says. "What defines a bad boy?" He turns it around on Bill, waiting for the answer. "Is it the guy who gets too many penalty minutes?" he asks, and I sit back in my chair. "Is it the guy who is the team enforcer?" He looks at Bill now. "Or is it when the media gives him that name that he's automatically pushed into the category?"

"I think it's a mix of all those things," Bill says. "What age did you start playing hockey?"

I can tell right away he's uncomfortable because his hands in his lap turn white when he wrings them together. "I started playing when I was seven or eight." He doesn't give any more than that.

"You were drafted by Dallas." Bill smiles. "A while ago."

"You saying I'm old, Bill?" Wilson laughs with him. "I'm not that old."

"Out of all your seasons, which one do you think landed you in the bad-boy category?" Bill asks, looking at Wilson. "Or at least when the media started calling you the bad boy?"

"Probably about four seasons ago," he says, trying to remember. "Or maybe even before that." He shrugs. "I got suspended for twenty games." He looks at him, and his tone is very monotone.

"You fought them." Bill looks down at his notes. "It got brought down to …"

"Fourteen games." Wilson fills him in. "It took a third party to come in and bring it down."

"What memory stands out to you?" I watch the screen as Wilson smirks.

"It had to be game four of the playoffs. I think it was three years ago against Toronto," he says, and you can see his eyes getting lighter. "I scored two goals in that game, and in the third period, I dived across the crease to stop a goal from going in when our goaltender got tied up."

"I remember that," Bill says. "That was a great day. It still plays on some of the spotlights."

"It's a little less of a story when we lost game seven in the next round," Wilson says.

"Your first game in the NHL," Bill starts. "What were your thoughts?"

"One," he says, laughing. "I got carried off the ice when I lost a blade on my skate." Even I laugh now. "Can you imagine my first game? I'm pumped that I'm actually playing, and then I fall flat on my face when my blade falls out. I'm sure someone was up in the press box saying who the fuck." His eyes go big now. "Sorry."

"It's fine. She'll edit it out," Bill confirms.

"I'm sure someone was in the box wondering how I even got on the roster," he says.

"If you could change the way the media spins the bad-boy name," Bill says, and I watch Wilson remain guarded, "what would you want them to do?"

"Well, one, why does anyone have to be a bad boy?" he asks. "In one game, I scored a hat trick, and then the other team tries to rough me up. I drop the gloves and knock him out, and all of a sudden, I'm the bad boy."

"I mean, I think you broke his jaw," Bill counters.

"So, if he would have broken my jaw?" Wilson leans back. "That would have been better?"

"Touche," Bill says.

"Every single time I've hit, it's been me hitting back," he says, and I just listen to him. "Okay, maybe not all, but most of them. They come on the ice trying to intimidate me, and then when I fight back, I'm the brute. I'm not defending myself. What I'm saying is that this bad-boy title was given to me by the media. They don't look that I had forty-seven goals and twelve assists and that I had a plus eleven on the ice. No, what they harp on is that I got into three fights." He shakes his head. "It's bullshit, really. Because then the press watches my every move. Every time I'm on the ice and shit goes down, they yell that I wasn't punished enough."

"What does your family think of this?" Bill says, and I sit up when I see Wilson's face go tight. "Surely, your mother and father …" It's then I see that his eyes are totally guarded. I can see his hands get tight and white. "They don't like the title you were given."

He looks in the camera, a smirk on his face. "And this is going to be another reason I get the name bad boy." He stands up and unclips the microphone. "You had a list of topics to avoid, Bill." He shakes his head. "Have a great day."

TEN

WILSON

"**W**HAT DOES YOUR family think of this?" Bill asks, and the minute he mentions my family for the second time, my whole body goes tight. I knew the minute I saw who was interviewing me that my off-limits were not going to be off-limits. He has a reputation for giving zero fucks about crossing any line. "Surely, your mother and father …" I rub my leg, squeezing so hard that my fingers are turning white. "They don't like the title you were given."

I look straight into the camera that the guy said would be pointed directly to me. A smirk fills my face, my heart pounding so hard in my chest, and the anger radiates through me. "And this is going to be another reason I get the name bad boy." I stand, trying not to show that my hands are shaking from the anger I feel. Unclipping the microphone from my shirt and then grabbing the box that they put in my back pocket. I place both on the table between us "You had a list of topics to avoid, Bill." I shake my head. "Have a great day."

I step down, and I can hear her heels clicking on the floor. "Hold on a second." She walks around the cameras, coming to stand in front of me. I look over and see that Bill hasn't moved from his chair as he sits there with a cocky smile on his face. His foot rests on his knee and his hands are crossed together, letting me know that it's Bill one, Wilson zero.

"Nope," I say, looking around for Richard, who is nowhere to be found. I get even angrier when I can't find him. He's a sorry excuse for an agent who gets ten percent for doing fucking nothing. He can't even be where he is supposed to be.

"Wilson." I hear her call my name, and I turn and look at her. "Why don't we take a fifteen-minute break?" she says, looking around. "Fifteen-minute break!" she shouts to everyone, and slowly, everyone walks away, including Bill, who just tosses the blue card with his notes on them on the chair he was sitting on. "Can I speak to you in private?"

I should just tell her to fuck off and storm away, but something in me stops me. "I don't think there is anything for us to say."

"Right this way." She ignores what I just said now and turns around, walking away from me. My feet move while my head screams out to continue walking out the door to my car. She walks into the closest office, and I follow her inside. It's almost a copy of the office I dragged her into not too long ago, but this time, the mood is completely different. I take one step in, and I don't bother closing the door behind me because I'll be leaving in a matter of minutes. "I think we just need to take a minute to calm down and regroup."

"A minute to calm down?" I say, laughing bitterly. "I need a minute to get the fuck out of here."

"I know you must be upset."

"Don't even pretend to know how I feel right now," I hiss.

She stays in the same tone as before, ignoring the fact I just hissed at her. "And if you have certain topics that you want to steer clear of, he should have respected your decision."

"One fucking thing." I hold up my finger, not even trying to stay calm. "It's not even something he doesn't know." I point at Bill. "It's not a new rule with me," I inform her. "My family is off-limits, period." I shake my head. "Not like you would know anything about that." A tightness forms in my chest. "Not everyone has someone to hold their hands while they go through things. Not everyone has someone to help fight their battles." I can see her eyes getting darker and darker. "We all don't have the perfect family like you. I don't have someone who is going to jump to my defense like you do, princess." The words come out almost like a dagger, and I know it's triggered something inside her when I see her eyes gloss over for a split second. I regret the tone the minute I see the change in her.

"One, I'm nobody's princess," she says, her voice going tight. "Nobody's family is perfect, Wilson, least of all mine. Now, if you want, I can talk to Bill and make sure he sticks to the rules, and we continue, or you can storm out of here like a child having a tantrum because you didn't get your way." We stare at each other. "The decision is yours. If you're not on set in the next ten minutes, I'll have my answer." She storms past me, mumbling "asshole," and out of the room. How did this go from me being in the right to me feeling like a dick?

"What the hell is going on?" Richard comes into the room, looking confused.

"Where the fuck were you?" I look over at him and see that he still has his coffee in his hand.

"I went to take a phone call." He takes a sip of the coffee. "It was an emergency."

"You're fired," I say before anything else. "Consider this your termination letter."

"Whoa, whoa, whoa." Richard holds up his hands. "Where did this come from?"

"It didn't just come," I tell him. "One, you got here late, and two, you were nowhere to be found when shit went down. You were supposed to be in my corner, and when I needed you, I was sitting by myself." I shake my head. "So there will not be a third time."

I walk past him as he stands there, not able to say anything. Even if he did, I'm not interested in hearing it. I pull out my phone, calling Nico, who answers after two rings. "Hello."

"Hey, it's Wilson," I say, looking around to make sure no one is around to hear this conversation. "Just giving you a heads-up."

Nico groans. "Why is it when you say that, my balls shrivel up? Nothing good comes from that sentence."

I try not to laugh. "I just fired Richard."

"Fuck," he groans. "Why?"

"We just aren't a good fit," I say, not wanting to get into the rest of the story.

"I'll talk to Becca," he says, and I look over at the set and see people getting into place. "I'll let you know what she says."

"I don't really need an agent," I reply. "No one is banging at the door bringing offers." Another thing that comes with the bad-boy title is sponsorships are few and far between.

"I'll keep you posted," he says and hangs up the phone. I can hear voices around me and walk toward it.

"You knew the deal, Bill." I hear her voice and look around the corner to see Bill and Frances in a face-off. "And you fucked it up. If he comes back to that set and you mention his family, I'll cut the segment myself." She turns and walks away, and I turn and walk back to the set.

The phone vibrates in my hand, and I look down.

Nico: Becca said don't do anything stupid. She'll call you tomorrow.

I walk toward the set, stepping around the cameras. Stepping up to the chairs, I pick up the mic and attach it back on as best I can. She walks back on set, avoiding my eyes. "Looks like we are back on." She claps her hands. "Let's go, people, and get this over with." She turns and walks past the camera guy and into the darkness. Bill comes out with his hands in his pockets.

"Well, I didn't think you'd stick around." He smirks, grabbing the papers that were in his chair.

"Yeah, well, I'm not doing it for your sorry ass." I sit down and look in the camera, hoping she heard that last part.

"Good to know," he says.

"You think you can do your job and not fuck up?" I ask, leaning back in the chair.

"It's funny." He chuckles. "I had that question down to ask you." I shake my head as the man comes out and calls the show, and Bill starts with his questions again.

This time, he sticks to the script, and after an hour, we are done. I get up, taking off the mic for the second time. Catherine comes over and takes the mic pack from me. "Thank you," I say to her, looking to see if Franny is around. I see her talking to one of the guys, and she laughs, and the burning in my stomach starts to come back. I take a step down, irritated and not even knowing why.

The guy spots me walking toward them. "Great segment," he says, and I ignore him, turning to her.

"Did you get everything you needed?" I ask when I walk next to her, and she finally turns to me, the smile on her face disappearing. My voice comes out harder than I wanted it to come out.

"We sure did," she says, being professional. "I'll let Richard know when it's going to air." I don't bother to tell her that I fired him. "And I'll be sending it to you a week before in case you want to change anything."

I nod at her. "Thank you." I turn, walking away from

her, ignoring the need to turn and get one last look at her. After today, I doubt she'll even acknowledge me when we do cross paths. The sun hits my face as soon as I walk out the door, and the way it clicks behind me lets me know it's over.

I get in my Land Rover and let out a deep breath as I head back to my house. Walking in, I head straight for the bedroom and fall on the bed. Closing my eyes, all I can see is her face when I called her a princess. "You fucked up big-time." I turn my head to look out the window at the sun shining high in the sky without a cloud in sight. The whole day, I feel like an asshole, which irritates me even more, and when I walk into the rink on Monday morning, I'm snapping at everyone who talks to me.

After the third time of snapping at someone, everyone gets the memo. I push harder than ever in practice. I know exactly why I'm cranky, but I don't want to admit it, not even to myself. Walking out of practice, I call Richard, who answers after one ring.

"Did you calm down?"

"I want all correspondence that you had between yourself and Frances," I tell him.

"I'll send it right over." I hear him clicking away on his computer.

"Good." I get into the Land Rover. "By the way," I say when I get the notification that the email came through, "you're still fired." I press the red disconnect button and pull up the email.

I scroll to the bottom where her information is—her name and her cell number. I click the number, and it pulls up a text message. I think of things to say, but only one thing comes to mind, and my fingers move before I can take it back.

Me: Sorry I was a dick.

ELEVEN

Frances

My phone beeps, and I look down. The number's foreign, so I have no idea who sent it.

945-227-9648: Sorry I was a dick.

I look down, laughing as I read the text over and over again. "Who the hell?" I do a quick search in my emails for that number, but nothing comes up. "Must be a wrong number." I place the phone down and look back at the monitor.

Now that filming was completed yesterday, I get to have fun with it. And by fun, I mean I get to edit it and then go through hours and hours of old plays to incorporate into the segment. I get to watch old fights that got him his name as a bad boy. I wish I could say I didn't have anything to work with, but there is something about Wilson that the camera just eats up. When he called me a princess yesterday, it was as if my body turned to ice. I hate when anyone thinks I have it easier than they do. I hate when anyone assumes things that aren't true. I hate it all.

He looked at me, and I saw the pain in his eyes, the turmoil he was going through by talking about his family. I don't know the story, and at this point, I don't care. It's done and gone. I made sure he never saw me sweat, and I stayed professional instead of blowing up and telling him to go fuck himself. I made sure he didn't get under my skin, but the truth was, it was all I thought about last night. So much so that I went down the rabbit hole and googled him. I found a picture from when he was drafted with a woman who looked nothing like him, but I assumed it must have been his mother. But there was no information there, and after an hour, I felt like I was invading his privacy, so I shut it down.

Grabbing my cup of coffee, I bring it to my lips at the same time as my phone goes off again. Turning it over, I see it's an email from Becca with the subject line of Wilson. I open the email and read through it. Wilson is no longer being represented by Richard but Becca, and all communication has to go through Becca. "Interesting." I set my phone down. Until this is finished, there is no reason to talk or think about him.

I block him out of my head for the next week and throw myself into my work. We are almost done with the finishing touches on the first show that will air next weekend. My stomach is in knots thinking about it. I spend fourteen hours at the office, coming home with just enough energy to shower and crash. I walk into the office wearing my black pants and a short-sleeved black silk top that I paired with white Alexander McQueen sneakers. "Is it dress-down day?" Earl asks me when he steps into the staff kitchen.

I look over at him. He's wearing his regular dress pants and button-down with loafers with tassels. "Are you trying to insinuate that I can't wear flat shoes because I'm a woman?" I pour a cup of coffee and turn to look at him. "That's pretty sexist, don't you think?" He puts his hands in his pockets, and his face gets all red.

"I should check the employee handbook." I try to hide the smile from my face with my mug. "To see if footwear is in there." I turn and walk out of the room but stop. "I'll also definitely make sure I ask HR about it. Wouldn't want to violate any rules." I smile at him as he glares. I turn around now. "Asshole," I mutter under my breath.

"Ava," I say my assistant's name. "Do we have an employee handbook?" Her eyes pinch together, and she leans back in her chair and folds her hands together on her chest. "Earl just asked me if it was dress-down day since I'm wearing sneakers."

She leans over, looking at my shoes. "Those shoes cost seven hundred dollars." She gasps, and I laugh. "I'll check and see what it says in the handbook."

"Thank you kindly." I walk back into my office and sit down at the desk. I'm editing some of the stuff for the show coming up when I hear a soft knock on my door.

My eyes look up, and my heart speeds up. "Hi," Wilson says, stepping into my office. "Can I come in?"

I shake my head to try to snap the fuck out of it. "Yeah," I say, getting up and looking out toward Ava's desk and seeing it empty. "Come in." I step around my desk, looking at him. He's wearing track pants and a sweater with the team logo on it, and as soon as I get a touch closer, I can smell his musky aftershave.

My core goes tight, and my stomach flutters when he smirks. "You're a hard woman to get in touch with."

"Is that so?" I ask, not sure what he's talking about.

"I went to the studio first," he says. "But no one was there."

"We only use the studio on taping days," I tell him, and he nods. If I didn't know any better, I would think he was nervous.

He looks around the office, the walls still bare, but I did add in a picture of me with my nieces and nephew. "I texted you," he finally says, and I look at him shocked.

"You texted me?" I ask, pointing at my chest, my hands getting clammy.

"I did," he confirms, his blue eyes just staring into mine, making my chest tight. "Sorry for being a dick."

I laugh and shake my head. "That was you?" I grab my phone and pull it up. "I didn't recognize the number."

"How many people would have sent you that?" He chuckles, asking me the question.

"Well, I have lots of male relatives," I tell him. "So it could have been a whole slew of people."

"But you didn't even text me back?" he says, folding his arms over his chest. I see that the ends of his hair are wet, and I wonder if he came here right after practice.

"I figured if the guy was really a dick and wanted me to accept his apology, he would have texted me back." I shrug. "Or it was a wrong number."

He takes a step toward me and stops right in front of me, and I have a hard time swallowing. "I like the way you smell." His hand comes up, and he grabs a piece of my hair and twirls it around his finger. "Like heaven."

I swallow, or at least I try to, but my whole body is on alert when he stands close to me. It's as if it knows what he can do to me. My head is trying to forget, but my body, my body is screaming out for him. "Good to know." That's all I can come up with, and even when I say the words, I'm surprised I'm not panting.

"Have dinner with me." His voice comes out low, and his eyes go from my lips to my eyes. "So I can make it up to you for being a dick."

My mouth goes as dry as the desert in the middle of the day. "I normally work late," I say honestly, and his hand drops from my hair.

"You have to eat dinner," he reminds me. I have to take a step away from him so my brain can get with the program.

"I usually eat at my desk while I edit," I inform him. "The show launches next week, and I really, really have to make sure that it's the best."

He nods his head. "That's fine," he says, and I have the need to go to him and wrap my arms around his waist. Which is weird because the only thing I ever wrapped around his waist was my legs when he carried me naked to the bed where he fucked me like a rag doll. My pussy clenches as I remember it for just a second.

"Condom," I panted out when he laid me on the bed

and reached down to finger me. "Now."

He turned to walk out of the room, and I watched his ass as he walked away. My hand went to my clit, and I played with myself as I watched him grab a condom out of his pocket. He walked back with the swagger that you just knew he had a big dick, and after sucking it and stroking it, I could confirm he could use the swagger. He crawled onto the bed, and my eyes were mesmerized as I watched him roll the condom on his cock. My hand goes from my clit into my pussy as it pulsed, knowing that in a couple of seconds, he'd be fucking me, and I could tell he was going to fuck me better than I ever imagined. "Spread." He stroked his cock, and I was jealous. He stopped stroking slapped my clit with it. "Your pussy," he mumbled and leaned down to suck my clit into his mouth. "Prettiest fucking pussy I've ever seen."

"Well, this pretty pussy needs a good fucking," I said, and his eyes turned so dark they looked like a sapphire.

"I'm going to." He didn't even wait to say more. Instead, he just slammed into me, and my eyes rolled to the back of my head.

"Um, hello?" I hear his voice, and I look over at him. "You okay?"

"Yeah, yeah, I'm fine." I can feel my cheeks turning pink

"Well, whatever you were thinking about made you smile," he says, and my eyes fly to his, wondering if he knows what I was thinking about. I also wonder if he thinks about that night. Does he remember the whole night or just bits and pieces? "So, dinner?"

I smile sadly. "I'm sorry, I just don't have the time." My heart thumps in my chest so hard it echoes in my ear.

He nods. "Well, then, I'll let you get back to your work." He walks out, stopping to look back. "Take care, Franny," he says, using the name I told him that only my close friends and family use.

I watch him walk toward the elevators, and only when he turns the corner and I can't see him anymore do I sit in the chair closest to me. "What the fuck was that?" I ask myself. Looking back, I suddenly hope that he won't take no for an answer. But it doesn't happen. The only thing that happens is I spend too long in that chair, and when I get back to my desk, the only thing I can think of is him. "Motherfucker," I mumble. "He called you a princess," I argue with myself. "And he's an asshole with a huge chip on his shoulder." I look at the computer screen, my head spinning. "Who cares? All you want is to fuck him again anyway," my head screams back. "The least he could do is give you a couple of orgasms, and then you can move on."

I'm about to counter my visible argument when I get a text, and my heart speeds up, thinking it's him. But one look, and I see it's from the WHO RUNS THE WORLD GIRLS chat I have with Vivi, Alex, Julia, Erika, and Jillian.

Alex: I'm in town next week, bitches. Wine night tomorrow at Franny's place. Who's in??
Julia: Me.
Jillian: I'm pregnant. I'll chaperone.
Vivi: I'll fly in with you, Alex.

Erika: Cooper just groaned reading this, so I'm in. I need a sitter.

Me: It's BYOB …

Jillian: Shit, can BYOB stand for bring your own baby? The guys are on a road trip.

Alex: Ask my parents to babysit.

Jillian: Oh, good idea.

"This is exactly what you need," I tell myself. "A drunken girls' night."

TWELVE

WILSON

MY PHONE RINGS the minute I step out of the shower, and I grab it. My heart slows down when I see it's just my mother. I don't know why I thought it would be her. It's been a week since I've seen her and asked her to dinner, which she turned down. I've never been turned down before. So, it was a kick in the nuts and also fucked with my ego, more than I will ever admit.

"Hello," I say, putting the phone to my ear.

"There he is, my son," she says, and my stomach burns. "My only son."

I wrap the towel around my waist and look at the bruise on my hip. We are in the middle of our road trip, and the games have not been easy in the least. Hence the bruise on my hip I got when I got speared in the side last night against Boston. I swear it took a minute for me to catch my breath, and once I did catch my breath, my gloves came off, and I knocked the guy on his ass. It did not end well, especially when they scored on the power play. "What do you need?" I say, not interested in this whole song and dance.

"Can't a mother just call her son?" she says, and I roll my eyes.

"She can." I walk out of the room, heading for my travel bag. Today was a travel day, so there was no skating, and tomorrow we play Pittsburgh and then Philly before heading back home. "But you aren't that kind of mother." She gasps out in shock, and I just shake my head. "You can cut the dramatics, Mom. I'm not in the mood."

"You are in some type of mood," she says. "A bad mood."

"Mother, I'm going to hang up unless you tell me what you want." I slip on my shorts when I hear a knock on the door.

"Fine," she hisses. "I was wondering if I can borrow some money from you." I open the door and grab the paper bag that is left there. I opted to eat in tonight instead of going out with the guys. "A couple of the ladies are going away for Christmas," she says as I walk back into the room and place the bag on the table. "And I wanted to join them, but I'm short."

"How much are you short?" I grab the black takeout container and sit in the chair.

"About seven thousand," she says, and I just shake my head. "It's a Mediterranean cruise leaving out of Greece. We are going to spend a couple of days in Santorini, and then it's two weeks on the cruise and then another couple of days in Greece before we fly back."

"How much is this vacation costing?"

"Seven thousand one hundred and eighty-five dollars," she says.

I laugh. "Basically, you need me to pay for you to go on vacation?" I point out as I take out the second black takeout container.

"I said I would pay you back," she snaps.

"How?" I ask, opening one of the containers to see it's a salad.

"I gave up everything for you." She starts sighing.

"Here we go," I say. "Glad you did it for love. Send me the trip details, and I'll send over the payment to the travel agent."

"You could just send it to me," she says, and I answer right away.

"Last time I did that, I paid for the trip twice," I remind her in case her memory isn't that good.

"Fine," she huffs out. "It can be my Christmas gift." I laugh even louder.

"So you aren't paying me back," I confirm with her. "Whatever, Mom, I have to go. Send me the agent details."

I put the phone down and disconnect before I grab the plastic fork and knife, then open the second container with my grilled salmon and steamed veggies. The phone rings again, and I answer it, expecting it to be my mother, and groan when I hear my ex Tiffany's voice. "You answered." What the fuck is going on today? Is today fuck-with-Wilson day? The two people I don't want to talk to are calling me, and the one person I would actually like to talk to isn't giving me the time of day.

"By mistake," I say, taking a bite of the salmon. "I thought I blocked you."

"Why are you being like this?" she sighs. "I don't understand."

"Well, if I'm so terrible, why the fuck are you calling me?" I ask her as I grab a piece of broccoli.

"We can start over," she says, and I laugh.

"I like my women like I like my coffee," I say. "Without a dick in it. Hence, why we can't start over."

"How was I supposed to know we were exclusive?" She sighs now, and I have to wonder what the fuck I found so great about her. She was hot on the outside and cold on the inside.

"You left me at the table to go fuck the waiter in the closet," I tell her. "While at a work function that I was attending for you." I close my eyes and laugh. "After I caught you with your coworker the day before. It was a lot of work for a three-day relationship."

"That was an accident," she huffs. "You said you forgave me."

"It was an accident to answer this call." I take another bite of the salmon.

"What about when you went off with my best friend?" She tries to bait me.

"You mean to change her fucking tire?" My voice goes loud. "Listen, Tiffany, I don't want to be an asshole," I start. "I mean, I'm an asshole, and it's a given, but I don't want to be a bigger asshole. Whatever this is or was, it's run its course."

"What if we are just friends who fuck?" she says, and I swear to God if my dick could run and duck for cover, it would.

"No, never going to happen. I have to go," I say and hang up, and this time, I do block her number.

The following morning, I get on the bus and sit down next to Cooper, who just side-eyes me. "You look like you're in a fantastic mood," he huffs.

"I fucking hate traveling," I say. "The beds suck so bad."

"So bad," he says now. "Two more games, and we go home."

"Four days," I correct. "Four fucking days."

"You think you're going to stay out of the box?" he asks, and I roll my eyes, putting my head back.

"You think you're going to be able to score a goal anytime soon?" I look over at him, and he glares. "What is it, four games with no points?" I put my hand on my stomach as the bus moves. "I may have fucked up the last game, but at least I got two points on the board."

"I bet you a hundred bucks I score a goal at the next game, and your ass will still end up in the box." He looks at me, and the bus stops.

"Deal," I say, getting up. "Now hopefully that will light a fire under your ass," I say, getting off the bus. Practice is a shitshow, and all of us are dragging our asses. When we get to the arena for the game, we suit up.

Getting on the ice, I know after the first shift that we have lost our steam. I know I've lost the steam, and the hits keep coming. I'm going to pass the puck, and my stick completely misses the puck twice. When I get back on the bench, no one has to tell me how much it sucked because I break the stick on my knee and pitch it in the back. "Relax," Martin hisses at me. "Don't go off the rails."

The equipment manager hands me another stick, and this time, when I get on the ice, I'm going to pass it to Cooper, but I'm cross-checked in the back. I fall to my knees in the front and then turn to pounce. I'm not the only one pouncing. Cooper is right there with me. I land a couple of punches at the guy's helmet, and my knuckles ache as fuck. Cooper drags another guy to the ice, and it takes three referees to pry them apart.

We both end up in the box, and I look over at him, then I look down at the knuckles that are bloody and look a little purple. "You had to try to be a tough guy."

"Fuck you," he says, looking ahead, taking off his helmet, and grabbing the water bottle that is there.

"You still haven't won the hundred bucks," I tell him, and all he does is laugh. We both look up at the Jumbotron as they do a replay

"You're such a pain in the ass," he says, laughing now, grabbing a towel and wiping his head. The rest of the game is cutthroat, and I end up in the box twice more, but we win the game in overtime. Cooper scores with three seconds left to go before shootouts.

"Someone owes me a hundred bucks," he says when he comes back into the room, and I toss my jersey in the bin in the middle of the room. "Pay up." He stops in front of me. I shake my head, grabbing my wallet and taking out five twenties to hand to him. "Wow, you actually carry money on you."

I just look at him. "Who doesn't carry money with them?"

"I have a wife and three kids. My wallet is their petty cash drawer," Cooper says, going to sit down.

"I can't remember the last time I actually carried cash," Michael adds in. "Actually, it was two weeks ago, and then Franny took it from me to buy a hot dog." He turns to Cooper. "You should pay your sister's debts."

He laughs at him, flipping him the bird, and I try not to listen to their conversation, but the minute they mentioned her name, my whole body woke up. "If she knew you wanted someone to pay her debt, she would kick you in the balls," Cooper tells him. "She doesn't want anything from anyone. I tried to pay her lunch last week, and she told the waitress that my card was fake and that the IRS was after me." I turn away chuckling and it just makes me even more curious about her. I know what she tastes like, I know what she feels like, I know that her pussy is tight as a vise, and she gives just as good as she gets. I know that when push comes to shove, she would fight me at every single turn. I know all of this, yet I also know that she hasn't heard the last of me.

THIRTEEN

FRANCES

I CLOSE MY front door behind me with my foot. Why is it that we always carry all the bags into the house at one time, instead of making two trips? I do this every single time. I run to the kitchen and dump the bags on the counter with red marks all over my wrist and my fingers. "Why didn't you make two trips?" my sister, Vivi, asks, coming into the kitchen. She got here last night with Alex, and we spent most of the day working side by side until I remembered the wine party that I was having and ran out to grab stuff at the grocery store.

"I literally called you and said come outside and help me," I huff at her, unpacking one of the bags.

"I said I was coming." She outstretches her hands. "And here I am."

"Fine, then you can unpack the bags, and I'll go take a shower." I grab a bottle of water and walk toward the stairs. My phone rings in my back pocket. I take it out and see it's my father. My heart speeds up, and I get suddenly nervous. "Hello," I say softly. He hasn't really spoken to me since he left. He did answer the text message that I sent him asking him about a recipe, but our relationship is stuck at a standstill.

"Hey there," he says, and I can tell from his voice he isn't sure what to say. "How are you?"

"I'm good," I reply, walking to my bedroom. "What about you?" I sit on my bed and look down at the water bottle, turning it in my hand.

"Good, good." He stops talking, and I literally hate this whole thing. "I got your email."

"Oh, good," I say, smiling now. "Did you get a chance to watch it?" As soon as I was done with the segment, I sent it to my father. It was something that I wasn't sure of, but I did it without even thinking twice or else I wouldn't have sent it.

"I did." He takes a deep breath. "It was really good," he says, and I can't help but smile. "You did good, Fran." I wipe away the tear that rolls down my cheek. "Knew that you would." I can't help but smile through the tears. I can't tell you how many hours I spent on that segment but what I can tell you is that at the end all I wanted was for my dad to see it.

"Thank you," I say softly. "That means a lot." I try not to sniffle or make him know that I'm crying.

"Seeing the old clips," he says and I can hear a smile in his voice. "It was strange."

"You didn't think I would do a segment on Uncle Max and not have you in there. I mean M&M for life, right?" I say softly, and his laughter makes me smile. "I miss you, Dad." I wipe the tear away.

"I miss you, too, Fran, and I'm sorry. I shouldn't have said what I said, and I should have supported you."

"Yeah, you should have," I agree. "And I'm sorry, too. For not talking to you about it."

"That's what hurt the most." His voice is almost in a whisper. "The fact that you made a life-changing decision without even talking to me hurt."

"I had to do it on my own," I tell him. "If only so I can know that I can do it."

"That's what you have family for," he reminds me. "You never have to do anything alone."

"Well, I promise that the next time, I'll talk to you first." I smile.

"And I promise you that the next time, I'm not going to be a … what was it that your mother called me this morning?" He laughs. "A buffoon." I can't help but laugh also knowing that my mother probably called him more than that.

"I don't think you were a buffoon, more like a donkey." We both laugh now. "So now that you're talking to me again," I start, "want to be a part of my show?"

"I'd love nothing more. We are coming down next weekend." I smile. "Set it up."

"Okay," I say with a weight lifted off my shoulders. "Done."

He hangs up, and I put the phone down. I don't know if things will go back to normal. But it's a step in the right direction. "I thought you were in the shower?" Vivienne says, coming in with a wineglass in each hand. "Why are you crying?"

"Dad called," I say, wiping the tears away. "It was nice talking to him."

She sits on the bed next to me now, handing me a wineglass. "Mom is going to kill him any day if he doesn't stop acting like a disgruntled child."

"She called him a buffoon," I inform her, and we both laugh, and I take a sip of wine.

"Grandpa called him worse on Sunday," she tells me, and I get up.

"Well, he's going to be on the show so." I shrug and smile. "Maybe this is a new beginning," I say hopefully, going to the shower.

After putting on my yoga pants and a big loose white sweater, I head downstairs with my empty glass of wine. I can hear laughing already, and when I walk into the kitchen, everyone is there. "There she is," Alex says, and I look at her outfit, tight jeans and a tank top with her red-bottom shoes. Looking around, I see all the other women are dressed like me.

"Why are you all dressed up?" I ask.

"Ugh," she groans out. "One, what if the house catches on fire and a hot fireman comes to save me?" We all laugh at her. "And two, what if I get into an accident driving home and the cop who stops me is hot?"

"Stop watching *Chicago Fire* and *Chicago PD*," Julia says, grabbing a chip from the bowl in front of her.

"Let's get the snacks set up in the living room so we can watch the game," Erika says, grabbing two bowls and walking toward my living room.

"Why are we watching the game?" Alex groans.

"I haven't seen my husband in a week," Erika complains. "This is the only way."

"I'll bring the wine," I say, looking over at Jillian, who just grabbed Julia's hand so she can feel the babies kick.

Jillian looks over at me. "Come feel," she says, and I walk over and put my hand on her stomach. "They are super active tonight."

"You did eat ice cream before we got here," Julia says, and when we finally all settle into the living room, we are all sitting around on the L-shaped couch. The coffee table is full of snacks, and when the doorbell rings, Vivi gets up to get the pizza.

She comes back with the four boxes, and we all look at her. "I ordered, and I was hungry. Sue me," she says, and Alex, Julia, and I remove the snacks, putting them aside so she can put the pizzas down.

"There he is," Jillian says, pointing at the screen, and we see Michael skate onto the ice. Cooper is right behind him, and I look over at Erika, who just smiles at the television.

"You know he can't see you, right?" I say, gulping down my glass of wine and refilling it. She flips me the bird, making me laugh.

"I really hope they win tonight," Jillian says, taking a bite of her pizza and putting the plate on her belly.

"Well, if they stop acting like assholes," Erika says, and I drink another sip of wine while taking a bite of my pizza.

"There is Wilson," Erika says. My heart sinks, and I look up at my big-screen television. He skates to the ice and smirks over at the guy he's in front of. I grab my wine and drink another glass as the puck drops. Things are uneventful for the first five minutes, and then someone slashes his wrist. The referee blows his whistle, and Wilson is exchanging words with the guy.

"He acts like he has the biggest dick in the world," Julia says, and I laugh.

"He doesn't have to act," I say, and when I hear the words come out of my mouth, I want to die. It's like whiplash when all heads and eyes turn to me. "What?" I say, grabbing my wine and finishing the glass.

"How do you know how big his dick is?" Vivi asks. She's sitting on the floor with her back to the couch.

"I sort of banged him." I act as if it's nothing, finishing another glass. "At the wedding."

"My wedding?" Jillian gasps. "Shut up."

"You banged him at the wedding reception or after the wedding?" Erika asks with a smile on her face.

"Please say you did it at the reception," Julia says from the floor, next to the coffee table, crossing her fingers on her two hands.

"Please don't say that," Alex says.

"Relax, it was in his room at the end of the night." I watch the television, and the camera goes to him on the bench, talking to the coach behind him.

"I'm in shock," Jillian says.

"It's not that big of a deal." I try to brush it off. "It was one night."

"Wait a second," Vivi says. "Isn't he one of the guys on your segment for *Bad Boys of Hockey*?"

My whole face goes red, or at least that is what it feels like. "He is, yes." Everyone's mouth hangs open. "Relax, we kept it professional. He's a dick." I point at the screen. "Who then asked me to have dinner with him." I swear you could hear a pin drop in the room. "I said no, obviously."

"Obviously," Vivi repeats.

"Hold the phone for a second," Erika says, putting up her hand. "You banged him, and then he asked you out, and you said no."

"That is correct," I say, pouring myself another glass. "I mean, he didn't really remember our night when he saw me at the bar after the game opener." I finish my glass in two gulps, placing it back down on the table, ignoring the need to look over at the screen.

The announcer screams goal, and we look up to see that Ralph has scored a goal. "Someone turn this fucking game off," Alex says, grabbing the remote and pointing it at the screen to mute the game.

"He forgot he banged you?" Julia asks, refilling my wineglass for me.

"Sort of. Until I reminded him we banged," I say. "But then when he came to the show, he didn't know I would be there."

"This is better than *90 Day Fiancée*," Erika teases. "What did he say?"

"Well, before he was a dick, he told me he remembers

what I tasted like." I try to roll my eyes and pretend it doesn't get to me.

"And I'm dead," Julia says, gulping her wine. "How good was it?" I look at her, and all eyes are on me.

"Good," I confirm finally. "Very good."

"Best." Erika sits back on the couch and folds her arms over her chest as if she knows something I don't know.

"Best," I agree.

"Dammit," Julia says. "Why didn't I get laid at the wedding?"

"Because you were doing shots with Alex and Dylan," Jillian answers. "And then you thought you were Drake and tried to sing karaoke." I roll my lips. "At. My. Wedding."

"Hey." Alex points at Jillian. "We made that wedding fun." Alex comes to Julia's defense.

"You guys tried to make the DJ play 'WAP.'" Jillian laughs.

"So we could do our choreographed TikTok routine," Alex says, and Julia holds up her hand to high-five her.

"Are you going to date him?" Vivi ignores the other conversation, and I look at her.

"I don't date," I remind her. "I bang. Which is why I'm moving on." Just saying the words feels funny.

"Maybe I should be a dance teacher," Alex says, and we all look at her.

"Just because you do TikTok doesn't make you a dancer," Erika reminds her.

"Well, I have to figure out what I'm going to do with

my life," she says, picking a piece of pepperoni off the pizza.

"What do you like to do besides shopping?" Julia asks her.

"I don't know. That's the whole thing," she admits. "I haven't found something that I like doing."

"You like doing foundation stuff," Vivi says of The Horton Foundation that our uncle Max started.

"Do you want to come to work with me?" I look over at her. "You used to like helping me in New York."

"Do you think I could just tag along?" She looks at me, and I nod.

We all look up at the television and see that Wilson just scored. He raises a leg and cocks his arm back and then up. "I can't see him and not know that he has a big dick," Julia says.

I laugh. "Me either," I mumble. "Me either."

FOURTEEN

WILSON

I SIT ON the plane and close my eyes. "Next stop, home," Cooper says from behind me. I turn my head to look out the window.

"Did you talk to Erika today?" Michael asks him, laughing.

"She was hungover from going over to Franny's house," Cooper replies, and my ears perk up at her name. It's sort of crazy how one mention of her name, and I want to know everything.

"They were going to my parents' house today," Michael says. "I'm supposed to head over there. Alex and Vivi are still in town. They leave tomorrow."

"Alex filled up my phone with videos," Cooper says, laughing. "The last picture I got was of Erika learning some dance on the floor about a bucket and a mop."

I laugh, thinking about the dance he's talking about. The plane starts to move, and I lean back, closing my eyes, and all I can see is Franny. Except it was from that night, the night that replays over and over in my head.

"Fuck, your cock is good," she panted out as she rode me in a reverse cowgirl position. My hands held her hips as she leaned forward and held my knees. Her ass bounced every single time she sat down. Her long hair hung down her back and swayed back and forth. I sat up as she sat down on my cock, both of us moaning as I got even deeper into her. My hand went into her hair as I pulled back her head to devour her mouth. She rotated her hips as she tried to lift herself to slam back down on me. My hand went around her and pinched her nipple. Her mouth let go of mine as she moaned, "So full." Her own hands came up to cup her tits, and my hand slid to her clit, going in little circles.

I pushed her forward, and her hands flew out. My cock never left her pussy as she squeezed it. "Your ass." I slapped one ass cheek as I pulled my cock out of her and slammed it back in. "Looks good riding my cock." I felt her hand on my balls and looked down to see one hand playing with her clit. "It looks better with my mark on it, though." I slapped her again, and this time, her pussy convulsed all over my cock.

"I'm coming." Her head fell forward, and I felt her coming all over my cock. Her pussy squeezed my cock every single time. She looked over her shoulder. "Thought you would be able to fuck me harder." She smirked at me and pushed back on my cock. I placed my hands up in the air and watched her fuck me. I couldn't look away as her pussy swallowed my cock. "If you want it done right,

you have to do it yourself." She pulled herself off me. "Time for me to ride." She tilted her head to the side and pushed me back. She threw her leg over me as she held my cock in one hand and aligned it with her pussy. She sank down it, and both of us moaned.

The plane landing wakes me up, and I look around, shaking the sleep away but not the memory. I can still hear her whispering in my ear. Everyone shoots up as soon as the plane stops, eager to get home to their families.

I don't say anything to anyone as I walk over to my Land Rover and head home. Parking my truck in the garage, I get out, grabbing my bag, and making my way into the house.

The blinds are closed as I walk up the steps to my bedroom. I dump my bag in the closet, unpacking it. I change out of my suit and grab a pair of jeans with a T-shirt.

I walk back downstairs to grab something to eat. Opening the fridge, I see that the cleaning lady did the grocery shopping for the week. Nothing catches my eye, so I grab a water bottle and walk toward the family room. I turn on the television and sit down, flipping through channels, and all I can think of is Franny. I wonder if she got drunk with the girls. I wonder if she did the dance. I wonder about all of it and look at my watch to see it's just past six.

Grabbing my phone and my keys, I walk out to the garage and make my way over to the Chinese restaurant. Walking in, I spot the menu and order five chicken dishes, five beef dishes, and five shrimp dishes, egg rolls, crab rolls, four different noodles, fried rice, shrimp fried rice, and chicken fried rice. The lady at the table just looks at me with her eyes wide.

"Lots of people," she says. I don't tell her that it's just for two or maybe even one. I sit down and wait. My head tells me this is a bad idea while my heart tells me to go get her. The lady comes out with four white bags filled with stuff. "Chopsticks inside," she tells me, and I nod, walking back out to the SUV.

I drive to her office and take a deep breath before getting out of the truck with the food. My palms are sweating, and I have to wonder if it's the heat coming from the bags of food or if my nerves are taking over. There is no one in the lobby, which irritates me since anyone can get to her. I press the number for her floor, and the nerves come in tenfold. The last time I was this nervous was the time I played my first NHL game. And even then, I think I was less nervous. I don't have any time to think. When I step out of the elevator, my stomach rises up, and I literally think I'm going to barf all over the place.

Looking around, I don't see anyone, and the lights are mostly off. I walk toward where her office is, and it suddenly hits me that she could not be here. My heart speeds up and my stomach sinks and then rises, and when I step in front of her office door, everything in me settles.

She sits behind her desk with her hair piled on top of her head. Her eyes are focused on the screen behind her black-rimmed glasses. I knock on the door softly, and her eyes look up, and I can't help the smile that fills my face.

"Hi." I step in, not sure what to do, and then I stop after two steps. "I," I start, but all the words are stuck in the back of my throat. "God, I didn't think this through," I say, laughing nervously as she takes off her glasses and puts them down on her desk and pushes off to stand. I take her in when she walks around the desk. She's wearing black pants with a black and white button-down shirt tucked into them. Her sleeves are rolled up to her elbows with her Rolex and love bracelet on. She's so fucking gorgeous. "I mean, I did, but I'm not here so much." I try to calm the beating of my heart by telling myself she's just another girl, but she's not.

She laughs. "What are you doing here?" Folding her arms over her chest, she probably sizes me up and down.

"You said you couldn't have dinner with me because you work late so …" I hold up the bags in my hands and take a deep exhale. "I brought you food."

"Oh my gosh, what?" she says, and I wish I could walk up to her and bend to kiss her lips. I wish I could dump the bags on the floor and fuck her on her desk.

"I can drop the food off," I say softly. "And you can have a feast all by yourself." I look down at the bags in my hand, taking another step out of my comfort zone. "Or I can stay and maybe we can have dinner together."

She shakes her head. "What do you have in there?" She points at the bags.

"Chinese food," I say, and then my mouth just stays

open. "Fuck, do you even like Chinese food?" I look up at the ceiling and close my eyes. "I've never done this before. I should have maybe asked you."

"You've never done what before?" she asks me softly, her eyes never leaving mine.

"I've never brought food to a woman before," I tell her honestly. "Especially without knowing if I was going to be eating it or not." I look at her, and I'm already here, so I might as well lay it all out there for her. "I was sitting down thinking about you." I don't tell her that all I do is think of her. "And I remember you said that you work late, so you couldn't have dinner with me, so I figured I would …"

"Show up with a hundred pounds of food?" She laughs, and the sound is music to my ears and my cock.

"It might have played differently in my mind," I admit, looking down.

"How did it play out in your mind?" She tilts her head to the side, and I wonder if this is a good sign. I mean, she hasn't kicked me out yet, so that is good, right?

"Well, in my head, I would bring you food, and you would be so grateful that you would let me taste you again." Her eyes go dark now. "Maybe you'd taste me."

"Did you have a plan B?" She takes a step forward, and the smell of her has my cock begging to let it out.

"Plan B would be you saying I could stay and have dinner with you," I tell her. "I mean, either is good. I'm not opposed to either of them."

"Well." She steps closer to me, and I can smell her,

and it takes everything inside me not to grab her face in my hand. "Since we are at my job, and I like my job." She looks around. "And I don't know if anyone is still here. How about we go with plan B?"

I smile now. "Really?" I ask her, shocked she would have dinner with me. "Wow." I don't even hide my shock. "Okay, good. Let's have dinner."

FIFTEEN

FRANCES

HE SMILES AT me so big it lights up his eyes. "Really? Wow." His voice comes out in a high pitch. "Okay, good. Let's have dinner," he says, shocked, and he isn't the only one. I'm shocked myself. This whole scene is shocking to me. Him showing up here with dinner. Me accepting to have dinner with him. It's just got my head going in circles.

"Do you think all that food will fit on this table?" I point at the little round table I brought into the office this weekend with two chairs. In my head, I would be able to sit and have a coffee and my meals there. In reality, I eat straight from the container at my desk.

"We can make it fit," he says, and I want to tell him to relax, but seeing him all nervous about me is, well, there just aren't words for it.

He puts the bags down on the desk. "I'll go get us something to drink." I turn to walk out of the room.

"Only water for me," he says, and I laugh, turning around.

"It's an office. Did you think we'd have a stocked bar?" I shake my head.

"Some offices have happy hour," he replies, and then I just stare at him. "Or do they go out for that?" He shrugs and then laughs nervously again. "Hey, I play hockey where we only drink on the off-season."

"Or at weddings." I put in and he laughs.

"Or if you win the Stanley Cup." He points at me. "You are allowed to get shit-faced for a month if that happens."

"I know a couple of people who won the Cup." He rolls his eyes. "They only got drunk for a bit of it."

"Then they didn't do it right," he says, and I laugh full-on belly laughs. "Go get the drinks. I'll set up the buffet." He motions with his hands at the four bags. I nod, walking toward the communal kitchen, and I grab two bottles of water. I also look around and check out other offices to make sure we are alone. Not that anything we are doing is wrong, but I don't want people to think he did the show because we are together. Seeing all the lights off in all the other offices, I walk back to my office, and the smell of Chinese food hits me right away.

The whole table is filled with containers. "Oh my God," I say, walking in. "You really did order all the food."

"Well, I didn't know what you liked." He looks down at the spread on the table. "So I took five of everything in the category." He walks over to one of the chairs and holds it out. "Sit."

"Such a gentleman," I say, sitting down. "You weren't a gentleman at that last game," I say, and his eyes shine, and I want to kick myself.

"You watched the game?" he asks. His hand remains on the chair, and the warmth of his fingers through my silk shirt sends a shiver up my arm.

"My family was over, and their men are on the team, so I had no choice." I try to pretend I didn't really watch the game.

Then he leans down until his head is next to mine, and I can smell him. "I like knowing you watched me." If I turn my face right, we would be face-to-face. I turn my head at the same time as he stands up and walks over to his chair. "You know what this is missing?" he says, sitting down, looking at me. God, his eyes are mesmerizing. "Candles."

"No to the candles." I look at the food and wonder if he'll notice if I don't eat any of it. "Dig in," I tell him and he grabs the closest dish to him and also the only dish I eat. He holds the container in his hand as he grabs a pair of chopsticks.

I look around nervously for something to pick at. "Do you like Chinese food?" he says, and I roll my lips. "You don't like Chinese food."

"It's not that I don't like it," I say now. "It's just, an hour after you finish eating, you're hungry again." I shrug.

"So you don't like any of this?" He chuckles.

"I like beef and broccoli," I say, and he looks down at

the container.

"Do you want some?" he jokes with me.

"No, I want the whole thing." He laughs and just hands it over. "You're just going to give it over, just like that?"

"I'm sitting down and having dinner with you." He holds the container for me. "Which is all I want, so if I have to give up this, I will. Having dinner with you is the only thing I wanted out of tonight." I swallow down the lump that has swelled from my chest to my throat and grab the container from him. "I almost opted for pizza," he says, and I nod my head and smile. "I'll know for next time."

"Oh, you think there is going to be a next time?" I grab a set of chopsticks and take a piece of broccoli. "That's cocky of you."

"One can hope," he says, grabbing the sweet and sour chicken. "So now that I know you prefer pizza over Chinese, tell me something else." I just look at him, not sure what else to tell him. He looks up as if he just discovered the best thing in the world. "We should do twenty-one questions."

I laugh at him. "Is that what we should do?" I tell him, instead of asking what I want to ask, which is when was the last time you had sex. Not that it matters, but has he had sex after me?

"We should." He nods, taking a piece of pineapple. "Favorite color."

"Pink," I say and look at him. "You?"

"I don't really have one, but I guess I like green." I

shrug.

"Interesting. I would have gone with blue," I reply. "If you could only eat one meal for the rest of your life, what would it be?"

"Easy, pasta," he says. "Hands down, you can have pasta every single day."

"Do you cook?" I ask him, and he nods his head. "What is the best thing you know how to cook?"

"It's not your turn." He points his chopsticks at me, and I roll my eyes at him. "It's your turn to answer what you would eat."

"Pizza," I say now. "It has everything. Carbs, sauce, meat, and cheese. It's a win-win for everyone."

"Favorite vacation spot?" he asks, and I put the container down.

"The beach," I say, "with crystal blue water. You?" I look at him.

"I like the beach as long as I'm not interrupted." He puts his container down and picks up another one. "But I also love just getting away from it all. Renting an RV and stopping when I want. Not talking to anyone."

"Have you actually ever done that?" I ask, and he laughs.

"No, but it's something that I want to do. I think I'm going to do it at the end of this season," he says, and I want to ask who he is going to do it with.

"They rent RVs," I tell him. "There is this place in California where you can stay in an RV, and all you see is the sand."

"Really?" he asks, and I nod.

"I saw pictures of it a couple of months ago," I tell him, and he takes out his phone. "What are you doing?"

"Making a note to check it out," he says and puts his phone away. "Okay, your question."

"What makes you angry?" I ask, and he looks over at me.

"When people assume they know me," he answers without thinking twice. "Everyone thinks they know me because I play hockey, but no one really knows anything about me."

"No one?" I say, swallowing. I don't know why I was expecting something else.

"I can say without a doubt that not one person knows all of me," he confirms, and just the way he says it, I'm sad for him. Sad that he has no one he could talk to. "What about you? What makes you angry?"

"People thinking I got this job because of my family," I tell him something I haven't told anyone.

"How did you get the job?" he asks me, his voice soft.

"Because I worked my ass off," I tell him, my voice getting just a touch louder. "Because I paid my dues and did what I needed to do."

"So, then, fuck 'em," he says. "Do you think you deserve to be in your position?"

"I do, without a shadow of a doubt, I deserve this position."

"Then all you have to do is show the haters." He puts down his chicken. "If you show them how much you kick ass, they won't be able to come back with an argument."

"That's good advice." I smile. "You going to take

the advice yourself?" He laughs now. "Stop throwing punches and put some points under your name."

"I'm working on it." He smirks. "It's a work in progress." He leans back in his chair. "Okay, whose turn is it?"

"If you could have a meal with one person, who would it be?" I ask.

"Well, you, obviously," he says with a smirk, and I roll my eyes. "Also, I'm not sure I want to answer that question."

"Why?" I ask, my interest piqued. "Tell me."

"It's weird," he says, and I just laugh at him.

"Weirder than showing up at my office with a hundred pounds of Chinese food?" I joke with him. His chest moves, and all of a sudden, a picture of him over me pops into my head. I blink away the memory and look at him. "Come on. I promise to never repeat it." I put my hand up. "This whole conversation will be our secret."

"Ugh," he says, rolling his head back, and then he looks at me. "Okay, fine, Cooper Stone," he says, and I open my mouth. "The OG."

I laugh at him. "See, that is why I didn't want to say anything." He points at me. "Because it's weird."

"It's not weird," I tell him. "And we are all used to it."

"When he came into the dressing room when Cooper was traded over, I swear to God I thought I would faint." He holds up his hand, and I can't help but laugh even harder. "Whatever."

"That is so cute," I tell him, and I want to reach out and hold his hand. "If you want, I can try to get you a signed jersey." He rolls his eyes now. "Your turn."

"Who is your hero?" he asks, and without even thinking about it, I answer him.

"My parents. Hands down, I want to be my mother as a mom. Hands down, and then my dad. It's been a touch rocky with him the past couple of months," I say, trying to fight back the tears. "He's just the rock in our family." I look down at my hands.

"I wish I had even one percent of that," he shares, and I look up at him. His family is off-limits, and I know this, yet he is talking to me about it, and I don't know what to say. "I never met my father." His words hit me like a kick in the stomach. "I mean, I think I met him when I was three or two." He looks up. "My mother was his paralegal, and well, one thing led to another, and out came me. Don't get me wrong, he took care of his 'responsibilities,'" he says, using his fingers for the quotation marks. "And when he died, he left me a huge chunk of money. I guess everyone parents in their own way."

"Wilson," I say his name softly, but he holds up his hand.

"It is what it is." He shrugs, and he gets up now. "Thank you for letting me stay tonight." I get up and walk over to him.

"Thank you for bringing me dinner," I say softly. "No one has ever done this before." I look up at him, my heart beating in my chest. I want to reach up and touch his cheek, but more than anything, I want him to kiss me.

"Well, then," he says. His hand comes up, and I'm

waiting for him to touch my cheek, but instead, he drops it just as fast as it rose. "I'm glad I came. Have a great night, Franny." He turns and walks out of my office.

I watch his broad back and firm ass walk away from me, and the only thing that comes out of my mouth is, "He didn't even kiss me. What the fuck?" I fold my arms over my chest. "What kind of bullshit is this?"

SIXTEEN

WILSON

I STEP INTO the elevator, and it's like the air just goes out of me. My heart races in my chest as my head falls forward. This whole night was something I would never have expected. I went with the intention to have dinner with her, and in the end, I told her things no one knows. And I mean no one.

The ping of the elevator makes my feet move out into the lobby. I look up, wondering if I should go back. I just left her there with all that mess to clean up. But after she told me about her family and I told her about my father, it was clear to me that we come from two opposite ends of the world. It also showed me that she probably deserves better. When she stood in front of me, and my hand came up, I wanted to cup her cheek and then bend to kiss her, but instead, my head told me to walk away.

I play the conversation over and over in my head. I see her smile, and I can hear her laughter as I drive home. My phone rings as soon as I park in my driveway, and I see it's her.

"Hello," I say, putting her on speaker as I sit in my garage.

"What the fuck was that?" I can tell she's angry. She also doesn't even give me a chance to say anything before she continues. "You didn't even try to cop a feel? You didn't even try to kiss me? What is this bullshit?"

I laugh. "One, I offered you plan A, but you chose plan B." I close my eyes, and I love her voice.

"I chose plan B, but you could have put in some of plan A in there," she huffs out, and I hear a door closing.

"Are you home?" I ask her.

"Yes, after I packed up the Chinese food and put it in the fridge, I came home," she says, and the clicking of her heels stops, so I know she took them off. "Now, don't change the subject, Wilson. What the fuck was that?"

"I didn't know it was okay to kiss you." I really wish I could go back in time and take the kiss that I wanted so bad.

"At the end of a date, you kiss or have sex," she explains. "One or the other."

I laugh now. "Are you sure about that?"

"No," she huffs out, and I get out of my truck and walk into my house. I wonder if she is undressing or if she's getting naked. "I have no idea. I don't date."

I laugh. "So how would you know how the date ends?"

"I'm assuming." I can hear clothes rustling. "I might have to ask my sister to be sure, but yeah. It's at least a kiss."

"Are you getting naked?" I ask, stopping in my tracks in the middle of the stairway.

"Yes, I just got home. I don't really like showering with my clothes on, so I have to get undressed, and I'm pent up and have all these hormones, so I might have to use my showerhead." My mouth hits the floor.

"Well, if this is going to be a phone sex call," I say, running up the stairs. "I'm here for it."

"Oh, no, you had your chance, buddy," she scolds, huffing out. "That train has left the station."

"I didn't even know my train was in the station," I say honestly. "I want my train to go into your station." And I can't help but laugh. I don't think I've laughed this much before. Just being around her, I can't help but smile and laugh.

"My station was open for your train, but instead, you decided not to roll it in," she says, her voice going up. "What do trains do when they just linger there not in the station?"

I close my eyes and rub my face with my hand. "No fucking clue, but can we get back to you being naked?"

"Sure," she answers, and I sit on my bed. "I'm really wet, and I am slipping in a couple of fingers."

I groan. "This wasn't such a good idea," I mumble.

"Then I touched my clit," she counters.

"I'm going to let you go," I say, looking down at my cock. "Good night." I hang up before she says anything and then my phone pings in my hand.

I see she sent me a picture and it's of her legs spread, but all you can see are her legs apart.

Fran: My train station is open.

Me: I'm going to google if we can die from blue balls.

Fran: You can't. It's just a discomfort.

Me: How did you know that?

Fran: I can't tell you all my secrets on the first date. Save this question for the next one.

Me: So there is going to be a next one?

Fran: Maybe. Time will tell. Good night, conductor.

I laugh and toss the phone over my shoulder and onto the bed. She's hands down the most open person I've met. She has the best smile, and every single time I talk to her, I want to continue talking to her. I take a cold shower that night as my hand fists my cock, and I call out her name when I orgasm.

The next day, I get up and head over to the rink for the morning skate. I don't text her even though everything inside me wants to, and when I slip on my suit jacket, I wonder if she will be at the game tonight. It's a Saturday night, and usually, it's full of families. I skate onto the ice and look up to see if I see her, and I don't, which throws me off when I feel a sense of disappointment. No one has ever been to my games before. Even when I was younger, my mother would drop me off and pick me up at the curb. I think the only time she came with me was when I was drafted.

"Don't forget. After-game get-together," Manning says, and I look over at him. "Across the street. Food and drinks paid for by Nico."

As soon as we touch the puck tonight, the other team

is looking to hit us. We end up winning by three goals. During the third period, the other team pushes more and the hits are harder. When I finally get off the ice, I walk to the dressing room. I undress and pick up my phone, pulling up her name. The picture of her legs is on the screen when Cooper comes to stand beside me, and I fumble with the phone and turn around.

"Don't worry there. I'm not interested in all the women you are texting," he says, and I want to tell him that I'm not texting women. I'm just texting the one, but I don't have a chance before Nico comes into the room and starts clapping his hands.

"Good game, boys," he says with a smile. "I want to see everyone over at the bar." He looks at everyone, and all I want to do is call Fran and go home. Maybe I can persuade her to come to my house, or we can go and get a bite to eat somewhere.

Walking to the shower, I hold my head down to get the water to pulse down over my shoulders. I take longer than I should, hoping no one is left here. Except when I walk out, Cooper and Michael are there. "I literally can't move." Michael gets up and grabs his jacket. "All I want is to go home."

"I'm going straight home," I say, pulling my boxers and pants on.

"Fuck, no," Cooper says. "If we have to suffer through it, so do you."

I look at him, my eyebrows pinching together. "Or," I say, putting up my finger. "We all fuck off?"

They both laugh at me, and neither of them leaves.

"You guys are assholes," I huff as I slide my jacket on and walk out with them.

The phone in my pocket is getting heavier and heavier, Cooper pulls open the door to the bar, and we can hear the laughing and dishes clashing as soon as we walk in. Nico is standing at the door, and he smiles when he sees us. "There is the best part of the line," he says, standing next to Manning.

"What took you so long?" Manning questions, looking around.

"This one," Michael says, pointing at me. "Was trying to bow out, so we had to make sure he suffered with all of us."

"Teamwork," I mumble, looking around.

"There they are," Cooper says. I look where he is pointing, and my eyes find her right away. She is sitting next to another woman, and she throws her head back and laughs. With all the noise around me, all I can hear is her laughter. "Come on, tough guy."

"I'm going to go to the bar," I say, trying to get out of it.

"Not a chance in hell," Michael says. "You'll bow out." He pushes me with his shoulder, and we walk over to the U-shaped table. She is sitting at the end of the table.

"There they are," the girl next to her says, and her eyes fly up and meet mine. Erika looks up and gets up to come over to Cooper. Leaving the chair next to Fran open, Michael walks over and takes the seat next to Jillian, then leans over to kiss her.

"There are empty seats over here," Ralph says, holding up his hand, and I walk over, sitting right across the room from her at the other end of the table.

"Thanks," I say, sitting down, and a waitress comes over and hands me a menu. The chair in front of me is pulled out, and Cooper sits down with Erika beside him.

"Is that the menu?" Cooper asks, and I hand him the menu at the same time as my phone vibrates on the inside of my jacket pocket.

I take it out and look down, seeing it's from her. I smile, and my eyes fly up to where she sits and she looks at me smirking and then turns her head.

Fran: So we meet again?

SEVENTEEN

Frances

I SEND HIM the text and then wait for him to check it. He reaches into his suit pocket, and I can't look away even if I wanted to. When Julia called me this afternoon and told me she was coming to get me and taking me out, I hesitated. But then she said the whole team would be meeting up later and that Jillian was forcing her, so she was forcing me. To be honest, as soon as she said the whole team was going to be there, she didn't have to twist my arm that much.

He looks down at the phone in his hand and smiles, looking up at me, and the minute our eyes meet, Julia calls my name. "Do you want something to eat?" She hands me the menu, and my heart is going a million miles a minute when the phone vibrates in my lap.

"Just a burger is good," I say, handing the waitress back the menu.

Wilson: So we meet again. How are you?

I smile and answer him.

Me: I'm great. You?

I press send, then put the phone down on my lap and look over at him. He is saying something to Cooper when he grabs his phone. I lean back in my chair, watching him as he smiles and types. He puts his phone down at the same time as it buzzes in my lap.

Wilson: Better now that I can see you.

I look up and see him staring at me, and he just winks and then turns his attention to the guy beside him. My palms are getting all sweaty, and my stomach is fluttering. I grab the glass of wine that the waitress puts down in front of me. After taking a gulp, I answer him.

Me: Do you come here often?

I laugh, putting the phone down and turning to Julia, who is having a conversation with Jillian. "Is it hot in here?" I say when my cheeks get hot after finishing my glass of wine.

"Lay off the wine, and then your temperature will go down," Michael says from beside me, and I punch his arm. "Ouch, what was that for?"

"It's my first glass." I point at the glass.

"It's her first glass here," Jillian says, laughing. "And it's not for you to tell her when or how much to drink," she tells Michael, who just puts his arm around her shoulder and shrugs. "She's single and ready to mingle."

"She is ready to mingle with anyone who isn't here." He uses his hand to motion the whole room. "She's off-limits." Julia and Jillian both share a smirk and look down.

I laugh. "Why am I off-limits?" Avoiding looking across the room.

"You just are," he reaffirms, and the waitress comes back over and drops a plate of appetizers in the middle.

"Good to know." I ignore the extra pounding in my chest as I grab my phone off my lap and look over to see him watching me again. His jacket is off, and his button-down shirt is pulled across his chest. His sleeves are rolled up, and you can see the watch on his hand.

He picks up his phone and texts me again, and this time, I look down and see two texts from him.

Wilson: Are you trying to pick me up?

Wilson: Stop staring at me like I'm your next meal.

I laugh at this, and Julia looks over at me. "Funny text?" she teases, and I look at her.

"Eat a chicken wing." I point at the plate, and she throws her head back and laughs. I grab her glass of wine, downing it.

Me: What if I was trying to pick you up? Would you say no?

Me: How am I looking at you?

I start to feel a bit flushed and turn to listen to Julia, Jillian, and Michael talk about I don't even know what. The truth be told, if I could, I would be over at his table talking to him face-to-face. Instead, I'm here on this side, trying to flirt with him through texts. My phone buzzes, and my hand flies out fast to grab it.

Wilson: Let's play twenty-one questions.

Me: Fine. Favorite position? Mine would be riding. But then again, I love doggy because you get deeper

***into me. But I also love missionary when you slam right
into me over and over again.***

I press send and grab the bottle of wine from the
table. Filling my wineglass, I look over at him. When he
reads the text, his eyes fly up to mine, and then he puts
the phone down, making sure no one is behind him. He
shakes his head, smirking at me, and I don't know if it's a
smirk that *it's on* or if the smirk is I know *I did you good.*

I grab my phone, and I'm about to text him back when
his text comes through.

***Wilson: As long as your pussy is on my cock, I'll
do whatever position you want. Give head or get your
pussy eaten?***

My stomach rises, and I swear my body tingles as I
read that. I can still feel his mouth on me.

***Me: Definitely sitting on your face leaning over
sucking your cock. Last time you jerked off? Mine was
this afternoon in the shower thinking about your cock.***

"What the hell are you doing?" Cooper snaps from
in front of me, and my heart sinks. I look up at him and
wonder how the fuck I'm going to explain this. "Are you
drinking the whole bottle of wine yourself?" I let out a
huge sigh of relief.

"Not the whole bottle," I say, pouring another glass.
"Just half." I take another gulp. "I'm with my family.
What the hell can happen to me?"

Julia puts up her hand. "I'd like to answer the
question." I glare at her, and she laughs. "Where is Erika?
She is more fun than you." She looks over to Erika who
is getting up from her seat and coming over.

"Take my seat," I tell Erika. "I've got to go to the bathroom." I grab my phone and turn to walk to the bathroom. I zigzag through the people who are all of a sudden all around our table. I try to look over at him as I pass, but four guys are standing in front, having a conversation. I walk down the hallway past the kitchen, and I'm about to push the door to the ladies' bathroom when a hand goes around my waist, and I'm pulled against someone. My body goes tense until I smell him.

He drags me to the closet at the end of the hallway. Once inside, he closes the door, then pushes my back against it. His hands go flat against the door beside my head, and my hand goes to his waist as we try to see each other in the dark room. The soft light comes from the outside through the window. "This afternoon." His voice comes out in a whisper, and he presses himself against me. His cock is hard as a rock. "When I took a shower." His head comes down, and my breath hitches when I think he's going to kiss me. My stomach flutters as my hands move from his hips up his chest. The heat is seeping out to my hand. "I pictured you in front of me." He moves his face to the other side, his nose touching mine as he does it. My pussy clenches, thinking about being naked in the shower with him. "My face buried in your pussy." His lips come so close to mine that I can feel his breath on me. "Your leg over my shoulder." He moves his face lower as he trails kisses along my jaw, his tongue coming out after. "But just before you come," he says. "I slide my cock into your hot pussy, and you come right away." I close my eyes and moan softly, gripping his shirt with my hands.

I lift my leg to hitch around his hip. "Like this," I pant out, arching my back, and I'm pissed I didn't wear heels tonight. When I was getting dressed tonight, I thought of dressing up a bit. Instead, I went casual with my black jeans and a white shirt. His hand goes down to my ass as he palms it and squeezes it, pushing me into him. "I need to."

"I know what you need," he says, his lips hovering over mine. "You need my mouth."

"Yes," I tell him, panting. "Your mouth," I say, my tongue coming out to lick the bottom of my lip the same time he does. Our tongues touch, and I swear the whole fucking place can crash around us, and I wouldn't give a rat's ass.

"Where do you want my mouth?" he asks, hovering over my mouth as he rubs his cock up and down the middle of my covered core. My whole body is on edge. I want his touch, I want his mouth, I want his tongue, I want him.

"Everywhere." I answer his question in a whisper right before he groans. His hand leaves my ass and the hand beside my head comes down as he takes my face into his hands. His mouth slams down on mine as my eyes close. His tongue slides into my mouth, my leg pulling him tighter toward me. He picks me up, and both my legs wrap around his waist as he moves his head to the other side, deepening the kiss. We're hungry for each other, making the kiss frantic. He lets go of my lips only to lower his mouth to my neck as I lean back to give him access. "I should have worn a dress," I pant out. "I need you." I rotate my hips on his cock, his hand leaving my face and traveling down to my tits where he pinches my nipples through the shirt. "Wilson." His name comes out as if I'm pleading with him to put me out of my misery.

His mouth finds mine again, my hand coming up from his chest to his face and into his hair as I wrap my arms around his neck. His tongue slides in mine, going around and around in a circle. We take the time to savor the kiss. I'm about to move my head to the other side when we hear voices, and both of us stop.

"He probably bailed." I hear my brother Cooper's voice laughing as he comes closer to the door. The sound of our breathing fills the room.

"He left his jacket?" Michael says. "He's not in the bathroom."

"He probably went outside to take a call," Cooper replies, and then the footsteps walk away from the door.

"This isn't finished," he says, putting me down. My arms leave his neck, and my body wants to scream out in protest.

"It better not be," I tell him, and he smiles at me, leaning down and kissing my lips softly. My hand comes up to cup the back of his head as I slide my tongue into his mouth. "I still need that mouth," I say when I let go of his lips.

"You'll get my mouth." He turns me, putting his hand on the handle of the door. "And more," he says before walking out of the closet, leaving me alone.

I wait for him to walk away from the door before

putting one hand to my stomach and the other hand to my lips. That has to be the best kiss I've gotten in my whole life. I kept remembering the way he kissed me that night, and nothing, and I mean nothing, came close to the kiss he just gave me. I would have let him fuck me in a closet as long as he didn't stop kissing me. My head spins as I walk out of the closet, and thankfully, no one is there when I do.

Making my way back to the table, I spot him sitting down to drink a bottle of water. I pull out the chair and sit down with Julia, the only other one at the table. "I'm going to guess that you got lost going to the bathroom."

I smirk at her and grab my glass of wine. "I wouldn't say I got lost at all," I say and grab my phone, looking around. Seeing that people are slowly leaving. Opening my phone to our chat, I send him one last message.

Me: So my place or yours?

EIGHTEEN

WILSON

"WHERE THE FUCK have you been?" I hear Michael say as soon as I pull my chair out and sit back down.

"Went outside to take a phone call," I say, avoiding his eyes and grabbing the bottle of water in front of me.

"Bullshit," one of the rookies says, and I look over at him, the panic filling me when I think he saw me drag Fran into the closet. When I saw her get up and walk, my eyes followed her every move. She was drinking wine, so I had to make sure she was okay. Or at least that was what I told myself. I grabbed her around her waist as soon as she got to the bathroom door. Her body went totally tense, but as soon as I pulled her closer to me, she melted into my arms. "You were probably out banging one of the waitresses."

I don't answer him. Instead, I just take another drink of my water. When I stepped out of the closet, I looked around until I found an exit sign. Pushing the door open,

I found myself in the middle of the alleyway. I took a second to take a deep breath and then close my eyes. I replayed the scene over and over in my head. I can't even believe that I lost control like that. I can't believe I was so careless about someone seeing us. But all I wanted was to taste her. All I wanted was to kiss her and then leave. One touch and I lost control. I rub my hands over my face and then drag them through my hair, holding my neck as my body calms down. I can still feel her lips on mine. The whole time I walked back into the restaurant, I kept telling myself it was a bad idea. Even sitting at the table and seeing her come back, I know I should walk away. But one look at her, and all I see is fucking perfection. She's so fucking perfect, inside and outside.

Watching her pull out her chair and take a water bottle, I wish that I was sitting next to her if only to be in her presence. She makes me want things I've never wanted before. She makes me want to be that better person. She picks up her phone, and a second later, it vibrates in my hand.

Fran: So my place or yours?

I look down at the phone, and everything in me wants to tell her where ever she is, is where I'll be. Her eyes come to mine, and the tightness in my chest becomes even tighter. The pressure feels like a semi-truck is crushing down on it. My hands get all clammy when I know what my answer will be, and my heart goes into my throat, making it hard to even swallow.

Me: Rain check.

I press send, my sweaty hand shaking, thinking she

might think I'm not interested in her, when in fact all I want is to be with her. But not for just one night, and I'm not sure what to do with these feelings.

The phone buzzes, and I almost laugh.

Fran: Is there someplace else you have to be?

Me: There is nowhere else on this planet I would rather be than between your legs.

Pressing send, I stand and grab my jacket. There is just so much going on in my head that I need to get away from it all and regroup. "Okay, guys, I'm out," I say, my hands fumbling with my jacket as I try to put it on. Tucking my phone in the inside pocket, I feel it vibrate again. "See you guys Monday." I walk out of the restaurant with my head down, my whole body aches to walk away from her.

I can hear other people around and see more of the team walking out of the restaurant while making my way over to my car. My head spins as I head home, and the nerves are still there just thinking of her. My stomach is in knots, wondering if I did the right thing. Maybe I should have just gone home with her, but then you're giving her what she wants, and what if she doesn't want me after?

Stepping into the house, I can smell something's off right away. *What the fuck*, I think as I step into the house almost as if I'm a stranger in my own house. "Hello," I say loudly and then stop when I see her purse at the front door next to her shoes. "What the fuck?" I walk up the steps two at a time and find her in my bed. "What the fuck are you doing?"

She looks over at me, smiling, and she has so much makeup on I can see it from the doorway and her hair is perfectly curled. She drops the sheet in front of her, showing me her tits. "Finally," she says, getting on her knees, and I hold my hand out to block my eyes from looking at her.

"Tiffany," I hiss. "Put some clothes on. And get the fuck out of my house." I look down, seeing her clothes, and toss them to her.

"I thought we could talk," she groans, and I hear her voice getting closer and closer.

"We already talked," I tell her.

"I know, but you haven't been answering my texts or my calls," she says, and I can hear her getting dressed.

"You would think that would be a sign I don't want to talk to you." I put my hands on my hips. Aggravated that this woman just let herself into my house and even more aggravated because the woman who I want in my house I left at a restaurant.

"You don't have to be such a prude," she huffs. "You've seen me naked plenty of times already."

"Yeah, I'm trying to erase those images from my head. I might try bleach for my eyeballs next." I turn and walk out of my room, hoping she follows me. I'm going to have to strip the bed and call a locksmith. I walk into the living room, but then I turn back toward the kitchen, thinking she would throw herself on the couch and try to hump me.

Opening the fridge, I grab a water bottle and lean against the counter, watching the staircase. She comes down a couple of minutes later, wearing tight white jeans and a top that shows everything off. I automatically go back to Franny and her tight black jeans that molded to her body. My cock wakes up seeing her in my head, and I chase away the thought in case Tiffany thinks my boner is for her. It's not.

"I can't believe you are treating me this way." She slides on her high-heeled shoes and comes into the kitchen.

"I can't believe you thought it was a good idea to break into my house." I just stare at her as she comes closer. I see all of her flaws.

"You gave me the code for your door." She takes out the stool and sits down. "I didn't break into anything."

"I didn't give you the code to use at your leisure," I say, taking my phone out to make a note about calling the locksmith. I see a text from Franny, and my heart speeds up, but I can't answer it."Not to just wander into my house whenever you feel like it."

"Give me a break." She rolls her eyes. "I wanted to show you how much I've missed you." Her attempt to purr out the words makes my skin itchy.

"Tiffany," I say, putting down the phone beside me. "Let's be real. We were having a good time."

"Well, I thought it was more." She folds her arms over her chest, pushing up her tits even higher.

"What's my favorite color?" I ask her, and she doesn't even take a second to think about it when she answers.

"Blue." I laugh.

"Wrong." I shake my head. "Listen, I'm tired. I have

to get up and pack tomorrow, so if you don't mind ..."

"Why don't I stay, and we can unwind together?" She smiles at me, thinking her smile will lure me back.

"I can honestly say that if you and I were the last two people on earth, I still wouldn't bang you." She gasps when I say this and shoots me a glare.

"Why, I never ..." She pushes away from the counter. "Have ever been so insulted."

"I find that hard to believe," I say. "Didn't your sister call you a raging cunt when you fucked her husband?"

"I was drunk." She throws up her hands. "It's not my fault she can't keep him happy." I push off the counter and walk to the front door, opening it for her.

"Well, best of luck to you and your future endeavors." I watch her walk to her purse, grabbing it, and I see that she parked her car on the street. I should have noticed it when I got home, but my head was swimming with thoughts of Fran.

"You'll regret this," she hisses. "No one tosses me to the curb."

"I mean ..." I shrug when she walks out. "Consider me number one," I say, slamming the door closed. But I don't know if it matters since she knows the code. Walking back to my phone, I pull up Google and ask him how to change the lock door code. After watching five YouTube videos, I finally manage to change it.

Turning off the light, I walk up to my bedroom and groan when I think about changing the sheets. Opting to just change out of my clothes and sleep in the guest bedroom, I'm slipping under the sheets when I grab my phone and see that she sent me a picture. My mouth hangs open when I see the picture is of a pink dick and what looks like pearls in it and two little pieces in the front to play with her clit. I zoom in, making sure that I saw right, and then my hands grip the phone so hard my knuckles go white. I groan and hang my head back when I read her text.

Fran: This could have been you.

NINETEEN

FRANCES

MY PHONE PINGS from the counter twice as I walk around to start my cup of coffee. Picking it up, I see one text from Cooper and the other text from Julia.

Cooper: Mom and Dad are down. Lunch at one! Wakey, wakey!

Julia: I'll swing by and get you for lunch since I have your car!

I don't bother calling Julia back. Instead, I call Cooper, and he answers right away. "You're up bright and early." He laughs, and I look over at the clock on top of the stove and see that it's just after nine.

"I couldn't sleep," I huff, grabbing the cup and pouring the coffee. I don't even bother adding milk, just drinking the hot liquid in hopes it wakes me up. "When did Mom and Dad get in?"

"Ten minutes ago. They texted you last night, but you didn't answer," he says, laughing. "Which is funny because you were stuck to your phone all night long."

"I wasn't stuck to my phone all night long," I retort, wanting to add I was stuck at some point to Wilson as he dry-humped me in the supply closet, but I don't. "Let me check," I say, opening the text and seeing it there. "Fine, they texted me." I walk back to my room and sit on my bed. The treasure chest of vibrators beside the bed. "I didn't know they were coming to town."

"Yeah, I think Dad has a meeting or something like that," he says. "We are meeting at Uncle Max's because Auntie Allison ordered all the food."

"Okay," I say. "See you there." I hang up the phone and look over at the chest. I look down at my phone and pull up his name. My eyes stare at the words rain check. I thought he was joking when he sent it. Then I saw him get up and put on his jacket and walk out, and I was dumbfounded. There was nothing I could have said. I stared at the spot where he disappeared to, waiting for him to come back, but the joke was on me when ten minutes later, he never came back. The whole ride home, I was flabbergasted. I kept looking at my phone, waiting for him to text me his address or ask me mine. Or say he was joking. I was waiting for anything. Even as I undressed and got naked, I waited. Then I finally caved and sent him the picture of the vibrator I took to bed with me. All it says is delivered; he never answered me back. "Fuck him," I say, tossing the phone on the bed, and it hits said vibrator that is still under the sheets. Grabbing the vibrator, I head for the shower, and even after I come twice, I'm still on edge.

I put away all the toys under the bed, and I'm slipping on my yoga pants when the doorbell rings. I grab my white short-sleeved top and put it on while rushing to the door. I don't know why I'm thinking it could be him. I don't even know why I care, but sadly, I do. Opening the door, Julia stands there with a bottle of water in one hand and iced coffee in the other. "I come bearing gifts." She smiles. "And from the looks of you"—she pushes her sunglasses on top of her head—"you need a double shot."

"Thank you," I say, grabbing the iced coffee and walking to the front closet. "How cold is it outside?"

"Well, it's October in Dallas, so a hundred." She laughs while I slip the jean jacket off the hanger and put it on. I also grab a Dallas baseball hat to wear and check myself one last time in the mirror. "Only you can pull off a baseball cap and yoga pants and probably get laid at the dog park."

I laugh at her, tying the laces to my white and black sneakers. "I don't have a dog."

"Exactly," she says, opening the door and stepping outside. I take one step out and then turn back to grab my sunglasses. "It's brighter than the devil's asshole."

"Good to know what the devil's asshole looks like," Julia says, tossing me my car keys.

After parking my car at the end of the driveway, I get out and stretch my legs. "I think staying at home would have been a good idea," I mumble when I walk into the house and can hear the voices already.

"I live for Sunday lunch with your family," Julia says.

"They put the fun in dysfunctional."

"They put something in something," I say, walking into the kitchen and coming face-to-face with my uncle Max.

"There she is." He takes me in his arms, kissing my head. "Your father was asking about you."

"Was he?" I say, letting go of him. He hugs Julia the same way he hugs me.

"Is Alex here?" I look around, wondering if she flew in for the weekend.

"Nah," he says. "She went to Montreal for the weekend." He looks at my aunt Allison. "I think she's interested in someone on the Montreal team."

I look at my aunt Allison, who just shakes her head. "Oh, I think she's definitely interested in someone on the Montreal team." I laugh at my own joke as I walk into the house, kissing the kids and finally coming face-to-face with my dad.

"Hey," I say softly, not sure how to act. We are talking more, which is a good thing, but we still aren't there.

"Hey." He hugs me much like my uncle did and kisses my head. I wrap my arms around his waist and lay my head on his chest. "How are you doing? You look tired."

"Yeah," I say, looking at my mother, who just eyes me. She comes over and only when she is standing next to my father does he let me go.

I put my arm around my mother's shoulder, standing beside her. "You look like you haven't slept." I'm about to answer her when my brother yells.

"That's because she drank last night," Cooper says

from the kitchen. Erika punches his arm. "Ouch, what was that for?" She mumbles something to him. "Like my parents don't know she drinks."

"I didn't drink that much." I roll my eyes and look back at my father, who just looks at me. "I was with Cooper and Michael." I put both my hands up. "And I'm safe."

"Stop looking at her like that," my mother tells him. "She's a grown woman who can take care of herself."

"Come and eat!" my aunt yells as the two chefs start putting serving dishes on the counter.

"It smells good." My hand drops off my mother as I walk into the kitchen and see the Italian food they made.

I grab a plate and walk over to one of the tables to sit down. Julia follows me with Jillian, who is getting so big. She's carrying twins, and even though she is a twin herself, she was shocked she would be able to have twins. She sits next to me, and my mother and aunt join us while the guys sit at the other table talking about the games that were on last night.

"Why are you so quiet?" Erika asks me, taking a sip of water.

"I didn't sleep last night," I answer honestly.

"Oh, no," my aunt says. "Are you okay?"

"Yes, I was sexually frustrated," I respond, and Erika chokes on her water. Ignoring her, I continue picking at the food. "Did you know that it's actually a medical condition?" I look at all the women who just stare at me, shocked that I would even say this at the table. Although they should know that nothing is off the table.

"I had no idea," Julia says. "Maybe that's what I suffer from also."

"What do you suffer from?" Michael says, coming to the table and leaning down to kiss Jillian on the cheek. For the first time, I'm jealous of it. The touch. The intimacy of it.

"It's called restless genital syndrome," I share, and he just looks like he's seen a ghost. "Have you heard about it?" I try not to laugh at his face, and so does everyone else, but they all fail.

"What the hell is wrong with you?" He stands up, putting his hands on his hips. "We're eating lunch." He looks down at Jillian. "Put your hands on your stomach so the girls don't hear her talking." He turns and walks back to the men's table.

"I don't know what it is," I say, huffing out. "I just feel off."

"When was the last time you had sex?" Erika asks, and I look at her.

"How long have you been married?" I look over at Jillian. My mother and aunt gasp out, and I laugh out loud.

"It's fine." I put my hand up. "I'll get it fixed."

"I really need to know if you see a doctor for this." My aunt Allison laughs. "Like, do you go to your gynecologist or your general practitioner?"

I shrug my shoulders, and my mother changes the subject and starts talking about I don't even know what. I don't even eat much. Instead, I just move the food around my plate absentmindedly, thinking back to last night and where it went wrong. Was it me? Was I too assertive?

"Come sit outside with me," my mother says, and I nod, getting up with my plate. After I throw the leftover food in the garbage and putting the plate in the dishwasher, I follow her outside. I see the kids running around, going to the tree house that my uncle had made. Every year, he adds another part to it. Soon, it's going to be as big as the pool guesthouse. "Let's sit over there." She points at a couch under the awning. I sit down, and my mother sits in the chair facing me. "So, what's up?"

"What do you mean?" I ask, and she leans back in the chair.

"You barely said anything at lunch. You're grumpy; you're tired." I start to say something, and she holds up her hand. "I don't want to hear about your restless vagina."

"Well, that's what's the matter," I say to her.

"Who is he?" She looks at me, and I don't know what to say.

"No one," I answer her. "We met a while ago, and our paths crossed again."

"You went back for a second date?" She tries not to smirk and fails, which leads me to glare at her.

"I don't date," I remind her.

"But you want to?" She says the exact thing my head says at the same moment.

"No, I don't want to date him." My head yells liar. "I want to have sex with him, and that's it."

"Um," she says, and I don't stop. The words fly out of my mouth like I have word vomit.

"We flirt all the time. Literally sexted me all night and then dragged me into a supply closet."

"Oh, my." My mother puts her hand to her mouth.

"Yeah, oh my is right. I almost had sex with him right next to a bucket and a mop." I get up, my energy and frustration pouring out of me. "He got me all hot and bothered and then asked for a rain check." My hands fly up in the air as I shriek out the last part. "A fucking rain check, Mom."

"So you aren't sexually frustrated," she summarizes. "You're angry he didn't give you what you wanted."

"It's the same thing." I cross my hands over my chest.

"It is not." She shakes her head. "I'm sure there have been men who have flirted and then walked away, and you were fine." I glare at her, not ready to admit she's right. "You, my girl, are upset because you like him."

I gasp when she says that, putting my hand to my chest as if she just shot me. "I do not like him," I say in a whisper. "How can you say that?"

She gets up and comes over to me, taking my face in her hands and smiles. "It's okay to like someone," she says, and I roll my eyes. "It doesn't make you less of a badass."

"Yes, it does," I say just to say. "And I don't like him."

"Did you think about him today?"

My glare becomes a death stare. "Yeah, when I put away my vibrator." She laughs.

"You know what I mean," she says softly, letting go of my face and holding one of my hands. "Did you think about him at all?" I don't answer her because the question and answer are moot. "Baby girl."

I shake my head. "I don't like him." I turn and storm off like a child who just realized her mother might be right.

TWENTY

WILSON

I TURN THE treadmill down as I cool down. I spent the last two hours running on this fucking thing instead of doing what I really wanted to do, and that was to call Franny. I tossed and turned all fucking night. The only thing going through my head was her and that pink fucking vibrator.

I stripped my bed this morning and tossed the sheets in the wash using extra bleach. I packed my bag for the road trip next week. Then came into the gym where I tried to run to clear my head, but nothing worked.

The phone rings, and I turn off the treadmill, going to the weight bench where I left my phone. Looking down, I see her name, and everything happens at the same time. The smile fills my face, and my heart speeds up. I sit on the weight bench and press the speaker button. "Hello," I answer, looking down, and my stomach flips up and then sinks just like the waves in the ocean.

"Don't you hello me, Brad Wilson. This is ridiculous," she hisses. "What the fuck is this bullshit about a rain check?" And I try not to laugh out loud. "You were perfectly fine dry-humping me in a closet, yet you won't take me home and fuck me?"

"How are you?" I get up, grabbing my bottle of water, and walk to my bedroom toward the bathroom.

"How am I?" she shrieks. "I am not well." I stop moving when I think she's hurt or not feeling well. I take a step and press the FaceTime button. The sound of ringing fills our conversation. "Are you FaceTiming me?"

"Yes." I wonder if she is going to accept it, but when I see the little white circle go around, I wait for her face to fill the screen. The minute I see her, a smile fills my face. "There you are."

"Here I am." She turns and puts her phone down, and I can see she is in bed with her head on her pillow.

"What's wrong?" I search her face.

"What's wrong?" She puts her hand out, groaning. "What's wrong? I'm suffering from restless vagina." I can't help but laugh out loud. "Don't fucking laugh, Wilson, you put me in this condition." She takes the phone in her hand and slaps her bed.

"Oh, baby," I say softly, watching her blue eyes, and I suddenly wish I was next to her. Fuck, it's not sudden, it's been all fucking day. Fuck, it's been since we had dinner together in her office.

"You are too late, mister," she huffs out. "That train left the station." I laugh.

"Did you actually?" I ask, and she just looks at me.

"You left me pent up with all the hormones," she says loudly. She sits up, and I can see she's wearing a white camisole, and I can see her nipples through it. "You left me on the verge of an orgasm, and what did you do? Nothing. What else was I supposed to do? All night, I had to bring out the chest and then even this morning in the shower, and even that didn't help."

"You dirty, dirty girl." I shake my head, and my cock goes hard, thinking of her pleasuring herself all night long. Thinking about her, I have to squeeze my cock to calm down. "Did you think about me?"

"No," she huffs out, and my mouth opens again. "It was a threesome with Chris Evans and Chris Hemsworth." I see her eyes twinkle, and I wonder if she is telling me the truth, but all I can do is laugh at the top of my lungs. "A good time was had by all."

"You liar." I stare at her. "You thought of me."

"And what if I did?" She stares at me. "Would that make you come here and do me?" It's my turn to groan.

"You think you are the only one suffering?" I ask. "I was hard all night long."

"Good," she says, satisfied. "I hope you catch blue balls."

I can't help but laugh at everything she says. "Does one catch blue balls?" I ask. "Maybe I'm suffering from restless dick."

"Or you're just a dick," she counters. "It could be that you're just a dick who likes to rub up onto women and then just leave them without that magical moment."

"Magical moment." I repeat the words. "I've never heard that saying before."

"Also, in case you want to use that restless dick, you should know that restless dick syndrome means when you take your cock and poke me in the back with it, and I don't wake up."

"Shut up?" I say, shocked. "You aren't joking."

"No." She shakes her head. "After I diagnosed myself, I searched just in case, I don't know, maybe you were perhaps suffering like I was."

"I was suffering," I tell her.

"Good," she says. "That makes it a bit better."

I laugh. "You think I wanted to walk away from you?" My voice goes low as I look into her eyes, and my stomach burns as I think about leaving her in that room. "You think that was easy for me?" I laugh nervously, not even sure I should admit the rest to her. "I walked out of that restaurant, and I could've sworn I had cement in my shoes. Every single step felt like I couldn't move. I drove home and was holding the steering wheel so tight my hands had cramps when I got home. I almost turned the car around ten times. Ten." I make sure she is looking at me. "Walking away from you, Frances, was the hardest thing I think I've ever done in my whole life." I shake my head. "Every single thing I've done in my whole life has been for my benefit and my benefit only. Not once did I ever think about anyone but me." I look down. "I like you, Frances." The words come out, shocking her and me at the same time. I knew I liked her the minute I didn't fuck her in that closet. I knew she was too good for that and she was too good for me.

"Ugh, obviously not enough to give me what I want." She chuckles as she sits with her back against her headboard. "I sent you a picture of my vibrator."

"I got it. Trust me, I got it." I laugh. "I even zoomed in to see what the bottom was."

"Rabbit ears," she answers me. "It hits the clit right as the shaft—" I hold up my hand, and she stops talking, trying not to laugh at me.

"What you should be looking up is if a man can die when no blood flow goes to his cock," I tell her, trying to get my breathing down as I try not to picture that vibrator going into her. Instead, I focus on one thing and one thing only—getting her to go out with me. "Let me take you out."

"Why?" she groans. "Why can't you just come over here and do me like you did the last time, except this time, don't fall asleep?" She smirks.

"Ahah." I gasp out. "I knew it wasn't because I couldn't rise to the occasion." She laughs, and her eyes light up as she lies down, her face going soft. "Why did you lie?"

"I did not lie," she says softly. "I wanted a third, and you weren't up to it."

"I was sleeping," I say now. "Did you try to wake me?"

"I did," she confirms now. "Nudged you."

"But did you suck my cock because I'm pretty sure if you put your mouth on me"—my voice goes soft—"I would have been up in more ways than one." I wink at her, and she throws her head back and laughs. I see her neck, and all I can picture is me marking her, biting her right before I suck her neck and sink into her.

"I'll remember that for next time," she says. I just look at her, taking her all in without a speck of makeup on her face and her hair looking fresh and washed like silk.

"Does that mean you'll go out with me?" I hold my breath as she stares at me.

She groans. "Fine, if it means we'll have sex after," she says, "then I'll go out with you."

"A date." I say the word, and she glares at me. I can't even believe I'm this nervous. My palms are sweaty, and my leg moves up and down as I wait for her to answer.

"I don't date," she states, and I roll my lips. "But we can have dinner." I smile at her, and I swear it's like I just climbed Mount fucking Everest. "And then we can have sex. If you want to just have sex, that is even better."

"Friday," I tell her. "I'll be home on Friday, and we'll go out."

"And then have sex," she inputs. "Right?"

"I'll call you tomorrow." She just closes her eyes. "Sleep tight, Frances."

"Brad," she says my name, and I don't think anyone has called me that in a long time.

"Yeah, baby," I say softly, and her eyes light up just a bit, and I like it.

"You better save some of that energy," she tells me. "You're going to need it."

I laugh at her. "Call you tomorrow." I hang up, putting

the phone down on the counter.

Turning the water on in the shower, I undress, and all I can think of is her. I grab the phone, wanting to call her back, but instead, I just put it down, and I wait for tomorrow. The first thing I do when I wake up is grab the phone and text her.

Me: Good morning. How did you sleep?

She answers me right away.

Fran: My vagina is still restless.

All I can do is laugh, shaking my head as I head out the door toward the plane.

Me: I promise to make it up to you.

Fran: You can bet your ass I'm going to make sure you keep that promise.

I put my phone in my pocket. "Oh, trust me, Frances. I'm going to keep that promise."

TWENTY-ONE

FRANCES

I WALK OUT of the office building when the sun is still out, and I smile when the phone beeps in my purse. "Wow," Ava says from beside me, and I look over at her. "I thought for sure you were a vampire and that once we walked into the sunlight, you would shine." I shake my head, laughing. "Seriously, you get here before everyone, and you leave way later than everyone else." We walk side by side toward our cars. "You must have big plans if you are leaving work early."

"My sister is coming down, and we are going to spend the weekend at the spa." The lie comes out of my mouth. What was I supposed to tell her? I'm going to fuck Wilson hopefully all weekend long?

"Fun." She stops at her car, pressing the unlock button and opening the door. "Have fun and let loose."

"I will," I say, stopping at my own car and getting in. "I plan to let it all loose." Putting my purse on the passenger seat, I start the car. The phone beeps again, and I reach into my purse, taking it out and seeing that it's from him.

Wilson: Tonight is the night. Pick you up at eight.

My heart starts to pound away in my chest. All week, he's been sending me a countdown to the date. And every single time, it takes me a good five minutes to get the nerves out of me. My stomach was lurching every single time I saw his name. It was annoying as fuck, and after thinking about it, I would go from nervous to pissed about it. I was a fucking mess, and I hated this feeling so much.

Me: What should I wear?

I press send and see the bubbles appear right away.

Wilson: Whatever you feel comfortable in.

I smirk, answering him.

Me: I'm comfortable with me naked and your cock in me. Shall we skip the dinner?

Wilson: See you at eight with clothes on.

Me: Buzzkill.

Starting the car, I make my way home, and I sit in traffic for a bit, which makes everything even worse because my mind is going around and around. I've never been on a date before. Like ever. I usually just head to the bar with friends, pinpoint a guy, and have fun for the night. I've never done the whole get dressed for one man in particular. I'm way out of my league, and I know I have to call in the cavalry, but even that makes me nervous because I don't want them to make a big deal about it.

After parking my car and locking the door, I walk into the house and call my sister, who answers after one ring. "Hey," she says, and I can hear honking in the background, so I know she's in the city.

"Hey," I say, going straight for the stairs toward my bedroom. "Are you busy?"

"No," she says. "Just had lunch with a couple of friends from college. I'm going to stay at the brownstone."

"Okay, I have something to say." I toss my purse on the bench in front of my king-sized bed. "And something to ask, but I don't want you to make a big deal out of it." I sit next to the purse and kick off my ballerina flats.

"Like now or after?" she asks, chuckling.

"Both. You can't give me a hard time now or after." I close my eyes, knowing that eventually I'll piss her off and she'll throw today in my face.

"Fine," she huffs, and I hear a car door close, and the sound of horns fades into the distance.

I take a deep breath and hold it when I say the words. "I'm going on a date with Wilson." I don't have to say more because she gasps in shock.

"I'm sorry," she says. "You are going to have to start way before I have a date with Wilson."

"Ugh," I groan out. "Just, I don't have time. He's going to pick me up at eight, and it's already six thirty."

"Fine," she huffs. "But tomorrow, I want the whole scoop."

"You'll get the scoop Sunday," I tell her. "I'll be busy tomorrow. Fucking his brains out." I get up and head over to the walk-in closet behind the wall that my bed is against. "See, I'm good at that. I know how to handle that. I just don't know about the whole date part."

"Why would you agree to go on a date with him if you don't want to?"

"Because the date will lead to sex, and the sex is what I want." I roll my eyes. "Can we focus?" I ask her. "What does one wear on a date?"

She laughs, and not just a little, a full-on belly laugh. A laugh that you run out of breath and then cry tears. "Forget I asked."

"No," she wheezes out. "I'm just, how can you be in your twenties and never been out on a date?"

"Bye," I say, about to hang up, and I know that if it's not her, I'm going to have to call Erika, and I know that Cooper is going to be there and well, ain't no need for any of the men in my family to know that I'm going on a date tonight. Ugh, just calling it a date gets my armpits sweaty and my stomach rumbling.

"Okay, fine," she says, and I hear the other car door shut. Then her jogging up the steps. "What do you need to know?"

"Well, one, what does one wear on a date?" I ask, looking at the clothes in front of me.

"You wear what you would wear when you are going out to a bar. Did he tell you where he is taking you?"

"He didn't tell me anything except to wear what I wanted," I say. "But I would like to wear something I can fuck him in his car with."

"So a dress would be your only option," Vivi says. "Or loose shorts you can push to the side." It's my turn to laugh.

"Oh, really?" I say. "Interesting little tidbit."

"It was in Greece. I was doing ouzo with Stefano while Uncle Mark and Auntie Vivienne went back to the house."

"You banged Stefano?" I shriek out. "Oh my God."

"I didn't bang Stefano, idiot. I banged the waiter in the bathroom." She laughs. "That was a good night. So I'm thinking you go with a skirt."

"I don't want to be that dressed up," I say, huffing out. "Like I want to look nice, but I don't want him to know I made an effort." I push one hanger against the other and stop at the little black dress I bought last year. I snap a picture and send it to her. "I'm going to wear this."

"Oh, that is sexy and flirty, and you can wear flats or even heels." I just nod my head, looking at the other wall that holds my shoes.

"I think I'm going to wear my red bottoms," I say, omitting that I wore them at the wedding, and it gave us the perfect height for me to bend over. "Okay, so I got the outfit. Got the underwear."

"Got yourself all waxed and exfoliated?" We both laugh out because I totally got myself waxed and ready for tonight.

"Okay, I think I'm good," I say. "Wish me luck."

"Godspeed." She laughs. "One small step for mankind, one giant leap for mankind." I hang up on her as she laughs her ass off.

I pick up the phone and send Wilson a text.

Me: Hair up or down?

I put the phone down and step into the shower to wash my hair. I shave my legs to make sure everything is smooth, and when I step out and wrap myself in a towel, I look down and see that he answered me.

Wilson: *Hair down. One hour.*

Putting the phone down, I grab my lavender oil and proceed to make my whole body silky soft. Ignoring the panging of my heart as I dry my hair and leave it loose. All I put on is mascara and a touch of lip gloss. The tiny lace panties are really a waste of time. It's like a floss really, the only thing is a small square. Grabbing the one-piece black dress, I slip it on and zip up the side, then walk over to the full mirror and fix myself.

The long sleeves are tight around the wrists, making the sleeves puff out a bit. The black lace is too dark to see through. The front goes down to the middle of my chest, each side with a built-in bra, but all you see is that I'm not wearing a bra. The waist fits perfectly, and then it flares out just a touch to my mid-thigh. The lace is see-through on the skirt, but it has a black slip under it. I slip on my black heels with red bottoms that are sky high and will have my feet begging to be let free in an hour, but they make my legs look like they go on for days.

The doorbell rings, and I take one more look at myself in the mirror before walking out to grab my black Chanel purse. I walk downstairs, and nothing could have prepared me for him. Not all the handbooks in the world. Not all the notes. Not all the conversations.

He stands there wearing black jeans and a black polo shirt. The scruff on his face makes him look even tougher. His eyes are crystal blue, and in his hand, he holds a bouquet of roses wrapped in lilac. He smiles huge when he sees me, and his eyes never leave mine. I can't help but also smile when he holds out the roses for me. "Thank you," I say, grabbing them. "Let me put these in a vase, and we can go. Come in," I tell him. He walks in, but I only take one step before his arm comes around my waist.

My back is pulled into his chest. "Hi," he says into my ear, and my heart beats so hard in my chest it's echoing to my ears.

My eyes go down to look at his hand resting on my stomach, and I turn my head to the side to look at him. "Hi," I whisper. Something is going on inside me, and I don't know what it is for the life of me.

His head bends down to kiss my neck. "You smell good," he says, his voice soft.

"Do I smell good enough for you to fuck me in the hallway?" I see the smirk fill his face. "Or on the couch? I'm not picky."

"You smell good enough." His nose rubs my jaw, and I turn my face, hoping he kisses me. "To eat."

"I'm good with that, too," I whisper, and my whole body feels like it's going to melt under his touch.

"Put the roses in water, baby, and we can go," he says, kissing my lips softly. His hand lets go of me, and I take a step forward, hoping like fuck my knees don't give out. My hands clutch the roses as I look for a vase.

"These are beautiful." I look down and smell them as I find a vase and fill it with water. I cut the ribbon off the roses and put them in the vase. "I love flowers."

"Good to know," he says. I look at him, and I swear he literally makes my heart skip a beat. I really need to get this date over with so we can have sex, and I can be over this whole thing.

I walk around the counter now. "Shall we go?" I say. We walk side by side, and he slips his hand in mine.

"Are you not going to bring an overnight bag?" he asks.

I walk out, locking the door. "Why would I bring a bag if I plan to be naked the whole time?" I walk by him as he stands there. "Hope you saved up your energy, Wilson." I lean over and kiss his lips. "I know I did."

TWENTY-TWO

WILSON

SHE WALKS TOWARD the car, and I watch her. Her short skirt sways back and forth, and all I can see are her fucking legs. When she opened the door, I could swear I had died and gone to heaven. She looks that fucking good. I couldn't peel my eyes away from her. The smile was worth everything. "Are we going?" she asks when she gets to the car. "Or are we just going to go back inside and get naked?" She turns to look at me, cocking a hip. "I'm totally okay with that."

I laugh and walk to her instead of walking around to the side. My hands fly to her hair, and I grip it in my hands and kiss her softly on the lips. Her tongue comes out to lick my bottom lip, making me groan. My cock goes hard, and she moves her hand to cup it through my jeans. The minute she touches me, I spring back, moving away from her touch. I don't trust myself with her. She makes me do things I've never ever done in my life. "Get in the car."

"You are no fun." With a huff, she puts one long leg into the car and then the other. "I should have bent over and shown you what you're missing." She reaches out and grabs the handle, slamming the door. I put my hands on my hips and look up at the sky. "If you are praying to God, tell him I'm in desperate need of an orgasm." I laugh, looking at her walking around the car and getting in. "Okay, you have me in the car," she says, turning to look at me, her legs cross one over the other and all I want to do is rub them, kiss them, have them wrapped around my neck. "Where are we going?" I start the car and pull away from her house.

"It's a surprise." I lean over to grab her hand and bring it to me. "How was your week?"

"Frustrating," she huffs as she slides her fingers with mine. "The countdown was a bit much."

I laugh. "I hated that every time I wanted to call you, the time difference messed it up." Playing West Coast games are the worst for the time change. The games were also brutal, but I was so excited about getting home I didn't even give it a second thought.

"Are you tired?" she asks me softly, and I look over at her. "I mean, I can do all the work."

"Good to know," I say, pulling up to the restaurant. I stop the car at the curb. "But I think I'll be good." I open the door. "I've been saving my energy."

"Now that is what I like to hear," she says, opening her own door and stepping out. "Where are we?"

"Well, you said pizza is your favorite thing to eat."

Standing next to her, I grab her hand in mine. "And well, this is the best pizza place in Dallas." Her fingers hold on to mine as we walk to the black door. I pull it open with my free hand and walk in with her right next to me.

I look at her as she looks around the place, her eyes taking in everything. "Where is everybody?" she leans in and whispers.

"I wanted it to be just us." I look around at the empty tables. "So I called them up and asked them what it would take to have it closed for the night." Her eyes go big. "I know the owner, Fernando, so I didn't have to twist his arm too much."

"Welcome," Fernando says, coming out of the kitchen and toward us. "We've been expecting you," he says. "Right this way."

I follow Fernando past the bar and into the private back room, one table in the middle of the room. While other tables are around, they are pushed against the wall with soft candles lit on them. He pulls out a chair for Franny, and she lets go of my hand and sits down. I pull out the chair in front of her and sit down. "Thank you." She smiles at him and grabs the white linen napkin to put over her lap.

"What can I get you to drink?" Fernando asks her.

"Whiskey on ice." She looks at me.

"I'll have water," I tell him, and she turns back to him.

"I'll have the same." She smiles at him, and he nods and walks away. "You closed down this whole place?" she asks again, looking around. "I can't even."

"I wanted it to be private," I start to tell her. "And

I didn't want anyone to interrupt us or for you to feel like you were being watched." I shrug. "And you finally accepted my offer for a date, so I had no choice."

"You are just full of surprises," she tells me, and Fernando comes back with the two bottles of water and also her whiskey.

"In case you change your mind." He smiles at her. "So we are going to do things a bit different tonight." He slaps his hands together. "It's called the tasting menu. We'll bring out small portions of all pizza and pasta." I look at her. "One at a time bite-size portions."

"I'm ready," Franny says to him, and he's already under her spell. "I'm here for all of it." He nods at her and walks away. Someone comes out with a basket with three small squares of bread with a little bowl of marinara sauce.

"So." I sit up, and I hate that I'm in front of her. I get up from my chair, and she watches me as I grab my chair and put it right next to hers. "Good choice?"

She turns toward me now. "Great choice." She leans in and kisses my lips softly. "Best first date ever."

I laugh at her. "You have nothing to compare it to," I tell her, and she shrugs.

"I don't, but I have stories from all the other girls in my life and this." She twirls her finger. "This blows those out of the water."

"Well, if you're keeping score …" I lean back in the chair, putting one hand on the back of her chair. All I did this week was search for date ideas. As soon as I was alone in my room, I would google best date advice. I googled what to do on a date to make her know you like her. The shit I searched was insane, and I made sure to clear my history as soon as I was done with it. If anyone knows me, they know I don't do that. I don't ever put effort into something that isn't me. It's just the selfish part of me. It's a part that for tonight isn't even available. "I brought you ten roses."

"Okay?" She turns, putting her hands on her lap. "Is that a good thing?"

"One rose means love at first sight," I tell her. "Two roses mean a shared and deep love. Three roses mean I love you." She puts her hand on the chair between us. My hand reaches over as my finger traces hers. "Six means I want to be yours. Seven says I'm infatuated with you." I smile at her. "Which is what I was going to go with until I saw what ten was. Nine roses mean eternal love and ten roses," I say, looking down at her chest rise and fall. "Ten roses mean you're perfect."

"Oh my God," she whispers, and I laugh.

"It's funny the things you find on the internet," I say when Fernando comes back and brings two plates with him.

"This is margherita pizza." He puts the plate down, and I see that there are two small square pieces. "And spaghetti with marinara sauce." He places the two plates in the middle of the table and then puts two empty plates in front of us, filling her plate and then mine. "I'll be back soon."

I watch her take a bite of the pizza and moan. She didn't even go for the fork and the knife; just picked it up with her hand and took a bite. "So good," she says, and I grab my own piece.

"How was work this week?" I ask, and she looks at me.

"Good." She puts down her piece and grabs her fork to eat some pasta. "We did the show yesterday with my father." She avoids my eyes.

"How was that?" I ask her, and I'm pissed I wasn't there for her.

She shrugs. "It's getting better. Still a little awkward, but at least he's talking to me."

"I don't have any experience with that, but I think it's a good thing," I tell her and she looks at me. I can see she has questions, so I laugh. "What do you want to know?"

"No." She shakes her head. "I don't want you to feel uncomfortable." It's the first time anyone has ever thought about how I would feel.

"It's fine," I tell her. "It's not really something that gets to me or that I feel anything about. My father passed away seven years ago. I didn't even know until his lawyer contacted me." She gasps. "There was no last conversation with him. No I should have been there for you. Nothing." I shrug. "He didn't even leave me a letter. Instead, there was a reading of his will where he left me money. It was the first time I was ever called his son." She puts her hand on mine. "We all make our choices, and he made his. Nothing I could have done or said would have changed anything. I thought about going to see him once when I got the contract with Dallas. When I was drafted." No one knows about this. "I wanted to just go to him and be like, look at everything that I did without you." I shrug. "I didn't. Instead, I say fuck him."

"Well, I hate to speak ill of the dead," she says, "but he sounds like a dick." I laugh at her. "Besides, you can give him the big F you by being better than him to your own kids."

"I don't even know if I want kids," I share with her honestly. "It's not like I know anything about raising a child. Look at how I turned out."

"No one knows what kind of parent they are going to be," she says. "It's kind of a YOLO thing." I laugh at her. "The first one is pretty much a test drive. Second, you fix all the kinks in it, and by the third, it's perfect." She closes her eyes. "Shit, that means Vivi is the good one."

I laugh and lean over now. "Nah," I disagree, my hand coming up to cup her cheek. "Your parents got it right on the second one."

Her eyes shine now. "You need to stop doing that," she says, and I just look at her confused.

"You don't have to woo me." She leans in a touch, rubbing her nose to mine. "I'm a sure thing."

I laugh, mimicking her and rubbing my nose to hers. "But wooing you is fun."

"Well, consider me wooed," she says, kissing the side of my lips softly. My cock strains to come out. I want to grab her and place her on the table and devour her. "Now we ate some food." She points at the plates. "We've had small talk." She kisses the other side of my lips. "Now the big question is." She licks my lower lip. "Your place or mine?"

TWENTY-THREE

FRANCES

"WE'VE HAD SMALL talk." I tease him by kissing the side of his lips. "Now the big question is." I lick his lower lip. "Your place or mine?" He's driving me crazy.

"We haven't even finished our meal," he says, rubbing his nose with mine, making my whole body shiver when he kisses me. This time, he slips his tongue into my mouth, but only for one second, and then he lets me go. "Besides, I'm going to need more food for all the things you want to do."

I grab the glass of whiskey and gulp down the whole glass. "You are going to push me to drink."

Fernando comes back with two more plates with pasta and pizza. "Can I get another glass?" I hold up the whiskey, and Fernando smiles and nods.

"This is good." Wilson takes a bite of pizza and holds the piece up for me. I lean in and take a bite, and he isn't wrong. It's really good.

"It's really good," I say, and he leans in and kisses the side of my mouth just like I did to him.

"So tell me about your week." He puts his hands around my chair, rubbing my arm with his thumb. I turn in my chair and cross my legs.

"It was good," I say with my foot against his calf. "It was nice having my dad on the set." His hand moves from around the chair to my knee.

My body shivers under his touch. "Explain to me what you do?" he asks me softly, and his fingers rub my knee. My eyes go to my knee as I want his finger to dance along my leg.

"Well, you saw the interview process." I try to focus on the conversation and not how his hand is touching me. He moves his hand from my knee to my hand, holding it in his. He slips his right hand in my right hand, and his left hand goes to my knee.

"I did," he says, and I look at him, his gaze fixated on me.

"That's the easy part," I say as his hand on my leg goes higher and higher each time. I try to control my breathing, but at this point, I'm surprised I'm not panting like a dog in heat. "The next part is my favorite," I tell him, his right hand playing in mine. "It's when I get to sit down and go through thousands and thousands of old games and interviews."

He looks at me, shocked. "Really?"

I laugh at him. "Really. I even found a couple of videos from when you were in high school."

"Did you really?" He smiles, and I nod. His hand

moves to the edge of where my skirt lies on my thighs.

"I did, and I even found an interview from your first NHL game." I lean forward to grab the glass of whiskey.

"I can't wait to see it." His hand slips under my skirt. I bring the glass of whiskey to my lips and uncross my legs, opening them for him. His hand moves higher until his finger grazes my clit. The linen napkin falls to my side, so I grab it in one hand and place it right where his hand is to cover up what he's doing.

I look over at him, taking a sip of the whiskey. "I can't wait for you to see it either," I say as his fingers graze my clit again. My whole body is going into overdrive. It's the little touch and graze through the lace that sends shock waves right to my core.

"Are we still hungry?" Fernando asks as he stands beside Wilson, who doesn't move his hand. His fingers graze through the lace that sends shock waves right to my core.

"We are good for dessert," Wilson says, looking over at me to see what I'm going to say.

"That sounds great. Is there a bathroom?" I ask, and he points to the other side of the room. I move the linen napkin from my lap and get up, making his hand fall to the chair. "I'll be right back." I lean down and kiss his lips.

Once I walk to the bathroom, I look at myself in the mirror. My cheeks are pink, and I wonder if it's from the whiskey. I turn on the cold water, putting my hand under the water, and then dabbing my cheeks. My nipples are even peaked and aching to be touched, and he did all that with just little touches on my leg and my hand. I shake my head now. "Two can play that game," I say and peel my panties down my legs, turning to walk out of the bathroom.

He sees me coming and looks over at me as I sit back down. "Did you order dessert?" I ask him as I lean over and toss my black panties into his lap.

"What is this?" He grabs the little black ball.

"Those are my panties," I tell him. "Since you liked playing and teasing me, I figured I would remove the barrier." I open my legs now, my skirt falling between my legs. I move my hands up my legs and slip it under my skirt. It's a good thing the lights are dim in the restaurant. "In case you're wondering," I say, slipping a finger into me and closing my eyes. Fingering myself twice and then opening my eyes, I see him lean over me. His eyes are dark blue as his chest rises and falls. "I'm wet." I move my hand slowly, and his mouth attacks mine. His tongue slides into my mouth at the same time as his hand roams up my legs, and his finger slips in alongside mine. I gasp, letting go of his mouth for just a second. He doesn't even give me one second before his mouth is down on mine again. My hand comes up to cup his cheek as I turn my head to deepen the kiss. Fuck, his kisses make me weak. I've never craved kissing this much. Never. Our fingers move slowly in and out of me. "Faster," I say when I let go of him for a second.

"No," he says, his tongue invading my mouth so I can't even talk. He swallows my groan as my orgasm approaches. I wish I could spread my legs more. Right before I'm about to come, his thumb flicks my clit, and it's the extra push I needed. He doesn't let go of my mouth as I moan out my orgasm. It feels like I'm crashing against the rock. All I want to do is moan, but I can't. He slowly lets go of my lips when my orgasm passes. "That's one," he says, pulling his finger out of me and then sucking it into his mouth. "Hmm." He kisses me now. "Better than I remembered." I look around seeing that no one is around.

"I told Fernando to pack up the dessert, leave it by the door, and to give us some private time," he says as I take my finger out of me. He grabs my hand, licking it clean, and I press my knees together, watching him. "You know what I've been dying to do," he says, and all I can do is look at him. "This." He slips his hand into the front of my dress, grasping my nipple between his two fingers and pinching it. "I think we should head out." He stands, and I can see his cock outlined in his pants.

I get up, holding the table. My knees are a little weak, then walking over to him. Standing right in front of him "You know what I've been dying to do?" I tell him as my hand comes out and palms his cock through his pants. "Suck your cock," I say, moving my hand up and down. "I couldn't get it down my throat the last time." I step even closer to him. "But I've ordered a bigger vibrator, and I've been practicing." One hand comes out to hold my hip, and he squeezes it. "So I'm anxious to see if I can take you all the way down."

His eyes close as I rub his cock, and if I knew that we were going to be alone, I would get on my knees in the middle of the restaurant. He must read my thoughts. "He's going to be back any second."

I lean in, whispering in his ear, "I've never fucked in public before." I nip his earlobe. "And I have to say the thought makes me wet." Chest to chest with him, I continue, "Feel how wet I am." His hand slips under my skirt as two fingers enter me roughly, and I want to put my leg up so he can have more access.

"You want me to fuck you on that table?" He pulls his finger out and then thrusts back in again. His back is to the door and his body is turned to make sure no one can see us. "You want me to sink my cock into you?" I nod my head as he finger-fucks me. "What kind of fuck do you want?" I watch his eyes turn dark. "Hard and fast?" His fingers are grazing my G-spot. "Or soft and slow?"

"Anything." My legs start to tremble again as I get close to coming. "Right there," I tell him, and he looks into my eyes. His fingers rub the spot over and over again, and I can feel the orgasm teetering. My nipples ache to be sucked, my pussy squeezing the shit out of his finger. "Right there," I say again, moving my hips to get him deeper. My eyes close to take in the orgasm that is going to come. My toes curl in my shoes, and just like that, he takes his fingers out of me. "What are you doing?" I grab his wrist, pulling him back to me.

"Shall we go?" He cleans one finger and then the next, holding out his other hand while waiting for me to walk forward. "Next time you come, it's not going to be on my hand." He bends and bites my nipple through my dress. I literally have to squeeze my knees together. "It's going to be on my tongue right after my cock fucks you."

TWENTY-FOUR

WILSON

"IT'S GOING TO be on my tongue right after my cock fucks you," I tell her between clenched teeth. I've never been so out of it for a woman in my whole life. When she tossed her panties at me, I thought I was going to come in my pants. Then she fucking fingered herself right there, and instead of stopping it, I helped her. Fuck, it was the sexiest thing I've ever seen in my life.

"You better fucking drive fast." With a huff, she puts one foot in the car and then holds her dress down so as not to flash anyone while she climbs in. "Next time, I'm bringing my little bullet with me so I can play with myself while you drive."

"Good to know there will be a next time." I wink at her as she groans and leans out to grab the door handle and slam the door shut. I walk around the car and get in, looking over at her as she pulls to put her seat belt on. Leaning in the back to put the bag on the back seat, I feel her hands on me. The button to my jeans open, and then the zipper is down in the blink of an eye, and her mouth takes my cock even before I know what is going on. Her hands are already pushing my jeans down over my hips. I can't move between the seats, and I don't want to because the heat of her mouth stops me from even breathing. I sit back down in my seat with her mouth never leaving my cock.

"Start the car." She lets go of my cock to fist the base as she takes it back into her mouth. "And drive fast." I start the car, and I take a second to think about just letting her suck my cock and enjoy it before I start, but she puts a foot on her seat, and her hands go to her pussy.

"You can play with yourself." I watch her swallow my cock as she looks up at me, and she's the hottest fucking woman I've ever laid eyes on. "But if you make yourself come …"

"Hurry up," she pants, "and drive the fucking car." Her mouth goes back to sucking my cock. I don't know how I make it home, and I'm thankful that the restaurant was seven minutes from my house. Or maybe I just drove really fucking fast, and I'm thankful no one was on the road. I had to think of anything but what she was doing, and only when I pulled up to my house do I close my eyes and take in the feeling.

"I'm going to come," I say, and all she does is take me deeper into her mouth as I come down her throat. I push the hair away from her face to watch her swallow my whole cock into her mouth. Pressing the button on the garage opener, I watch the door open.

I park my car in the garage, and she sits up, her fingers wet with her juices from playing with herself the whole time. "Turn around and put your back against the car door." She unbuckles her seat belt and does what I ask. "Good thing you wore a dress," I say. "Now put one foot on the dashboard and another on my seat." I don't have to tell her twice. Her skirt falls around her. "Show me your pussy." Her eyes on me, as she first pulls the top of the dress to the side, showing me her tits. Her nipples are pebbled and itching to be touched, and then she lifts her skirt. Her pussy glistens in the darkness of the car, and my hand comes out to feel how ready she is for me. One look at it, and I bend my head, my tongue licking up her slit. "Fuck," I say, moving my head from side to side. "So much better than I remember." Her hand goes into my hair as she holds my head to her. "You need to come so we can get inside, and I can fuck you in my bed." She just moves one hand to her nipple where she tweaks it.

"I need more." She's frustrated because she can't open her legs more. "Harder." I lick up one more time and then lick my hand before turning it and smacking her clit with it. Her back arches. My hands go to her tits, squeezing them, then pulling and twisting her nipples. She moans, and I turn to open the door and step out, pulling up my pants before walking over to her side. She gets out of the car, and my hand wraps around her waist as she wraps her legs around my waist. Her mouth slams on mine as she tastes herself on me. I walk into the house, and as soon as I see the table, I want to stop and put her ass on it and fuck her. Except my head has other plans, and I make a mental note to fuck her there tomorrow.

Walking up the steps as she bites my lower lip, she rubs her chest side to side on my shirt, and I can feel her nipples. "Jesus fucking Christ, Wilson, if you don't stick your cock into me, I am going to fucking just take it from you," she hisses when I throw her on my bed. I pull my shirt off with one move and walk over to the bed, bending down. She gets up on her elbows and looks at me as I open her pussy lips and suck her clit into my mouth. Pulling her legs to the edge of the bed, I flick my tongue over her clit repeatedly. Her hand goes to the back of my head and pulls me to her. "Fingers," she orders me. "Cock." Her head goes back. "Anything." My thumb plays with her clit as my tongue slides into her over and over again. My head goes side to side as I suck her into my mouth. She opens her legs even more. "Cock," she says. "In my mouth."

With a smile, I get up and kick off my shoes to undress. It takes her two seconds to toss her dress to the side, and all she is wearing are those fucking shoes. Same fucking shoes as the first time I fucked her. I crawl onto the bed by her face as she takes my balls into her mouth, and she fists my cock. I lean forward and slide two fingers into her, my balls vibrating while she moans, and I finger-fuck her as fast as I can. I can tell she's getting close, and she comes all over my hand. Wetting me and her hips thrash up. She lets go of my cock to moan out as she comes. I fuck her through her wave, and only when she's done do I take my finger out of her and slap her clit, making her back arch again. "That was," she says.

"Condom." I reach over, grabbing a condom from the side table and tearing it off. She turns her head toward the door as she plays with herself, watching me roll on the condom. Her finger plays with her clit around and around in a circle. "You better not fucking hold back on me," she says once the condom is on. I rub it up and down her slit, sliding my cock into her. We both close our eyes and moan. Her pussy squeezes my cock, and I open my eyes to see her smirking as she does it again. "Move that cock, Wilson." I put one hand on her hip and another on the back part of her leg as I fuck her harder than I've ever fucked anyone in my life. The sound of skin slapping fills the room along with our moans every single time she tilts her hips, and I go deeper and deeper into her. I lean down to take her nipple into my mouth, biting it and then sucking it. "So good," she says, her hand going to her clit as she plays with herself. My hands hold on to her hips as I slam into her over and over again. "I'm coming," she says, and she doesn't have to tell me twice because my cock is being strangled by her, and when she comes, I fuck her through it until I bury myself in her and follow her. I lower myself on her as her legs wrap around my hips and my face is buried in her neck.

"That was …" she says as both of us try to get our breathing back to normal. But nothing with her is normal. Both of us are covered in sweat. "That was good."

I lean on one elbow and look at her. "Just good?"

She kisses under my chin. "If I tell you that it could be better"—she tries to hide the smile—"does that mean we get to do that again?"

"You're lying," I say. Turning to the side, I slide out of her and immeditatly reach pulling her beside me.

"How big is your tub?" she asks me as she cuddles into my chest, and I look down at her. She rolls away from me, standing up and looking around the room. "Can I go?" She points at the bathroom.

"Baby," I say, getting up with her. "You can go wherever you want in this whole house." I walk to her, bending to kiss her lips. She turns, and I smack her ass as she takes off the shoes finally and walks with me to the bathroom. She passes the his-and-hers closet, her eyes looking around.

When we walk into the bathroom, she whistles. "Very nice." She smirks as she walks past the double vanity set to start the bath. "Do you have bubble bath?"

I just look at her as I take off the condom. "No."

"What?" she asks, surprised. "How do you not have bubble bath?"

"I've never even used that tub," I answer her honestly, and she gasps.

"Didn't your girls like baths?" She laughs, not even caring that I've had other women. Usually, it's something you always tiptoe around. I look down. "Wilson." She calls my name. "We obviously had other partners." I don't look up at her because the thought of her with someone else eats away at my stomach. She puts her hands on my hips. "I'm assuming you weren't a virgin the first time." She wraps her arms around my neck. "I'm okay with you having a past." She gets on her tippy-toes. "Now, do you have body wash?"

"Yeah," I say, pointing at the shower.

"Good, I'll try to make a bubble bath and you go get a condom." She pushes me out of the bathroom, and when I walk back in with two condoms in my hand, she is leaning over the edge with her hand in the water, but all I can see is her pussy. I walk up to her and rub her ass with one hand before I drop to my knee as I lick her. She hisses out my name, "Wilson." Then she lifts one of her legs and places it on the edge of the tub. I stand as she gets in the tub, and I follow her. She puts her head back on the edge of the tub as I sit in front of her. Her knees bend as I move between her legs, and she lifts her hips out of the water. My finger rubs over her pussy, and it's the most intimate moment with her. Neither of us says anything as she turns around, and I roll on the condom. She holds my cock up as she sinks down on it with her back to me. "I'm so full," she says, my hands going to her tits as she fucks me. Her head turns to the side, and my mouth covers hers as I let her take over.

For over twenty-four hours, we have had sex in every single part of my house. From the bedroom to the bathroom to the kitchen. Even the guest room when I gave her a tour. I just couldn't keep my hands off her. Even during the middle of the night, I had to touch her. I keep her with me until Sunday morning, dropping her off while she wears my shorts and a T-shirt. "I'll call you later," I tell her, and she grabs the handle of the car, avoiding looking at me.

"Okay." She gets out of the car, holding her dress in a ball with her shoes. "I had fun."

I laugh out at her. "Yeah, it was fun." She closes the door as I watch her walk into the house. I want to get back out of the car and take one more kiss, but I don't. Something is going on, and I can't explain it. I don't even understand it. I get to the rink and send her a text.

Me: Want to get dinner tonight?

I put my gear on and get on the ice, the lack of sleep definitely showing, and when I skate off the ice, I'm about to pass out. I grab my phone, seeing that she didn't answer me, and I'm wondering if she's sleeping. I shower and make my way home, not hearing from her the whole night. I spend the entire night with the phone in my hand, wondering if I should text her again. I sleep less than I did the night before, only because every time I turn and reach out for her, she isn't there.

I'm pissed when I walk into the rink on Monday morning, and everyone knows it. I'm pissed that I let myself feel something for once, and all it's come up with is nothing. Practice is a waste of time, and when I get out of the rink, I send her another text.

Me: Hey, you okay?

I try to play it cool, but it's not. She doesn't answer me all day nor does she answer me the next day. I do the stupid thing by driving by her house and seeing that her car is there so I at least know that she's okay. For two days, I've been on the edge. Two days, I've been holding my phone in my hand, waiting for her to throw me a bone. What the fuck was I thinking? I ask myself when I suit up for the game.

I sit on the bench, looking up at the stands and

toward the lodges to see if she's there. I shake my head, wanting to kick myself. When the coach calls my name, I fly over the bench, and all the frustration comes out of me. Their top defenseman takes the puck and starts up toward center ice, and I come in smashing him with a hit. The puck goes loose, and they skate to the puck when someone comes out and tries to push me down. "Pussy," I say to him as he holds his stick in both hands and pushes my chest. My gloves fly off as he grabs my shirt, and I fall to one knee for just one second before I grab his shoulders and pick myself up. I land a punch with my right hand, and he falls to the ground. I know I should let it go, but I don't. I give him an uppercut, and he falls to the ice, and I land two more punches before the referees pull us apart.

"That's going to cost you," the referee says to me, and all I can do is laugh because I don't have nothing anyone wants anyway.

TWENTY-FIVE

FRANCES

I SIT UP on the couch as soon as I see the hit from
Wilson. The throw blanket that I put on me falls to the
side. I got home from work twenty minutes ago exhausted
and decided to turn on the television. I was just going
to see what was on, but my head knew that I would be
changing it to the hockey game. The past two days have
been what I would like to call the most hell I've been in,
in all of my life. I have been on edge the whole time, not
sleeping, not eating, and my phone feels like a grenade
in my hand every single time I pick it up. My fingers go
straight to his texts as I read them over and over again.
The last three have gone unanswered, and every single
time I read them, I want to answer him, but I don't know
what the proper thing to do is. Every single minute he's
on my mind. Every single time I close my eyes, all I do
is see his face. Every single time I picked up my phone,
I wanted to call him. Every single time I took a shower,

I thought of him. He was in my every fucking thought, and I was so out of my comfort zone I had no idea what to do. I would climb out of bed in the morning, and the only thing I wanted was to wish him good morning, but instead, I pushed the thought from my head. This isn't what I do. I usually just dip, but with him, I've spent two nights with him. Two straight nights of fucking bliss. When he dropped me off, I felt like I left a piece of me with him, which was stupid.

I turn the volume louder when I see the gloves being dropped. My heart goes to my throat as I watch him land three punches and the referee goes to him. I stand, my whole body filled with nerves as I walk closer to the television, thinking that if I get closer, I would be able to see more. "What the fuck?" I say when instead of taking him to the box, they take him straight to the bench. I've seen enough hockey games in my life to know that it's not a good thing. I listen to the commentator talking as they replay the hit over and over again.

"It was definitely a late hit," one of the guys says, and as they replay it, I watch Wilson's face. It's filled with anger and rage. In all the time we've been together, I've never seen that face. Not even when he jumped out of his chair during the interview and walked out. My heart starts to pound in my chest as I watch it over and over again. I pace the living room floor as I try to listen to what is going on.

Grabbing my phone, I go online to see if the press is talking about it yet. I type his name in the search bar and press enter, and his picture comes up with his Wikipedia page. I look up when I hear horns and then see that Michael scored a goal, but I don't even pay attention as I try to look at the bench and see if Wilson is there.

I keep refreshing his name on Google, but all they have is the hit video. There is speculation that the players' safety board is going to be looking into the hit. I look at my watch and then up again to see that the game just ended. I rush into my bedroom, tossing my phone on the bed and then slipping on my jeans. I grab my phone and my purse, running to my car. I don't even take a second to think before I'm parking in his driveway, right in front of the garage door he drove into five days ago. Getting out, I walk to the front door and ring the doorbell. I look around, seeing no one outside, and all I can hear are crickets. I ring the doorbell again and then knock on the door.

Would he ignore me? I think to myself. I don't see why he wouldn't since I've ignored him for the past three days. I shake my head and try to look inside the windows. "This is one step above stalking," I say to myself as I walk to the side of the house and open his back gate. "I hope he doesn't have this place wired up and the cops show up to arrest my ass," I mumble as I walk into the back and see no lights on in the house. I take the phone out of my back pocket and call him. It goes straight to voice mail as I look up at the dark sky. "What did you expect?" I say, walking back to the front of the house. "Just leave," I tell myself, but instead of getting my ass back in my car, I walk back to his front door and sit down on the stoop. I take my phone out again and call him, and it goes straight to voice mail again.

I open the text thread.

Me: Hey, are you okay?

I wait to see the message go through, but instead of blue, the bubble turns green, and all it says is sent instead of delivered. I gasp out in shock. "Did he block me?" I don't have to wait long for my answer because I see his headlights shine on the house, and then hear the garage door opening. I walk toward the car as he parks next to me in the driveway. My whole body is shaking, and I don't know if it's from nerves or happiness that he's so close to me. The minute I see him step out of his car, my heart speeds up, and I'm thankful he's okay. He's dressed in a suit, but he carries his jacket in his hand. His white button-down shirt is open at the collar and rolled up at his elbows. His hair looks like he ran his hand through it a hundred times and my fingers itch to touch him. His eyes meet mine, and it's like a car crash to my chest.

"What the hell was that?" I point toward the street when we come face-to-face in front of his open garage door.

"What are you doing here?" he asks me, confused, and walks right past me into the garage.

"What am I doing here?" I repeat to him as I follow him inside. I know this house as good as I know my own house, and I've only been in it twice. The memories of him putting me on the counter in the kitchen crash into me. He stops in front of the fridge, opening it and taking out a bottle of water. His eyes are guarded and dark as he leans against the gray counter. The three lights that hang from the ceiling light up the whole room.

"So." He looks at me, and I hate that he feels like a stranger. I hate that I'm not standing in front of him. I hate that his knuckles are red and swollen, and I'm not kissing him better. "What are you doing here?"

"Did you block me?" He laughs, and it's not a nice laugh; it's a bitter laugh.

"You ghosted me." He points at me, and I can hear the hurt in his voice.

"I didn't ghost you," I say, but I totally ghosted him. I know it, and he knows it. "I was busy."

He smiles, and it's not a smile that gives you that warm and fuzzy feeling. It's a smile that he knows I'm fucking lying. "Well, I definitely blocked you." He pushes away from the counter, and I try to swallow past the lump in my throat. It's one thing to ghost him but another to be blocked.

"Why would you block me?" I ask, my voice low.

"Same reason you would ghost me." He shrugs. "Now, if you'll excuse me, I've had a hell of a night." He walks by me, and I can smell his cologne, and my stomach rises up. "Close the garage door on your way out," he says, going to the staircase.

"Okay, fine, I ghosted you," I finally blurt out to stop him from walking away from me. I throw up my hands. He looks over at me, and I finally admit to myself that I like him. "I didn't want to ghost you, but …"

"But I have a reputation." He points at himself. "And I don't want a relationship." He points at me. "Trust me, I got the message loud and clear." He shakes his head, looking down and then looking up at me.

"I don't know what I'm doing either. I don't know what this shit is." I point at me and then him. "But I can admit that I like you, and I like being with you." Admitting this to him is excruciating. Putting your feelings out there and knowing that at any moment he could be like yeah, no, thank you.

"So I'm sorry that I didn't answer you," I say softly, and then I shake my head as the tears start to sting at my eyes. "I didn't know what to do." I take a deep breath and exhale. "But I do know that you're better than that guy on the ice." I take one more look at him before I turn and walk out of the room. I have to get away from him, my hand grips the door handle, and right before I pull the door open, I hear his voice.

"Why did you come here?" he asks, and when I look over my shoulder, he stands exactly where I was standing right before I turned to walk out.

"Because I was worried about you," I tell him the truth. "Because I wanted to make sure you were okay."

"I'm fine." He puts his hands in his pockets, and I just look at him. "Thanks for checking on me."

"You're welcome," I reply, taking one more look at him and then turning to walk out of the garage. I walk down the steps, and everything in me is yelling to go back in there. I press the button to close the garage door, and the minute it starts to close behind me, everything in me is yelling to stay. But then my heart starts to speed up, and I swear my heart is going to come out of my chest. It's pounding so hard in my chest that I have to take a second and breathe. Putting my hands on my knees, I take a breath and look over my shoulder at the garage door as it seals itself shut.

TWENTY-SIX

WILSON

I WALK TOWARD the stairs, and I hear the garage door close. My whole body goes ice-cold, and instead of running up the steps to my bedroom, I'm running toward the front door. I run out and see her hunched over. Everything in me stops, and I mean everything. "Frances," I say her name, and she looks up at me. When I pulled up and saw her car, I was so fucking shocked. My heart became so full in my chest, but then in the blink of an eye, it was gone. I couldn't believe it, but the shock faded and was replaced with anger. I was pissed that she spent the past three days ghosting me. I was pissed that I brought my personal life onto the ice. I was pissed that I was tied up in knots the whole time, and when I saw her, she looked more fucking beautiful than she did before.

"I think I had a panic attack," she says, getting up to standing. But she takes one breath, and then she starts to pant and bends again. "I'm fine," she affirms. "It's fine.

It'll be gone in a minute." My feet move toward her, and for the second time tonight, my heart stops. The first was when I pulled up and saw her car there. It was as if it was a sign from above. It's like I fucked up, but someone, somewhere, was throwing me a bone for the first time in my whole life. When I got off the ice, I went to my phone and blocked her number and then proceeded to pitch my phone against the wall. It's safe to say—wall one, iPhone zero.

"Frances." I walk over to her and squat beside her.

The tears in her eyes are gutting me. "I'll leave," she says, and all I can do is tuck her hair behind her ear.

I put my hand on her cheek. "Breathe," I tell her softly.

"I'm trying to breathe, Brad." She uses my name, and I know she's pissed. "Go away," she says angrily, trying to shake my hand off her face.

"You came to me," I remind her.

"Yeah, when I thought you were in trouble." She starts breathing fine, and I don't know if she notices or not. "But now that you're fine, I don't want you near me."

"Is that so?" I smirk at her. "So if I kissed you right now." My thumb moves over her cheek. "You wouldn't like it."

"I never said I wouldn't like it." She stands up, and my hand drops to my side. "It wasn't about that," she huffs.

"What was it about?" I ask her as we stand face-to-face, my hand still tingling from touching her face.

"It was about," she starts to say and then stops as I tilt my head to the side.

"You were scared?" I say, watching her every single move.

"Oh, please," she huffs out, rolling her eyes and crossing her arms over her chest.

"I'm scared," I admit, and her mouth opens in shock. Stepping closer to her, I hold her hips as I pull her to me. Her hands go to my chest, and my whole body wakes up. "Never really cared if anyone liked me or not."

"I like you," she says softly, looking down as her finger plays with my collar. "That is the whole problem."

I laugh. "Why is that a problem?"

"I don't know." She shrugs. "I just don't know what I'm doing."

"Neither do I." I put my finger under her chin and lift it so she looks at me. "I don't know what I'm doing either."

"I don't know the rules of what to do and what not to do," she says softly, and there is a vulnerability in her that I haven't seen before.

"We make up the rules." I wrap my arms around her waist now. "Rule number one is you don't not answer my text." I hold up one finger at her, and she smirks but then turns back serious.

"Rule number two should be not blocking the other person." She counters my rule with her own, holding up two fingers.

"So, what do you say?" I rub her nose with mine. "Can we try this whole relationship thing?" My eyes look into hers, my heart stopping, waiting for her answer.

"What if I fuck up?" She moves her nose side to side

with mine.

"What if I fuck up?" I ask her the same question. "As long as we are respectful of the other person."

"Fine," she says, and I swear my heart wants to explode out of my chest. "As long as we are honest with each other. Like if you get on my nerves." I pull her tighter to me, and she wraps her arms around my neck. "Like you being a stupid idiot on the ice."

"I was angry," I tell her. "And I haven't been sleeping."

"Are you going to be suspended?" she asks me softly, and I shrug.

"Last I heard, probably two games." It was the last thing I heard when I walked out of the room while the coach was yelling about me being a horse's ass. Not only did I let my coach down but I also let my team down, and that was the worst. While I got dressed, I refused to make eye contact with anyone. I never even said a word, just grabbed my stuff and got the fuck out of there.

"You're better than that," she says. She's given me something else I've never had. No one has ever really been in my corner.

"Can I kiss you now?" I ask her, not sure if we have to wait more before kissing. "I've never had a make-up after a fight before." I lean in, kissing her lips softly. "I've never had a fight."

"I think a kiss would be good," she says, kissing my lips softly. "Followed by a couple of orgasms."

"That," I tell her, picking her up, and she wraps her legs around my waist. "I can help with," I say before her lips come to mine, and she opens her mouth as our tongues dance with each other. I turn and walk back into the house. Our kiss never breaks as I walk up the steps to my bedroom. She lets go of my mouth, pulling the shirt over her head, and I see she isn't wearing a bra.

I suck one of her nipples into my mouth as she moans out. Biting and pulling back, and her head falls back. "I missed you," she says in a whisper as we get to my room and fall with her on the bed. My hands go to her face as I push the hair away from her, she looks at me, and I get another kiss from her. My tongue fights with hers as her fingers pull my shirt out of my pants. She starts unbuttoning the first button, and when it's open halfway, she lets go of my mouth and bends to bite me right next to my nipple.

I hiss out when her hand slips into the front of my pants, my mouth bending to hers as she unbuttons my pants and pushes them over my hips. Her small hand fists my cock as she jerks it up and down. She lets it go, and my cock cries out for her to grab me again. "I need you in me," she says, unbuttoning her own pants, and I take over for her, getting on my knees to help her pants off. She sits up and swallows my cock into her hot mouth. She bobs her head up and down my cock. My hand slips into the front of her pants, passing her panties before sliding my finger down her slit. Her pussy already wet, I slip a finger into her, and she stops sucking my cock to moan out. I want to finger-fuck her fast, but the restriction of her jeans makes that really hard.

"I need your pants off." I move away from her. "Lift your hips." She moves her hips up, and I peel the pants over her hips. When she has one foot out, I fall on her, my mouth sliding into her mouth.

The both of us moan now as I stand. She leans back and plays with herself as she watches me pull off my own pants along with my shoes and shirt. One hand pulls at her nipple while she sticks two fingers in her. I grab the jeans stuck on her leg and pull them off, her fingers coming out to rub her clit. She's so fucking sexy as she bends her legs to the side, I climb back on the bed and lie down. "Sit on my face."

"You don't have to ask me twice." She throws one leg over my head and sinks her pussy onto my face. She falls forward, and her mouth takes my cock. I lick up and down, slipping in a finger with my tongue. She moves her hips over my face, my mouth sucking her clit. She takes my cock all the way into her mouth as she uses her hand to jerk me off. My fingers are drenched with her juices as I slide my finger up and slip it into her ass. "Yes," she says, letting go of my cock for a minute. She pushes back on my hand, and my fingers fuck her pussy and her ass. "I'm going to come," she says, and I pick up my speed, and my cock vibrates in her mouth as she moans out her orgasm.

"Get a condom," I say, flicking her clit with my tongue. She leans over to the side table and takes one out. I expect her to get up and hand me the condom, but instead, she rolls the condom down my shaft.

"Time for me to ride," she tells me, straddling my lap and holding my cock in one hand as she positions her pussy right over it. "I've been dreaming of this for the past three days," she says as she slides down my cock.

TWENTY-SEVEN

FRANCES

THE PHONE RINGS beside me, and I pick it up to see his name. "Hello," I say, the smile filling my face when I hear his voice.

"So she answers," he jokes, and I just laugh at him and lean back in my chair.

"For the record, I never not answered your phone call." It's his turn to laugh.

"You just ignored my texts." I roll my eyes.

"I see you have a working phone." I look out of my office and see people leaving. Turning my wrist I see that it's just after five.

"Yeah," he says. "Just got it. When are you going to be home?"

"Usually around eight." I get up to go stand by the window and look out at the sunset. "But I can leave the office in about thirty minutes."

"Do you want to come and have dinner at my place?"

"That depends," I say. "What does dinner entail?"

"Well, usually it includes food." He laughs, and I love the sound of it. "But I can slide in something else."

"I'd very much like you to slide in somewhere." My voice goes low.

"Come over when you finish work and bring a bag." I hear a car honk. "I'll be waiting for you."

"See you soon." I hang up the phone and walk back to my desk. This morning, I woke up to his hand cupping my tit at the same time as he slid his cock up and down my slit. He fucked me hard and slow, and I loved every fucking second of it.

When I went to him last night, I didn't have any idea what I was doing. The good news was neither did he, and when he touched me, everything inside went into place. We couldn't keep our hands off of each other, and even during the night, when I would open my eyes and look over at him, I had to get closer to him, which followed with him fucking me fast and hard. I would be asleep by the time he got back from getting rid of the condom.

I finish what I'm doing and walk out of the office twenty minutes later, stopping at my house and getting a bag. This morning, I rushed back home to make sure I walked into the office at my regular time, and instead, I could have spent an extra hour with him. I park in the same spot I parked last night and get out, grabbing my bag as I walk to the front door. My hand comes up to ring the doorbell. He opens it two seconds later, dressed in shorts and a T-shirt. "Why didn't you come right in?"

"Hello to you, too." I stand in front of him, tilting my

head back, waiting for him to kiss me. He puts the hand not holding the door around my waist, pulling me to him as he slams the door behind me.

"Hi," he says softly, right before his lips find mine. I drop the bag by my feet, wrapping my arms around his waist. His tongue slides with mine, and I swear I feel fucking flutters in my stomach. He lets go of my lips and kisses my nose. "You look good." His eyes roam from my shoes to my top. "Sexy as fuck."

I laugh as he lets me go. "Glad you approve," I say, looking down at my dark brown pants with a black top.

"Going to have to fuck you in those shoes later." He slaps my ass, and I look down at my leopard red bottoms.

"I might let you," I say, slapping his ass. "Now, where is this dinner you made?"

"I didn't say I was making dinner." He puts his arm around me as we walk into the kitchen. "I said come for dinner. I got takeout."

"Good enough," I reply as he walks over to the stove. He grabs the two containers from the oven, placing them on the counter.

"I got salmon or chicken," he says, looking over at me. "Which one do you want?"

"I'm good with either," I say. "Where do you want to eat?"

"We can eat at the counter." He points at the island where the stools are. "Or we can eat at the table outside." I walk to him and stand beside him, kissing his neck.

"Let's just eat at this counter so we can eat, and then you can give me my dessert," I tell him, cupping his cock that is at half-mast.

"I mean, we can skip dinner and go straight to dessert." He lifts me up by my waist and sets me on the counter. My legs open for him as he comes in, and I kiss him. His hands come up to cup my tits.

"I really need to wear dresses more often," I pant out when he lets go of my lips and starts to kiss down my neck. My stomach decides it's a good time to rumble, making us both laugh.

"Why don't we eat, and then we can do dessert?" he says, picking me back up and placing me on my feet.

"Ugh, fine," I say and then realize the only thing I ate today was a bagel this morning when he packed it for me. I grab the hot containers in my hands. "Hot, hot, hot," I say, walking over to the counter and placing them down.

"Wine or water?" he asks, walking to the fridge. "Or whiskey?"

"Water is good." I sit in the chair and wait for him to come to me. He drops two water bottles on the counter and goes over to grab the forks and the knives. He sits next to me. "So, how was your day?" I ask, and he just shrugs. "What did Nico say?"

"Not much to say," he responds, grabbing the plate closest to him. "Suspended two games." He looks down. "It was a stupid play, but what's done is done. How was your day?"

"The same," I say, biting into the salmon. "I was searching for interviews all day long."

"Can you do that working from home?" he asks, and

I just shake my head.

"If I miss a day." I take another bite, looking down at my plate and avoiding his stare. I can see him looking at me. "The old men would have a field day."

"What do you mean?" he asks me, and my stomach gets tied into knots. I stab a piece of potato and pop it into my mouth. I look away from him, not sure I want to say the words.

"If I say the words out loud, it's in the universe and means it's a problem," I admit, looking sideways at him. He just waits for me and gives me the time to say things. He isn't pushing me to tell him anything; he isn't doing anything except waiting and giving me space. "It has not been easy."

"What does that mean?" he asks me, and I just shrug, looking back down into my plate.

"They are set in their ways, and it's not easy to change. Especially when the change is coming from a woman who is half your age." I swallow down the lump in my throat. "So every single time they can fuck with me, they do. From pointing out how my outfits are not appropriate, to trying to go over my head and change the way we film. It's been a battle since the first show and it's only gotten worse, even with the ratings going up. They just kick you down and I'm not going to let them win." I try to make it seem like it doesn't bother me or they aren't getting under my skin. But truth be told, I came so close to telling them to fuck off, but then they win.

"You better not," he says, then he laughs. "Those poor

schmucks have no idea what they are in for."

I smile. "Really?" He nods and smiles at me. In the past six months, I've heard the same thing from my family members, but hearing it from him just fills me up. I look at him, his eyes lighter in the light, and my heart skips a fucking beat. It's just like everyone told me it would be. It's exactly what they described, it's exactly what I knew I would never feel, yet with him, I can't help but feel it. It's the exact thing I was avoiding, but it pulls me to him.

"I've watched the shows." He admits to me, and I can't help but feel proud. My blood and sweat go into that show and I'm glad it shows. "They were the best I've seen. From the interview to the clips. You are doing good, Frances."

"Thank you," I say softly. "Maybe after hockey, you can do motivational speaking." I nudge him with my shoulder and he just laughs.

"Can you imagine? That would be the worst thing for everyone."

"What do you think you'll do after hockey?" I ask him and he shrugs.

"I have no clue, honestly." He leans back in the stool. "I've been giving it a lot of thought lately. I can just retire and be good."

"Well, what do you do in the off-season?" I ask him.

"Travel, train," he says, putting one hand on the back of my stool. "Relax."

"Have you thought about doing a hockey camp?" I ask him, and he laughs.

"Who is going to send their kids to a hockey camp for me to coach?" He laughs, but I can see it bothers him. "I can teach them how to fight."

"Stop." I put up a hand. "You're a great player, and your stats speak for themselves. Okay, maybe not a hockey camp for you to coach, but what if you do special guest. Drop in to different camps and speak to the kids. Sort of, don't do what I do."

"I mean, I guess I could do that," he says.

"My uncle Justin," I tell him. "He runs one for underprivileged kids."

"That's what I would do," he says. "Help out kids who can't afford it."

"So do it," I tell him, and he rolls his eyes at me.

"It isn't that easy." He pushes and gets off his chair.

"Yes, it is," I tell him. "It's that easy. You get in touch with hockey coaches and ask them to nominate kids to be part of the program." He stares at me from the other side of the counter. "If you want, I can help you start it up."

"You have enough on your plate," he says, and I look at him.

"Yeah, I do, but," I say, pushing myself from the counter. "I know someone who doesn't, and I think this is just what she needs. My cousin Alex has no idea what she wants to do, but I know she loves to help those in need. Last year, she helped with The Horton Foundation, and she killed it. If you want, I can ask her. She's coming down this weekend, and maybe you can meet her and see."

"And you are worried about some old guys stopping

you," he says, pushing off from the counter and coming to me. "Are you full?"

"No." I wink at him. "I left room for dessert. But I want to shower first," I tell him, and he smiles. "I can join you."

"Actually, I'll shower first, and then you can get in," I say, walking to my bag and running up the stairs. I close the door and undress as fast as I can, showering in record time, wrapping myself in a towel, and when I open the door, he's sitting on the bed watching television. "Your turn."

"We could have saved the water." He gets up, walking to me and bending to kiss me.

"Hurry up," I urge. He walks away from me, and I see him peel his shirt from his body. He doesn't even close the door, and when he takes off his shorts, my knees get weak. He's got it all, the perfect chest, the abs are on point. His ass is thick and so are his legs and his cock is a masterpiece that I would love to get molded. "Has anyone ever asked you to get your cock molded?" I ask, and he looks at me with shock. "I see an activity in our future." I laugh, turning to walk to my bag.

I grab the white lace string thong I have, slipping it on, and hear my phone ring from downstairs. I grab one of his button-down shirts, then run down to get the phone seeing that Alex has just tried to FaceTime me. I call her back and her face fills the screen.

"Hey," I say when I see her.

"Hey yourself," she says, and I can see she's sitting in bed. "You look good. Have you done something to your hair?" she asks, and I walk to the couch and sit down.

"If you count being pulled during sex a hairstyle, then yes I have," I say, and she laughs. I look up to see Wilson walking down the steps in his white boxers.

"Where are you?" she asks, her face coming closer to the screen.

"At a friend's," I say, not sure what to call him.

"Does your friend have a name?" she asks, laughing.

"He might, listen, when you come down this weekend." I change the subject, crossing my legs. "We have to have coffee."

"Sounds good," she says. "By the way, tell your friend he needs to start pulling on the left side, the right side is higher." I laugh and disconnect the call.

"Is that my shirt?" he asks, stepping to me, and I look down.

"It is," I tell him as he stands in front of me, his cock hard. "Is that my dessert?" I ask, my hand coming up to cup his dick. I pull his boxers down, and his cock springs out. "Hmm," I say, taking his cock to the back of my throat and gagging a bit. One hand goes to fist his cock while the other hand is going to the middle of my legs.

He moves my hair away from my face so he can watch me swallow his cock, his hips move, fucking my mouth. "I need to get in you," he says, pulling his cock out of my mouth and sitting on the couch now. "Ride me, baby." He holds his cock up. I slip the shirt off my shoulder and straddle him, pulling the thong to the side. He looks at me. "I owe you," is all he says when he rips them away from me. "Better," he says, slipping two fingers into me, my head falling back as he finger-fucks me.

"Move," I say, panting, needing him in me. The both of us are not even paying attention as he holds his cock up, and I slam down on him.

"Fuck," he hisses out as his hands come up to cup my tits. I move my hips up and then down over and over again. "This feels," he starts to say. "Like heaven."

I bend my mouth to his as he tweaks my nipples, and I have to let go of his mouth while I feel like I'm going to come. "I'm right there," I pant, moving up and down. My head goes back as I come on his cock. My juices run down his balls as I slam back down over and over again.

"I'm going to come," he says. I just nod at him as I lean back, putting my hands on his legs. His thumb goes to my clit as he plays with it, and we both come together.

I collapse against his chest. "Fuck, how does it get better than the last time?" I ask him, and he just stares at me. "What happened?"

He sits up now, his cock going deeper in me. "We didn't use a condom."

My eyes go wide as I jump off him as if you just doused me with ice water in a bucket. "On my God," I say, looking at his cock and seeing that there is no condom there. "Oh my God." I point at his dick.

"I was going to say something, but then you just slammed onto my dick," he says, looking at me and he's not even freaking out.

"Don't blame me." I put my hands on my hips. "You had your fingers going. I was in a daze." I put my hand on my head. "I'm on the pill," I say to him. "But, um."

He gets up now. "The last person I was with is you," he tells me. "I got tested last month."

"Well, I haven't been tested," I tell him. "But you were the last one I was with."

"So, then, it's fine." He kisses my lips.

"But, um." I put my hands on his chest. "Is this?" I try not to sound suddenly needy, and he laughs.

"Is this what, Frances?" He says my full name, and I glare at him. "What do you want to ask?"

"You're an ass," I hiss at him and turn to walk away. I don't take two steps before his hand is around my waist, pulling me to him.

"I better be the only man." His cock pushes into my back. "Because you're the only woman I want in my bed."

His words fill me with an emotion I don't know what to do with. "Maybe," I say, trying not to laugh. He spins me around and tosses me over his shoulder. His palm comes up and slaps me right on the ass. "Brad Wilson." I call his full name, shocked that he just manhandled me with a blink of an eye. He carries me up the steps two at a time, and by the time he's done with me, I'll tell him anything he wants.

***

"Look at what the cat dragged in," Vivi says when I walk into the lodge on Saturday night.

"Trust me, no one has been dragged anywhere," I say, looking around at the full lodge. "I went willingly." I wink at her, putting down my black purse on the table. She sits with Alex and Julia, who just smirk at me. Their eyes are asking all the questions, and I know once I sit down, the questions will come. I also know I'm not sure what to answer her, not that I'm not sure about Wilson because, well, I want to keep him to myself. "Where are Mom and Dad?"

I look around and see them with my uncle Max and aunt Allison. "Hey," I say once I get close enough.

"Franny." My mother smiles as I hug her and then go to my father.

"How're you doing?" he asks me as he hugs me, and for the first time in a while, it feels like the old days. "You look good."

"I feel good," I say to him, smiling, and he doesn't let me go, putting his arm around my shoulder.

"Dallas agrees with you." My uncle Max bends to kiss my cheek. "Why haven't you been over yet?"

"Leave her alone," my aunt says. "She's a single woman."

I look down, and I'm about to say something when everything happens in slow motion. Everyone's phone goes off at the same time. I look over to the table with my sister, who looks up with her mouth open. I turn my head to my father, who looks down at his phone. I turn to look up at the television screen with a ticker at the bottom, which almost makes me fall to my knees.

Wilson is once again caught in another scandal, but this time, it's rated R. Sex tape leaked with none other than his teammate's sister.

TWENTY-EIGHT

WILSON

"WELCOME BACK," NICO says when I walk into the arena. "Ready for tonight?" It's my first game back after suspension.

"As ready as I'll ever be." I smirk at him and walk down the hall toward the locker room.

"Look who's back," Manning says to me as I walk into the room. "Just in time for my big game."

"You didn't think I would miss the big one thousand, did you?" I walk to him, holding out my hand, and he comes in to shake it and pulls me to him.

"Glad to see you back," Manning says. I walk over to my spot on the bench, taking off my suit jacket. I can still smell her on me from when she hugged me, the smile coming to me right away just picturing her smiling at me. I can still feel her kiss on my lips, right before she jumped out of my car. We drove to the arena together, but she got out before I parked, and I have to say I hated every fucking thing about it. We will definitely talk about what the next step is, and by that, I mean when she wants to talk to her family about us seeing each other.

My head is down, the chatter from the guys is all around me. They talk about the game and what they are going to be doing afterward. But all I can think about is her, the fact that in such a short period, I've fallen for her, and I have no idea if she feels the same.

"Gentlemen," Michael says, walking into the room and going to sit down at his spot. "I don't know about you guys, but I would love to kick Dylan's ass tonight." He mentions his cousin who is the best in the league, who plays for Montreal, and is playing us tonight.

I hear commotion in the hallway, and I have just enough time to look up to see Cooper rushing back into the room, followed by his cousin, Dylan. I hear Dylan yelling for him to calm down, but the rage on his face has me turning to face him just before he grabs me by my shirt and pushes me against the wall behind me. Michael springs into action, trying to get Cooper off me. Manning jumps in on the other side, and all I can hear is the way my heart is beating in my chest.

Everyone in the room springs into action, and it's a clusterfuck. The media is there filming, and I can hear the sound of clicking around me, so I know pictures are definitely being taken. Nico is trying to get through to us as I look into Cooper's eyes. "My sister," he hisses, and my heart sinks. My heart speeds up so fast I'm surprised it's not coming out of my chest. Knowing he knows, the only thing that goes through my head is getting to Franny to give her the heads-up. To warn her that he knows, fuck, fuck, fuck. "You fucking piece of shit."

"Enough," Michael says, pushing Cooper away from me, but he never lets go of my shirt. It's fisted in his hands, and when they finally pull him off me, the shirt rips off me. He then rears his arm back, and in a blink of an eye, he punches my face. I can taste metal in my mouth, and the side of my face burns. The whole room is quiet, and everyone, and I mean everyone, is watching. Our team, the Montreal team. The coaches, the trainers, and the fucking media, you could hear a fucking pin drop on the carpet. When I turn my head to look up at the television screen hanging in the corner of the room, my eyes read the red ticker at the bottom before my eyes finally take in the whole screen.

Wilson is once again caught in another scandal, but this time, it's rated R. Sex tape leaked with none other than his teammate's sister.

"What the fuck!" I roar as I see images of Franny and me fill the screen. Not just Franny and me but Franny and me from last night on my fucking couch. The rage rips through me so much my whole body is shaking. My hands are clenching into fists, and I push Cooper off me. It takes me two steps to get to the television. I grab the hockey stick by the door and smash the television with it. The screen turns blue after the first shot, and when I hit it again, it turns off. I smash the television until the stick breaks in my hand.

"Out!" Nico roars. "Everyone, fucking out. If you aren't with Dallas, you need to get the fuck out of this room." Dylan looks at Michael, who nods at him and walks out of the room. The rest of the media starts to walk out also, clearing the room.

I take one look at Nico and shake my head, charging for the door. "I'm going to your office," I tell him from beside him. "She's in the box."

"On it." He looks at Cooper, pointing at him. "You need to rein it the fuck in," he hisses.

Cooper puts his hands on his hips and glares at Nico. I know that if I was him, I would tell Nico to fuck off, but Cooper has more control than I do. I open the door, and the media is like flies on shit with questions, one after another.

"Did you film that?"

"Did you leak the tape yourself?"

"Did you know she was Cooper's sister?"

"How long have you been with her?"

I ignore all the questions as I walk toward the end of the hall, opening Nico's office and stepping in. Slamming the door behind, my heart hammering in my chest as I pace the room. Every single time I hear voices, I stop and look up at the door. I know right away when she's close by because I hear the press calling her name.

"Frances, did you know he was taping you?"

"Frances, are you dating him?"

Nico opens the door, and she walks in, followed by Cooper at her back. My heart stops in my chest when I see her. I don't know what I'm expecting, but what I'm not expecting is the anger on her face. She walks to me, and all I want to do is make sure she is okay. There are so many words going through my head and so many things I want to tell her, but the only thing that comes out is her name in a whisper. "Frances," I say, hoping to fuck she doesn't tell me to fuck off. Just the thought of that makes my heart stop in my chest.

She stands in front of me, touches the side of my lips, and I hiss. I raise my hand to touch it and feel the wetness. Looking at my thumb, I see it's blood, which is why I tasted metal. "Who did this?" she asks me, and then turns around with lightning speed to look over at Cooper. "Why would you do this to him?" she asks, and Nico steps into the room.

"You guys have one minute." He puts up one of his fingers. "One. Then I want the two of you"—he points at Cooper and then me—"in that locker room. You need to get on that ice and pretend nothing is happening. I know it's not going to be easy, but the press is already having a field day with this."

"I want you to get out of here," I tell Franny, who just looks at me and pffts out in defiance. All I want is to grab her face and kiss the ever-lovin' fuck out of her.

"Not a chance in fucking hell." She shakes her head.

"Are you fucking serious right now, Franny?" Cooper says, his voice not low, and I'm about to take a step forward, but Franny beats me to it.

"Are you fucking serious right now, Cooper?" She folds her hands over her chest. "What the fuck is wrong with you? Why would I leave to give everyone the satisfaction that I'm running away?" She looks at Nico. "Their minute is over."

Cooper just glares at her and then storms out of the room. I don't hear the press, so I know that Nico probably had them kicked out. "I'll give you guys one second," he says, stepping out of the room.

"Franny," I say, my voice breaking.

"No." She shakes her head. "Now you need to get your ass in that room and go out there and fuck shit up." She smiles. "And by fuck shit up, I mean go score goals and not Rocky Balboa." My heart settles into place seeing her smile. She walks to me and puts her hands on my shoulders. "Now give me a kiss and go get 'em, tiger."

I laugh, holding her face in my hands. "You really are perfect." I kiss her softly and then let her go when I hear a knock on the door.

"Time's up," Nico says. "I need you in the room." I nod at him. "Frances, I'm going to take you back to the lodge." She nods at him. "But I need to speak to the team."

"Take your time." She takes her phone out. "I have something to take care of."

I walk away from her, and every single step I take, there is pressure on my chest. "It's going to be a shitshow," Nico says from beside me. "The press is out there going nuts."

"I have no words," I tell him. "Except when I find out who leaked that fucking footage." My mind goes straight to Tiffany. "I'm going to bury them." My hands fist, and the rage comes to me now, rage like I've never felt before. Walking into the room, I stand right in front of Cooper, who stands up. Everyone is on alert. "I let you have one shot at me," I tell him, "but if you touch me again, you can bet your ass I'm going to fight back."

TWENTY-NINE

Frances

I LOOK DOWN at the phone seeing the email that has just come in.

Taken care of. Call Ma later.

I'm about to answer the email when the door opens, and Nico stands there. "Ready?" he asks, and I put the phone in the back pocket of my jeans. When I walked into the arena tonight, the only thing I was worried about was that I would slip and mention Wilson's name. Never in my wildest dreams did I think a sex tape would up that.

"I'm sure my father is having a coronary," I tell him as we walk out of his office. When Nico came to get me, it was a minute after the footage was aired. I was standing there with everyone else, watching the screen speechless. So many things were going through my head. So many thoughts, but the only thing that really went through my head was making sure that Wilson knew I was okay. I knew that he would be surprised also, and I knew that he would worry about me and not himself. He may have this big strong façade, but he's put me first since we started all of this. "Thank you for taking me to see him," I say as we get into the elevator. "He would have been a mess if he had to worry about me."

"I just hope they don't kill each other out there," Nico mumbles, and I laugh.

"Well, this is one way to tell my parents I'm dating him," I joke with him as we walk out of the elevator, and he walks me back to the lodge, stopping at the closed door.

"You ready?" He puts his hands in his pockets, and I tilt my head to the side. "Do you want me to stay with you?"

"I'll be fine," I say, and the minute I step in, it's on.

My father looks like he's been pulling out his hair. My mother sits with Allison beside her with tears in her eyes. Uncle Max sits on the chair watching my father, and I can bet you money he's making sure that my father doesn't fly off the deep end.

"What did I miss?" I smile as I look at the couch where Vivi sits with Alex. Julia, Erika, and Jillian all sit at the square table in the corner. They smile at me, and I am thinking it's for encouragement.

"You have some nerve." My father looks at Nico, and he stands there looking at him. "Taking her to see him and stopping me."

Nico laughs. "You put yourself in my shoes, Matthew. If this was going on with your team, would you let anyone get close to them?" My father glares at him because it's the truth. "When he's not in the arena, then you can talk to him. But here." He points at the floor. "This is my house, and you are a guest."

"Fuck you," my father says to Nico, and Max gets up, putting a hand on his shoulder.

"He'll be fine," my uncle Max tells Nico. "I'll come find you in a bit for a press release."

"A press release?" I say, shocked, and all eyes turn to me. "For what exactly?"

"How could you do that?" my father says, his voice cracking.

"What? Have sex?" I look at him. "I'm pretty sure you and Mom have done it at least four times."

"Frances Grant," my mother says with clenched teeth, and I'm sure she is trying to smooth everything over.

I look over at her, seeing her sitting on the stool wringing her hands with nerves. "I'm not going to apologize for having sex." I stand tall with my shoulders back even though my stomach is in knots, and I'm one second away from throwing up. I really wish I had a shot of tequila for this, or whiskey, to take the edge off and give me courage for this fight. "I'm not going to apologize for being intimate with a man I'm seeing." I look at my father and mother when I say that.

Vivi gasps behind me. "You're seeing him?" I turn my head to see her trying not to laugh while all the women's eyes go big. "I thought it was just sex."

I take a big breath in. "Yes," I admit, swallowing, and I look over when I see Erika push away from the table and come to me with her glass of wine. "I'm seeing him." She hands me her glass, and I down the whole thing in two gulps.

"Not anymore, you aren't!" my father roars, and Max laughs at him. My mother gets off her stool and comes over to stand beside my father. My blood runs cold with his words. The nerves from before are replaced with the fear that after all of this, I might lose my father.

"This is déjà vu all over again." My uncle Max laughs, shaking his head. He comes over and stands beside me. "You need to calm down and listen to her."

My father runs his hands through his hair now. "She needs to stop being calm." He puts his hands on his hips. "And see the bigger picture." His voice goes soft when he turns to look at me. "This is going to ruin you." His voice shakes, and I know it's killing him.

"This is not going to ruin me," I reply softly. "Kim Kardashian had a sex tape, and she is a millionaire." I want my father to see I'm okay with this.

"She's actually a billionaire," Vivi says from the couch, and my parents glare at her. "But that is hearsay. Go on." She puts out her hand.

"Well, for one," Alex says, holding up her finger and making her parents groan, "I've watched the tape."

"Who hasn't?" Vivi says from beside her.

"Not that one. The one with Franny," Alex says. "And Wilson."

"Alexandra," my aunt Allison says through clenched teeth.

"What?" Alex looks around the room. "I wanted to

see how long it was. It's not like I sat there watching it frame by frame. I skimmed it." She shrugs. "Twice."

"Dear God." My uncle Max puts his hands on his hips and looks up at the ceiling. He pinches his nose and then looks at my aunt, who just shrugs.

"I will say your body is banging." She looks at me, and I can't help but laugh. "And high-five on the eggplant. You did good." The parents groan while the young ones laugh. "It could be so much worse. It could be a threesome." I'm the one who holds my mouth. "Bet you're happy it was one-on-one, huh, Uncle Matthew?"

"Dad." I walk to him and take his hands in mine. "I promise you that I'm okay. I promise you that I'm going to be okay." The tears flow, and it has nothing to do with the sex tape. It has to do with standing here in front of my father, seeing the pain on his face. He's the first man I've ever loved and the man I put on a pedestal. He's the man who would fight to his last breath for his family and those he loves. I know this is killing him, but I need him to know I'm going to be okay. "I promise you that if I'm not, you will be the first person I'll call to make everything okay." I smile at him through the tears. "Did I want everyone to see us? No. Did I want people to see my nipples? Probably not." He closes his eyes. "But c'est la vie."

"For the rest of your life, this is going to be out there," he says softly.

"It's not like I murdered someone, Dad."

"It's my job to protect you." His hands come to hold my cheeks, bringing me to him and hugging me. I wrap my arms around his waist as he kisses the top of my head.

"You can't protect me from everything," I tell him and Max laughs from beside us.

"Don't anger him just when he's starting to think rationally." Max slaps my father on the shoulder. "You did good. I'm proud of you. When we get home, I'm going to put a sticker on the chart for you."

"Fuck you," my father says to him, not letting me go.

"Sorry." Erika puts up her hand as if we are in a classroom and she needs permission to talk. "Forgive me." She looks around the room at everyone. "But we seriously need to think about a press release."

"Oh my God," I say, stepping away from my father and walking over to the bar. "How about mind your business?" I suggest, pouring myself a shot of whiskey. "I'm sure by tomorrow it will be old news."

"How about …" Alex puts up her hand. "If you watch it, you're a pervert."

"You watched it." Julia points to her, laughing. "Twice."

"For research purposes." Alex throws her hands up. "But those other people are probably watching it to get off to." She motions jerking off with her hand.

"This child of mine," Max says. "She's going to put me in the grave."

"Oh, please." Alex gets up. "You still got lots of time left in you, Dad." She walks to me and grabs her own glass.

"So we are going with it's private, or you're a pervert?" Nico asks, and I take a shot of whiskey.

"How about it was a private moment between two people that was never intended to be shared?" I point out, looking at Erika.

"That works." She takes out her phone and looks at me. "Your brother would like a word with you when he's off the ice."

"My brother can dream on." She looks at me, shocked. "Until he apologizes for punching Wilson in the face, I have nothing to say to him."

"He did what?" my mother says at the same time my father puffs out his chest. "That's my boy."

"Not okay, Dad," I say to him. "Wilson did nothing to deserve that."

"Can we just focus on one thing?" Nico says. "I'm going to get with Erika and draft up something."

"I trust Erika with anything," I say. "Whatever she thinks we should say, we say it. But in no way do I want the finger pointed at anyone, especially not Wilson."

"We are on the same page," Nico says. "Now I have to get down there. The period is almost over, and I don't want to leave them alone." He looks at me. "I'll tell him you're okay."

"Thank you." I take another shot of whiskey. "What a fucking day," I mumble to myself before turning around and looking at the screen that shows Wilson. He looks angry, and the side of his lip is bleeding again.

"Do you want to get out of here?" my father asks, and I just look at him.

"The press is going to be all over the place, and I think for the rest of the night, you should lie low," he says. "I would be telling anyone else that."

"Your father is right," my uncle Max says. "God, that hurt to say. It's like acid in my mouth." We all laugh at him. "But the press is going to be all over him."

"I'll take you," Vivi says, getting up. "They expect her to leave with you." She points at my father. "But if we just duck out now, no one is going to notice."

"Fine," I say, taking one last shot. "Let's get out of here."

"I'll take you guys down," my father says, stepping forward.

"No, the minute they see you, they're going to be on her," Max says. "Alex, go with them."

"Gladly." She gets up. "I have lots more questions to ask her."

I just shake my head and look at my father. "I'll call you as soon as we are in the car," I say. He nods his head, and I know this is probably the hardest thing for him. I walk to him. "Thanks, Dad." I kiss his cheek. "For not freaking out more than you did."

"I must be getting soft," he replies, laughing. "I'm waiting for a call. You take her straight home." He points at my sister, who salutes him.

"Ready?" Vivi asks me as she puts her hand on the door.

"I'll be fine," I say to her as I walk out of the lodge with Alex and Vivi on each side of me.

"Yeah, besides," Alex says from beside me. "They've already seen her butt-ass naked." Vivi gasps, and I laugh. "Too soon?" We make it to the car without anyone noticing us. I take out my phone and send Wilson a text.

Me: Call me when you're out.

THIRTY

WILSON

THE HORN BLOWS, letting us know the game is over. I'm the first to jump up and walk into the locker room instead of going on the ice to meet the goalie and greet the crowd. That was the longest game of my whole fucking life. I don't even know how many shifts I played. I don't even know what the score was. The only thing I kept doing was looking up to see her in the lodge. But I never saw her, not once, and it ate at my stomach.

Nico stands at the locker room door with his hands in his pockets, waiting for us. The phone is in his hand, and I don't even want to know what he did about a press release. I have no idea what is even going on. Nico nods at me just like he did the last two periods. He pulled me aside during the first and second period to let me know she was okay but nothing else. I walk over to my spot and start to undress. By the time I sit and get my skates off, the whole team has followed me in here. "Locker room is closed for the press!" Nico shouts, and I look over at Manning, shaking my head.

"Why?" I stop untying my skate to look over at Nico. "This is Manning's one thousandth game," I say. "He deserves to fucking talk to the press."

Manning laughs. "You're kidding, right? This is the best thing in my opinion. I owe you a bottle of scotch." I just look over at him, shocked. "It's a big game, but even though I said no, Nico set up a ceremony after the next game so the press can be all over my ass for that."

"That is great marketing," Nico says to Manning. "You should take over PR when you retire."

No one says a word the whole time we undress. Everyone is on eggshells, and I hate that it's because of me, again. I shower in record time and then walk out of the room toward the car. The press is there, but I don't say anything to them as I take off. I dial her number right away, and she answers in the middle of the first ring.

"Hello," she answers, and all the pressure on my chest is lifted for a bit. It's like a feeling of peace comes over me, just from hearing her voice.

"Hi," I say, pulling out of the lot. "I just left. Where are you?"

"Home," she says. "But I'm leaving, and I'll meet you at your house."

"Wait," I say before she hangs up. "What if the press is there?"

"So, they see me walking into your house," she says. "I'll wait for you in the backyard until you get there."

"No!" I shout, looking at the phone. "The code to the

front door is zero six zero five.”

“Got it. See you there.” I’m about to say something else, but I stop myself. She hangs up the phone, and the pit in my stomach is back, knowing I’m going to have to do something that I don’t want to do. Something that will probably haunt me for the rest of my life. I get to the house before she does, and I’m glad to see no one is waiting for me. Walking into the house, I toss my phone onto the counter and look at it, seeing more messages than I know what to do with. The phone has been ringing off the hook and vibrating since I got in the car. I know that I should go online and see what the fuck is going on. I know that I need to call Becca, hoping she feels sorry for me and we think of a press release. I know that I should be doing all of these things, but I can’t do anything until I see her. My whole body is filled with anger, and I’m afraid I’ll do something that would make this whole situation even worse if I go online. Although I don’t know how it can get worse.

Shrugging my jacket off, I undo the top button on my shirt, feeling suffocated in it. My mouth is getting so dry as the minutes tick by. I walk to the kitchen and grab a water bottle when the front door opens and then shuts.

I look toward the hallway and see her walk in, wearing the same thing she wore when she got dressed here this afternoon. My eyes roam her face as I look for any signs of tears or anger or anything. “Hi,” she says, coming to me, and my heart stops beating in my chest. Her hand comes up to touch my lip, leaning in to kiss me, and my whole body goes stiff. She notices right away when my hand doesn't move from the water bottle to hug her. "What's wrong?"

I avoid looking into her eyes because I'm afraid she'll see the truth, but for the first time in my whole life, I'm going to do the right thing for someone else and not myself. I have to say it fucking sucks. "We need to talk," I say, and she steps away from me, and my hand squeezes the bottle I'm holding because I was going to pull her back to me.

"Oh my God." She shakes her head and walks around the counter to glare at me. "You're going to break up with me, aren't you?" She laughs bitterly.

"Break up is a stretch." I shrug. "Were we really together?" My heart sinks and then rises to my throat.

She stares at me from her side of the counter. "Fuck you, Wilson," she says, and the back of my neck burns. "You don't get to pretend you're an asshole."

"Trust me, sweetheart." I smirk. "I'm one hundred percent an asshole, and I never have to pretend."

"Are you finished?" She doesn't move from her spot. Her eyes are a darker blue, never leaving mine. I take her in, and every single time I see her, she gets even more beautiful.

"Finished with what?" I ask her.

"Finished trying to pretend you don't care." She calls me out on my bullshit. "If you aren't …" She pulls out the stool at the counter and sits down. "Just let me know when you're done and when we can really have a conversation."

"There is no conversation to have!" I shout, angry

that she is so fucking calm and levelheaded right now. Instead of freaking out and screaming, she's calm, cool, and collected. "We had fun, and we have to part ways."

"Did you talk to my father?" She puts her hands in front of her and folds them together. "Or my brother?"

"No." I shake my head. "Your brother didn't say a word to me the whole game." The team made sure we never sat next to each other or were on the same line. "And I never saw your father." Every single time I sat on the bench, I looked up, hoping she would be there, but instead, I saw her father staring straight at me. I couldn't see his face, but I could imagine that he looked at me with hatred. Little did he know I hated myself for putting her in this situation.

"Good," she says. "So tell me why you want me gone?" I start to open my mouth, but she stops me, leaning back. "And if you give me this song and dance about how it was just fun and all that shit, I'm going to come over there and throat punch you." I want to smirk at that last comment.

"Fine," I huff, knowing she will see through all the bullshit anyway. "It's the only fucking thing I can do to get you away from this scandal."

"What fucking scandal?" She throws up her hand.

"You were fucking naked on television!" I shout at her. "What more do you want from me?" I point at myself. "For my whole life, I've worried about one person and one person only because well, no one gave a shit to be honest. But now …" I take a deep breath. "Now I have to make sure you are okay before I am. So there you have it."

She pushes away from the counter and walks around it to my side, and I know that if she touches me, all this fighting will be down the drain. If she touches me, I'll forget all about being the good guy for once and then just be the selfish bastard that I am. "Maybe in a couple of months, we can try again."

"That's not going to work for me." She stands in front of me now, not touching me. "Because one, I hate when someone tells me that I can't do something." She smiles. "It just pushes me to do it harder. And two." She takes a step closer to me, and I don't move. I don't even think I breathe. "I don't want to try again later when now is working for us." She lifts her hand to the corner of my mouth. Her finger softly touches me, and my stomach sinks and then rises. "I like this whole dating thing," she says. "I like this whole spending time together."

"Frances," I plead, but I don't know if the plea is for her to go or to stay.

"Wilson." She says my name in the same plea that I said hers. "Tell me that you don't want me here, and I'll go," she says. "Tell me that this is just a game to you, and you'll never have to see me again." *Tell her*, my head shouts at me, but my heart, fuck, my heart is pounding so hard in my chest. "That's all you have to do." She rubs my nose with hers. "Is tell me that you don't want this, and I'll leave you alone." My hand comes out to hold her hip. "So what's it going to be?"

"Why can't you just listen for once?"

"What fun is that?" She laughs and then lowers her

lips to mine. "So …" She kisses me softly. "What's it going to be?"

"This was supposed to go the complete other way," I tell her the truth. "You were supposed to be pissed and not rational." I swallow as my other hand comes up to rub her cheek. "You were supposed to come in here and call me names and walk away."

"Not a chance," she says. "You're going to have to try harder to get rid of me, Wilson." She leans in and kisses me again. "Because I'm not going anywhere."

My other hand comes up and holds her face. "Stubborn, stubborn, stubborn woman," I say as my lips crash down on hers. Her tongue comes out and meets mine, and here in the middle of my kitchen, I silently tell her that I love her.

THIRTY-ONE

FRANCES

HIS HAND COMES up and holds my face. "Stubborn, stubborn, stubborn woman," he says right before his lips crash down on mine. My tongue comes out to meet his, and my body settles into his. The last time I kissed him, his body went tight, and I knew something was up. "So stubborn?" he asks when he kisses me softly.

"I've been called worse." He laughs, and I can finally see the light back in his eyes.

"You need to call your parents." He leans in and kisses my neck. His arm goes around my waist, pulling me closer to him and palming my ass with his hand. "And plan a time and place for a meet-up." It's my turn to go stiff.

"Um, why?" I ask, placing my hand on his chest as I play with the button of his shirt. My body fills with nerves.

"So I can talk to them." He looks at me. "I need to tell

them my side." My stomach flutters when I think about him going to talk to my parents to somehow protect me.

"Before you talk to them," I say, "can we talk about us for a minute? What the hell happened?" I ask him the question that I've been asking myself this whole fucking time.

He stands and shakes his head, rubbing his hands over his face. "I have no idea." He looks me straight in the eye. "The only thing I saw was what they showed on television. I haven't even seen the tape." He puts his head back, looking at the ceiling.

"It's from when we were in the living room," I tell him, and his eyes turn so fast that if I wasn't looking at him, I wouldn't have seen it. He storms out of the kitchen and walks to the living room. He walks to the couch, ripping the cushions off. Then goes to the side table and tosses the remotes onto the floor. He tosses everything around the couch to the floor. "Get my phone," he says as he flips over the coffee table. "So we can see the angle."

"It was straight ahead," I tell him, looking at the couch and then looking at the fireplace right in front of the couch. Picture frames line the mantel, and I walk over to them, studying each frame. "This is it." I pick up the picture of him in the middle of the ice from the winter classic and turn the frame over to see the USB slot.

"What are you, James Bond?" He rips the frame out of my hand. "I didn't put this here," he says with his teeth clenched. He is so angry that he has a white-knuckle grip on the frame.

"Well, someone did." I look at him.

His eyes go big now. "My ex," he says, and my blood turns to ice. I knew he wasn't a virgin, but the thought of him with someone else is just too much for me to bear.

"When was she here last?" I ask, and the heat runs up my neck as I wait for him to answer the question. I mean, we said we were exclusive not long ago, but before that, nothing tied us together.

"A couple of weeks ago," he says, and I try to maintain my poker face to make it seem like I don't care. "She was naked in my bed when I got home." His hand goes tighter around me when he says the words. "I kicked her ass out of the house and didn't even sleep in the bed that night until I changed the sheets."

"What was she doing here?" I want to kick myself for even asking him. I shake my head and hold up my hand. "Forget I asked. It's none of my business."

"Of course it's your business," he says. "She wanted to talk about getting back together."

I take a step away from him, trying to joke about it. "Great." I smile at him, but inside, my heart is racing, and I feel like I'm going to throw up.

"I told her it was never going to happen." He puts his hands on his hips. "And it had nothing to do with you or us."

"Good to know." I look around to see if I can sit anywhere because my legs are suddenly feeling weak.

"We were together three days." I hold up my hand again.

"Can we not?" I say when he stops talking. "She might have had that camera in the house longer than you think." I look around now. "And there could be more."

His eyes roam the room now. "They could be hidden anywhere." His voice is a whisper as he looks at the frame in his hands.

"Can you imagine how many hours she has of you getting nasty with women?" The words feel like acid in my mouth.

He glares at me. "I've not gotten nasty with anyone but you." His voice is tight, and his hand is still clutching the frame.

"Are you sweet-talking me?" I laugh, trying to get him to relax a bit but still scared he might turn around and break up with me because of his ex. Not that I'm going to go easily and without a fight.

"That fucking …" he says, tossing the frame onto the floor and smashing it with his foot. Over and over again.

"I think the camera is broken," I inform him, and he just looks at me, his eyes filled with pain.

"I'm sorry," he says, "for putting you in this situation."

I walk to him and put my hands on his hips, and he tenses. "You didn't know." I swallow down when I see his eyes are filled with tears.

"Before we do anything, I need to know you're with me," he says, and I smile and look down.

"I wasn't the one who was breaking up with you. So you have to be sure you are good." My hand comes up to touch his chin. "Like no more dipping because the water is too hot."

He grabs my face in his hands. "People have seen you naked." His voice cracks. "You've been fucking violated."

I roll my eyes. "We got it taken down four minutes after it was up," I tell him. "And it's being monitored."

"What?" he asks, shocked. "How?"

"My cousin, Stefano," I tell him. "He is a hacker of sorts." I try to avoid his eyes since not many people know, especially not the family. They just think he's in computer science, but he's actually trying to create some sort of currency on the dark web.

"I'm sorry, what?" he says, shocked.

"It's not something he puts out there, but he's sort of a badass when it comes to computers."

"And he was able to get it down?" he asks, and I can see the moment he feels just a bit of relief.

"He did and he also put like, I don't know, a Google alert on it, so if someone tries to upload it again, it'll alert him. Then he'll tell me, and we can go from there." I pull out my phone. "This is the IP address where it came from."

"I'm going to go pack a bag," he says, his voice soft. "We are not staying here tonight." I look around at the mess in his living room.

"I'll come with you and see if I can spot any other hidden video cameras." I follow him up the stairs, and he looks fucking defeated. His head hangs as he walks into his walk-in closet. I walk over to the side tables that he has and look for anything.

"Who does one hire to come and make sure there aren't any cameras in your house?" he asks me when he walks out of his closet with his bag still empty. "Like, this is fucking crazy."

"I have to say." I walk over to the other side of the bed and check in the drawers. "As the first guy I've ever dated, it's quite an adventure." I wink at him. "Are you almost done?"

"I'll pack for a day and then come back," he says, and I walk over to him and kiss his lips. We walk out to the garage as we make our way to my house.

"Welcome to my home." I smile, and he tries to smile back. "Why don't you take a nice hot shower?" I suggest. "And then we can head to bed."

We walk into my bedroom, and he stops. "You have two walls of mirrors beside your bed." He stares at the back wall in shock.

"It's not what you think." I walk to the mirror and press the button beside it for the mirror to move to the side. "My closet and bathroom are behind here," I tell him, and he follows me.

"We are going to put a chair right in front of the mirror, and you're going to ride me." He slaps my ass, and I look over at him.

"That's my man," I say, and as soon as I say the words, I panic. Is he my man? How is one declared one's man? "So there is the shower," I mumble my words, and he just wraps his arms around me.

"Come and take a shower with me," he says, his voice soft, and his lips find mine as he kisses me. His tongue slides into my mouth as he peels my shirt from me. I unbutton his shirt and push it off his shoulders. Neither of us says a word as I bend to kiss his pec and then his neck. We undress each other piece by piece. I wash his chest and then his back, kissing him after I wash him and rinse off the water. He does the same thing to me, except he takes my nipples into his mouth. One side, then the next, and I'm craving his touch. I fist his cock while I clean him, our eyes both watching. He stops me right before he comes and turns to me. He starts to wash my stomach, the suds running down to my legs, and his hand slides between them. I open my legs a touch as his finger slides along my slit and then in me. I gasp and close my eyes for a second, and when I open them, he's looking at me. "You're beautiful," he says softly, his mouth coming to mine. My tongue licks his lower lip before his tongue meets mine. His fingers thrust in and out of me gently as I open my legs more. "So fucking beautiful," he repeats once he lets go of my lips and looks down to see his fingers buried in me. He takes his fingers out of me, and I groan, wanting him back in me. But he has other plans as he turns me, and I arch my back, thinking he's going to finally take me, but all he does is wash my back. My hands reach around me to play with his cock as he teases my ass. His hand goes over my ass, sliding into me. My breath hitches, and I want to feel him in me.

"Wilson." I'm breathless when I speak, and his hand pulls out of me. I look over my shoulder at him, and he bends to kiss my lips.

Opening the shower door to step out, he holds his hand out to me, and I take it. He dries me off and then himself, grabbing my hands again, I follow him to my bed. Truth be told, I would probably follow him anywhere. I stand in front of him beside my bed, and he whispers the words again. "I need you."

I get on the bed and open my legs to him. Holding out my hand, he puts one knee on the bed and rests in the middle of my legs. "I need you," I tell him, my heart hammering in my chest as I look at him in the darkness. My eyes search for his. "Please," I whisper.

THIRTY-TWO

WILSON

"I NEED YOU," she says, and I want to tell her that I'll give her whatever she needs. She searches for my eyes in the dark. "Please." She arches her back and whispers to me. I rub my cock up and down her slit and then slowly slide into her. The sounds of our moans fill the room as I slide in and out of her. I fall forward, rubbing my nose along hers as I move inside her. Our lips graze each other every time I thrust up. Her legs move up, and she arches her back and tilts her hips, making me go deeper. I take her lips with mine as I thrust into her. Her hands come up to grip the pillow under her. "Wilson." She lets go of my lips to pant out my name. "Faster."

"No." I slide into her softly again. My eyes look into hers, and I slide in and out of her, taking all the time in the world. I want this moment to last. I want this moment forever.

"I'm right there." She tries to speed up my thrusts by

moving her hips. "Right there."

My mouth covers hers as she comes on my cock, pulsing over and over again, and when she finishes, I let myself go. I thrust into her hard and then come with her arms wrapped around my neck and her legs wrapped around my waist.

I fall to the side and take her with me. She kisses my chest as my arms wrap around her. The words are on the tip of my tongue, but instead of saying them, I roll away from her to go to the bathroom. When I get back into bed, she is softly snoring as I pull her to me. "Good night, Frances." I kiss her head, and in a couple of seconds, I'm snoring with her.

The smell of coffee wakes me up, and I blink several times when the sun hits my eyes. It takes me a couple of seconds to remember where I am. Her smell is all around me, and when I reach for her, my hand comes up empty. Getting up on my elbow, I look over and see the bed empty. "Frances." I call her name and don't hear her anywhere. I get out of bed and go to my bag, grabbing a pair of boxers.

I can hear her voice coming through the house when I step out of the bedroom. I walk down the steps. "I'm not kidding, Dad, you say even one wrong thing, and I'm out." I follow her voice. "Trust me, if he didn't ask to sit down with you, I wouldn't be doing this." Making my way into the kitchen, I see her wearing my T-shirt as she puts the milk away in the fridge. "Good, so we are on the same page. I'll see you in about an hour." She turns and sees me there. "I love you, too," she says and places the phone on the counter in front of her. "Good morning."

"Hey," I say, walking around the counter and taking her in my arms. Her face lies on my chest. "How long have you been up?"

"Not long." She doesn't move from my arms but instead wraps her own arms around my waist. "Did I wake you?"

"No." My arms drop to my sides as she walks over and grabs the two cups of coffee in her hands.

"I was going to wake you up once I made you coffee." She hands me one of the cups in her hand. "I called my father." I lean into the counter and look at her.

"I heard," I say softly, taking a gulp of the coffee. "You don't have to come with me." I watch her face. "You guys just started talking again. I don't want to be the one who puts a wedge back into it."

"Wilson." She glares at me. "If you think for one second you are going to sit down and have a conversation without me, you are sadly mistaken." She shakes her head.

I laugh, knowing she wouldn't listen to me. "Let's get dressed and get this over with." I walk back upstairs with her.

"What are you going to wear?" she asks when she steps into her walk-in closet.

"My combat uniform." I laugh, grabbing my bag and tossing it on the bed. I don't even know what I packed last night. I just threw things in my bag. "Why?"

"Because I want to walk in there as a united front," she says, sticking her head out of her closet.

"And going in there with matching outfits will show them that?" I grab my black pair of jeans.

"It can't hurt." She shrugs. "Black jeans, got it." She turns back to the closet and comes back out with tight black jeans on with holes in both knees. "What about a shirt? What did you pack?" She looks into the bag. "Too bad you didn't bring any shirts with your name on it." I laugh at her. "Wear a white shirt." She walks back into her closet and comes back out dressed like me.

"Is this good?" she asks, and I nod my head.

"You can wear a potato sack and make it look sexy." I kiss her neck, and half an hour later, we are walking out of her house. She puts the address in the GPS, and it shows us that it will take seven minutes. My stomach starts to move up to my throat as I pull up on their street. My heart speeds up so fast I hear it echoing in my ear, and the back of my neck gets hot. Parking on the street, I turn off the car and get out. She waits for me and grabs my hand as we walk up the driveway toward the front door.

I have never in my whole life been as nervous as I am right now. Not during my first NHL game, nor at the reading of my father's will. Nothing, and I mean nothing, can prepare you for the minute you meet the parents of the girl you are seeing. Especially after they see you butt-ass naked banging their daughter.

"Maybe this isn't a good idea," I say right before I hear the locks on the door click, and the door swings open. Her father stands there holding the door in one hand, and he just stares at me. We've met a couple of times, but it has been under completely different circumstances. His eyes go to me and then to Franny and then to our hands linked together.

"Hey." Franny moves into the house and pulls me with her. She stops in front of her father and kisses his cheek. "We're early."

"Matthew." I hear a woman's voice as she comes down the stairs, and I look up. "Can you let them in the door?" She smiles when she gets to the last step and comes over to us. "Come in." She stands in front of Matthew and pushes him back when she steps back. "Hi, honey," she says to Franny, who bends and kisses her mom. "You must be Wilson." She smiles at me, and her smile is genuine and without judgment. "I'm Karrie." She holds out her hand, and I have to drop Franny's in order to shake her hand.

"Nice to meet you," I say. "You have a lovely home." The minute the words come out of me, I want to kick myself. Who the fuck talks like that?

"Why don't we sit in the family room?" she says, waiting for Matthew to walk, and when he doesn't, she takes his hand in hers and pulls him.

We sit on the couch facing them as they sit on the opposite couch. I'm so nervous my hands are sweaty. I rub them up and down on my legs to dry them. Matthew just stares at me without saying a word, and I don't blame him one tiny bit. "Thank you for seeing me," I start, looking from Matthew to Karrie.

"So what did you want to see us for?" Matthew says, leaning forward and putting his elbows on his knees.

"I wanted to have an opportunity to tell you both that what happened last night will never ever happen again." I swallow. "I would never ever disrespect Frances like that." I shake my head. "I know what it looks like, but you have my word that it wasn't me."

"Of course, it wasn't you," Frances says to me and then looks at her parents. "You have to realize it wasn't him. What motive would he have?"

"That's what I've been trying to figure out the whole night," Matthew says, and I can tell that he hasn't slept. His eyes are bloodshot.

"I am a lot of things," I start, "but a liar isn't one of them. Besides, Frances is mine, and I don't share what's mine." Karrie looks over at Matthew, who just side-eyes her. "It was my ex-girlfriend," I start to say. "I mean, the label girlfriend is used liberally. We dated." I stop talking because they don't need to know the details. "We found the camera that she hid last night in a frame." I look at them both. "And I'm going to be talking to a lawyer about what my options are."

"Oh, no, you will not," Franny says. "Fuck no," she says, angry now. "You will not give her the time of day." She shakes her head.

I look over at her. "Franny, she can't get away with this."

"She did this for a reaction." Franny gets up now. "She knew it would get to her, and you would call her. Trust me, I know. I'm a girl." She folds her arms over her chest.

"I don't give a flying fuck what she is expecting," I

say, my voice staying calm. "What she did …" I shake my head, the rage flying through me.

"It's taken down," she counters.

"And what if she leaks something else?" I stand, looking at her. I can't believe we are having this conversation in front of her parents. "We don't even know if there are more cameras in the house." I throw up my hands. "It's either I go to the lawyer, or I go to her house and I'm pretty sure if I do that, I'll blow it up." I shrug. "So I'm going with the one that will not land me in jail."

"Or you just ignore it and move on," she says to me. "It's probably already yesterday's news."

"It's eating me up inside." I point at my chest, trying not to raise my voice. "That you were put on display for the whole world to see." I step to her, putting my hand on her cheek. "There's this burning in the pit of my stomach." I rub her cheeks with my thumbs, my voice going soft. "So much that the rage comes next, and all I want to do is punch something."

"I don't want anything to happen to you," she admits finally. "What if she's waiting for you and makes up lies and stories?"

"I can't not do anything, Frances," I tell her. "You have to meet me halfway here. Let's go see a lawyer and see what he says."

"Fine," she finally says, rolling her eyes, and I bring her face to me to kiss her softly.

"Holy shit," Matthew says. I look over at him, and my hands fly off her face as if someone had lit them on fire.

"This isn't a joke or a onetime thing?" He looks at me and then at Franny, then back at me again.

We stare at each other, and I shake my head. "It's not."

THIRTY-THREE

FRANCES

I WATCH MY father and Wilson have a stare-off. My heart pounds in my chest because one, we just had an argument in front of my parents. And then two, he just kissed me in front of my parents. Not just a kiss on the cheek, either—a kiss on the lips. In. Front. Of. My. Parents.

"This isn't a joke or a onetime thing?" my father says, looking at Wilson, then at me, and back at Wilson.

I watch Wilson when he shakes his head and says, "It's not." I swear my knees get weak.

"What do you need from us?" My father gets up, and I look over at my mother, who has tears in her eyes. I start to breathe a touch heavy, and I know I need to sit down.

"I need to …" I turn and walk out of the room toward the bathroom. After closing and locking the door, I exhale the big breath I was holding as I drop my head back onto the door. "Oh my God," I say with my eyes closed, the stinging of tears starting to form as my heartbeats start to slow just a bit. "I love him," I mumble to myself. "How in the hell did this happen?" I turn to look at myself in the mirror. "I love him," I repeat, and I think I'm going to be sick. I wet my hands with cold water and pat my cheeks as I fight off throwing up and tears at the same time.

The soft knock on the door has my head turning to the side. "Franny." I hear his soft voice, and I blink away the tears. As I look at myself in the mirror, I see the tip of my nose is a touch red before I open the door. His eyes search mine. "Are you okay?"

"Yeah," I reply, pushing down the lump in my throat. Opening the door, I step out. "I just needed a little bit of a breather."

He slips his hand in mine, and instead of walking back to the family room, he brings us to the kitchen where my mother and father are making coffee. "I just ordered breakfast," my mother says, looking over at me, and I can tell she has been crying. I don't have time to ask her what's wrong because Vivi comes into the kitchen.

"What did I miss?" Vivi looks around the room. "All guests accounted for." She smirks. "No casualties." My father rolls his eyes. "Dad, are you going soft on me?" She walks to Wilson. "We haven't met formally." She holds out her hand. "I'm the good sister."

"She's also my only sister," I mumble to Wilson, who puts his hand out to shake my sister's and puts his other on my lower back.

"So what are we talking about?" she asks, going to

stand next to Mother. "By the way, I can't find the video anywhere."

My mother gasps. "Relax, I was just going to report it." She turns and winks at Wilson and me. "Luckily, no other videos turned up." She walks to grab a cup of coffee. "I also have your name as a Google alert, so as soon as one pops up, I'll be the first to know."

"I need to find someone who can do a sweep of my home to check for any hidden cameras."

"I know someone," my father says, taking out his phone from his back pocket.

"Of course you do," Vivienne says and rolls her eyes. "Who don't you know? It's like you're the Godfather."

I'm on pins and needles the whole time. My mind's in overdrive as I play out the past couple of weeks, trying to pinpoint when I fell in love with him. Even when we go back to his house and meet with the people to discuss the camera we found, I stay quiet and just observe.

That night when we slide into bed, he turns to me. "Are you okay?"

"Yeah," I say, trying to put on my poker face. "I'm just tired." He searches my face and then takes me in his arms. I fall asleep listening to the sound of his heart, and when I get up the following morning, it's to him bringing me coffee.

He bends to kiss my lips, sitting on the bed beside me. "How did you sleep?"

I take a sip of coffee. "Good, except the couple of times I woke up to your cock in me."

He smiles at me. "You kept rubbing up on me."

I smile at him. "Too bad we don't have a camera as evidence." He glares at me. "Too soon?" I sit up to kiss his lips. "Do you have to go to the rink today?"

"Yeah," he says, and I get out of bed and head to the shower. He jumps into the shower when I get out, and when I walk into the walk-in closet, the phone beeps from my bedroom. I slip on my gray pants with white and black lines. Grabbing a black short-sleeved cashmere shirt, tucking it in with a black blazer. I pick up my white sneakers and then change my mind and opt for black ballerina flats.

When I turn, I find him leaning against the doorjamb, watching me with his white towel around his hips. His eyes are crystal now. "I have to get going, and there is no time for whatever it is you are thinking." I kiss his lips and grab my phone, walking. "I'll call you later!" I shout out to him from the front door before walking out of the house.

I stop to get another coffee and a sandwich before walking into the office, and for once, there are a couple of people in before me. I stop and look at my watch to make sure it's not later than it is, grabbing my phone to double-check when I see the email.

Emergency board meeting requested.

I look around, then walk into my office. Sitting down, I turn on my computer. I see Earl coming in and going straight to his office. A couple of the other men walk in and go to his office. My phone beeps again at the same time as Ava comes into the office.

Board meeting in ten minutes.

"What is going on?" she asks, and all I can do is look out at the men huddling together. "I have no idea," I say with a sinking feeling in my gut. "But I don't think it's a meeting to shoot the shit and talk about our weekend."

I stand and head toward the boardroom. The men are all sitting facing that one chair in the front that is unoccupied. "Gentlemen," I say, walking in and pulling out the chair. "What is this meeting about?"

"It's come to our attention," Earl starts, "that there was a sex tape." The minute he says the words my back goes straight up. "Circulating." I look at the men as they all stare at me. "With you in it."

I tilt my head to the side. "You mean something that was shared without my consent?" I say, and as I look at the members, a couple of them can't look me in the eye. I know what this is. They are here to ambush me and fire me. Well, they've come to the wrong fucking girl. "Is that what you're talking about?" I look straight at Earl. "I never pegged you as the voyeurism type."

"We've held a vote," he says.

"You held a vote with whom?" I ask, putting my hands on the table. "How was I not included in this vote?" No one says anything. "So basically, I was prosecuted without being able to defend myself."

"What can you say? We all saw it. We know it was you," Earl snaps. "You can't deny it, and we can't have the station associated with you."

I laugh at them, and I'm sure a couple of them are surprised. "You guys are a joke." I stand with my head held high and my shoulders back. "First, I'll have you know firing me for having sex is discrimination." I hold up my hand when Earl starts to speak. "And I have grounds to file a suit against you for sexual harassment."

"That's preposterous," Earl says.

"Is it?" I stare at him and make sure he sees that he doesn't scare me. "I have kept extensive notes of dates and times when my wardrobe was discussed. But I'll cut to the chase. I'm not going to give you the pleasure of firing me because I quit." A couple of them look at me in shock with their mouths hanging open. I turn and start to walk out. "And just so there is no mistake, all my shows are no longer allowed to be used by this station."

"You can't do that. We own those shows," Earl says, getting up.

I smile having the last laugh. "That's where you're wrong. The station may have aired the show, but they belong to MFG Production." Looking around the table, I continue, "Which I own. Have a nice day, gentlemen."

I walk out of there with a smirk on my face, putting the production name into the contract was done at the last minute, and for once, I'm glad I listened to my father.

"How did it go?" Ava asks nervously.

"I quit," I say, and she gets tears in her eyes. "Ava, I would like you to come work for me. It won't be the same salary, and I'm going to have to see about benefits." She just stares at me. "Can you give me a week to come to you with an offer?"

"I would like nothing more," she says with a smile.

I look around the office now, the office I thought

would bring me so much joy. "Guess I need to clear out."

"Why don't you let me take care of it?" Ava says. "Don't give them the satisfaction of walking out with a box." She looks back at the men who are watching. "I promise I'll pack it myself." She steps forward and turns her hand, showing me a USB key. "I backed up all your files."

I smirk at her. "Look at you." I hold out my hand, and she slips me the USB key. "I'll call you later." She nods at me, and I grab my purse, walking out with a smile.

Stopping at the flower shop on the way home, I pick up eight roses and put them in a vase as soon as I get home and I start making my plan.

The phone rings, and I pick it up, a smile coming over me when I see Wilson's name. "Hello, you."

"Hey," he says softly, and I hear a car door close. "What time will you be home?"

"I'm home already," I say, leaning back in the chair.

"Already?" He laughs. "Everything okay?"

"Yeah, I just decided to work from home." I avoid telling him about what went down, knowing he'll blame himself. "Are you on your way?"

"I'll be there in twenty," he says and then disconnects.

I turn off the computer and walk downstairs to grab a glass of water when the door opens and slams shut. "Why is your front door unlocked?" He comes into the room, and I can't help but smile when I see him.

"Hello to you, too, sunshine." I laugh with the glass in front of my lips.

He glares at me, and then his eyes go to the flowers.

"Who the fuck sent you those?" He puts his hands on his hips, and I walk around the counter

"Someone is either hangry or cranky." I wrap my hands around his waist. "You didn't even give me a kiss." I look up at him, and he bends his head to kiss my lips. "Now the front door was open because I know you don't have a key, and those flowers"—I point back at the flowers—"I bought for you." I kiss under his chin. "Count how many I bought." I get on my tippy-toes.

"Eight," he whispers.

"Do you know what eight roses stand for?" I wrap my arms around his neck and look into his eyes as he puts his hand on my hips. "It means I support you, no matter what."

"Frances," he whispers. "I …" His hand comes up to touch my face. "I …" His voice trembles, and my stomach soars as his fingertips trace my face.

"You?" My voice almost cracks. He's about to say something when the doorbell rings, followed by a knock on the door. "Hold that thought." I walk away from him toward the front door.

The doorbell rings again, and the banging gets harder. "Jesus," I say, swinging open the door and coming face-to-face with my father.

His face is filled with rage, and my heart sinks when I think another tape leaked. "They fucking fired you?"

THIRTY-FOUR

WILSON

I STAND BEHIND her as the banging starts, and when she swings open the door, Matthew is standing there. His hair looks like he just ran a rake through it, and his face is filled with rage. My body goes cold, and my hands form fists beside me. At the thought of another video being out there in the world, I'm pretty sure I look the same way Matthew looks. "They fucking fired you?" he shouts at Franny, and my chest tightens.

"Would you like to come in?" she asks, and he walks in. He just looks at me, and maybe from the way my face is, he realizes that I didn't know. "I need a drink," she says, walking past both of us and going to the kitchen. We watch her walk out before we look back at each other.

Matthew doesn't move, and neither do I. "She didn't tell you?" I shake my head.

"I just got here," I reply and then look up at the ceiling. I want to kick myself for not even asking how her day was. When I got in the car and called her, I was so happy to hear her voice after the day I had that I didn't even bother to ask. "But no, she didn't tell me."

He puts his hands in his pockets now. "Take a couple of seconds to calm down and then." I look at him and glare. "They tell me counting to ten helps." With a chuckle, he walks away from me, slapping my arm.

I don't count to ten. I don't even count to one before I storm back into the kitchen and see her standing at the island with a glass of whiskey in front of her mouth. I don't even try to hide the anger in my voice when I finally say, "You got fired because of me." Her eyes come to mine, and if she doesn't take my breath away with her beauty, she takes it away with the sass that I know will come.

She puts the glass down in front of her, looking at me square in the eyes. "No." She shakes her head. "I quit because of me." She points at herself and then smirks, and I really wish I could kiss her right now. I also really wish we hadn't been interrupted before I told her that I loved her. My eyes go to the flowers she bought me. She got fired yet still stopped to buy me flowers to let me know she supports me. She isn't just perfect. She is one of a kind.

"That is so much bullshit," Matthew says, and I turn to look at him. "We are going to call my lawyer and see if we have a case." She glares at him, and my eyes go big.

"You didn't even want me to take the job." Her voice goes higher, and I know she's not only pissed; she's fucking angry. "You literally stopped speaking to me because I took the job."

"I swear to God when I get a hold of Tiffany," I say, shaking my head. "I'm going to fucking …" I continue between clenched teeth. "Fucking sue the pants off her," I say instead of what I really want to say.

"Getting her pants off is what started this whole thing to begin with." She winks at me, and I walk to her.

"Why didn't you tell me?" I ask, my voice going low. "You should have told me."

"Because there was nothing much to say." She turns toward me, and I bring my hand up to rub her cheek with my thumb. She smiles at me and then turns back to her father, my hand going around her waist. "Honestly, I didn't even think about work. I walked in this morning and was summoned to some board meeting. Only when they started did I realize it was about the sex tape."

"So you did get fired because of me." I look down at her as she rolls her eyes at me and grabs her drink to take another sip.

"One, I didn't get fired," she says between clenched teeth while glaring at me. She looks at her father, and I swear I see a sparkle in her eye. "I wouldn't let them fire me. Pfft," she says, picking up the glass of whiskey again. "Pompous asses," she mumbles.

"I'll go to the board and talk to them," I say, getting closer to her. "I'll explain what happened."

She looks down and then looks up, and I can see her struggling and blinking away tears. "I don't want you"— she points at me and then turns to point at her father—"or especially you, doing anything." Matthew and I share a look.

"You loved that job." My eyes roam her face as she looks down at her whiskey in front of her. Her hands are nervously turning the glass around and around in circles.

"It's been fucking miserable," she says, her eyes avoiding us. "I've been miserable." She looks up at her father, and her face shows defeat. "Every time I wanted to do something, it was always a tug-of-war with all of them. I just …" She takes a deep breath. "It's been a fucking struggle, and I was at my wit's end." She finishes the whiskey in the glass. "They did me a favor by pushing my back to the wall." She shrugs.

"Those sons of bitches," Matthew finally says, and we both look at him. He puts one hand on his hip while he runs his other through his hair, shaking his head. "They came to me before they hired you." I don't know why, but I pull her closer to me.

"What are you talking about?"

"They wanted me to buy the station and merge it with the New York station that your grandfather gave me," he says softly. "But I told them no, and I still remember him saying that he was going to make sure I bought the station."

"Oh my God," she hisses, shaking her head. She pours another shot of whiskey in her glass. "All this fucking time." Her voice starts to go higher. "I thought they hired me because I was good enough." She grabs her glass of whiskey and downs it in one shot.

"You are good enough," Matthew says, but she just looks down at the empty glass of whiskey in front of her.

"Your father is wrong," I say, and she looks up at me. "You aren't good enough for them." I smile. "You are too good for them," I say, kissing her head. "Way too good for them."

"You are the best thing that station had going for them." Matthew walks to the counter to get closer to her. "Your show pulled in triple the numbers than the sports show that plays during the day. And that was their best show to date."

"Well, then it's a good thing that all the shows I've produced belong to MFG Production." She claps her hands. "They thought they had a sucker." She shakes her head.

"Say what?" Matthew says, laughing.

"All the shows were shot by MFG Production." She looks at her father and then me. "I own MFG Production." She smirks. "Matthew Franny Grant," she says, and my eyes go big. "I started it when I signed the contract. I knew that if what I created took off, they would own my shit for life. There was no way I was going to allow that to happen." Matthew throws his head back, and the laughter roars through him.

"Now that's my girl." He points at her. "With that said, we are expanding into the Dallas market." He smiles at her as her eyebrows pull together. "I'm going to be spending time here and figured why not." He shrugs. "I want to offer you a job."

"No," she says right away, and Matthew just stares at her, not sure what to say. "I'm not going to take a pity job."

He laughs. "It's not a pity job," he says, and she rolls her eyes. "I told you I watch the show, and I told you how good it was."

"You have to tell me that. You're my father." She folds her arms over her chest. "What were you supposed to say? It sucked?"

"You should take the job," I urge, and she looks up at me. "At least listen to what kind of job it is."

When she doesn't say anything, Matthew begins his pitch. "You can do what you want, to be honest. You'll have the creative control to produce your own show. Exactly like you did for them."

She stares at him, and I can tell she wants to say yes, but she stops. "I'll think about it."

"Good enough," Matthew says, tapping the counter in front of him. "You start Monday." He turns around and walks out of the room.

"What just happened?" I ask, and she shakes her head, trying not to laugh.

She looks up at me, smiling, and all the sadness is gone. "I just landed a job."

THIRTY-FIVE

FRANCES

"WHAT JUST HAPPENED?" Wilson asks me, and I shake my head, trying not to laugh.

"I just landed a job." I turn away from him, running to the door to stop my father before he leaves.

"Dad!" I shout after him and find him with one hand on the door. "I'm not working for you," I tell him when he turns to look at me. Admitting to him how miserable I was had to have been the hardest moment in my life. Even harder than telling him I was moving away.

"Why not?" He turns to look at me.

"I won't work for you, but"—I hold up my hand, smiling—"I'll work with you."

He just stares at me. "I want MFG Production to have its own division." He crosses his arms over his chest. "I have ideas on shows that we could do from the winter classic to off-season training with the guys. I want to have my own team and run it my way."

"Are those your terms?"

"Those are the big terms." I fold my arms over my chest, mimicking his stance. "I'm sure I'll think of other things."

"I'm sure you will." He smirks. "Accepted. You start Monday." He turns to walk out but then stops. "Proud of you, Franny." My feet move toward him, and he opens his arms. I put my face in his chest as he wraps his arms around me. "I still want to sue those motherfuckers," he mumbles in my hair, making me laugh away the tears.

"Well, how about we don't sue them and instead make their shows tank and then wait until their stocks fall low and buy them?" I suggest as I step away from him, and he roars with laughter.

"That's my girl," he says, putting his hand on my cheek.

"Why does it feel like you guys are Doctor Evil?" Wilson says from behind me. My father and I share a look, but neither of us says anything because Wilson's phone rings.

"Maybe you're getting fired also," my father says. "Then I can snap you up for New York." I roll my lips as Wilson shakes his head and looks down at the phone.

"Hello?" he answers. "I can be there in ten minutes," he says to whoever is on the phone and then hangs up. "The team that is sweeping the house is done." He looks over at my father.

"Sweeping the house?" I ask him, confused.

"Looking for bugs and cameras," my father informs me. "Did they tell you if they found something?"

Wilson shakes his head. "I'm assuming it's why they want to see me." He puts his phone in his pocket.

"Do I need my purse?" I ask, and he shakes his head, so we all walk out together.

"Call me after," my father says, getting into his SUV.

Wilson opens the car door for me, and when I get in, he leans in and kisses my lips. "We have to table this conversation," he says, coming back for another kiss. "FYI." He closes the door, and I watch him walk around the car and get in.

"I don't understand what conversation needs to be tabled," I tell him as he starts the car, and I turn to him.

"One." He looks over his shoulder as he backs out of my driveway. "You didn't tell me about work." He holds up his hand and then puts the car in drive. "And two, you didn't tell me about your job."

I laugh, shaking my head. "One and two are the same thing." I lean over and kiss his cheek. "It wasn't a big deal."

"It is a big deal." He grabs my hand and holds it on his lap as he makes his way to his house. He parks his car, then turns to me. "I want to know when you have a shitty day or a good day."

I can't help but smile at him because, to be honest, no one has ever really asked about my day. Sure, my mother and father when I was in school, but it's just *how are you doing?* "Fine." I put my hand on his cheek. "Duly noted." I kiss his lips. "I had a shitty day at work and quit my job." I look into his eyes and smile. "But then I got another job that is even better."

"You're crazy." He kisses my lips. "Did I mention that?"

"Oh, baby …" I wink at him. "You haven't seen anything yet." I reach for the door and get out. I wait for him in front of the car, and he reaches for my hand. "Now let's go find out if your ex-girlfriend booby-trapped your house."

"Can we not call her my ex-girlfriend?" he says under his breath as he opens the front door of his house. "Or better yet, let's not call her anything."

I'm about to answer him when a guy and a woman start coming down the stairs. "You're here," the man says and smiles at me. "I'm Damon, and this is Louise."

"Nice to meet you." I nod politely at them.

"Come with me." He motions with his head toward Wilson, who never releases my hand as he walks toward the living room area. But instead of going to the living room, the man turns to the kitchen. "This is what we found." He points at another frame similar to what I found in the living room.

"One frame?" Wilson says, picking the frame up.

"Yes, in the bedroom facing the bed," Louise says, smirking and looking at Wilson.

"Are you sure this is it?" Wilson looks around. "Do you think she put bugs anywhere else?"

I put my hand on my forehead and close my eyes, laughing. "She was a jilted lover, not a black ops Navy SEAL trying to get government information." Wilson doesn't even crack a smile. Instead, his jaw gets tight. "Too soon?" I look at Louise and then Damon. "I'm sure they do this stuff all the time."

"We do." Louise nods. "We once found a recording device in the toilet paper roll."

"Wilson, she was a woman who wanted to tape you having sex with her." I shrug. "What she wasn't expecting was for you to be having sex with someone else." I wrap my arm around his waist. "It's okay." I look at Louise. "I got lucky, I guess."

She laughs. "If you need anything else, call us." They both shake Wilson's hand and then mine before walking out of the house.

He walks over to the frame and picks it up. "Okay, I'm going to ask a really stupid question," I say, and I don't know if maybe it's the whiskey I drank or the fact that this day started off shitty and is going to end really, really well. "Didn't you notice that she put different frames up?" He glares at me. "I'm just asking. If someone came into my house and put new frames out, I would notice."

"Frances," he says my name. "Look around. Do you think I know where all this stuff is bought?" He walks over to the counter and picks up the paper towel roll. "Do I look like someone who would know where to find this?"

"That," I say, pointing at it, "is marble. And you can buy it on Wayfair."

"Well …" He puts it down. "I didn't."

I walk around to go to him. "Okay, what's wrong with you?" I put my hand on my hip. "Why are you so cranky?"

"Because," he huffs, pointing at the counter. "This is

fucked up."

"Agreed." I nod. "But you can't change what happened. You just learn better for next time," I say, and my stomach suddenly feels like someone poured acid down it. I try to make a joke of it by walking to him and wrapping my arms around his waist. "I promise that when we do a sex tape, I won't leak it."

"When?" He smirks at me.

"Well …" I look up at him, and my whole body shivers. He's the hottest guy I've ever laid eyes on. He's all that and a bag of chips as my aunt Vivienne would say, in her French accent. But it's more than that. It's the way he makes sure I'm okay. It's the way he brings me coffee in the morning when he wakes up before me. It's the way he chooses ten roses because I'm perfect. It's the effort he takes to get to know me and not because of who my family is but because he wants to know me. "I never got to see the OG." I kiss under his chin. "So I say we set it up." I wink at him as he smiles. "And then watch it later."

He puts his hands on my hips and lifts me to the counter, his hand then going into my hair. "Frances." His lips come down to kiss me. His tongue slides into mine as I wrap my legs around his waist. "I don't share what's mine," he says, letting go of my lips. "And make no mistake about it, Frances." His fingers come out of my hair to rub my cheek. "You're mine."

"Is that so?" I ask, smiling. "Does that mean that you're mine?" I laugh, leaning in and kissing his neck. "I mean, as someone who hasn't dated in her life, is that how it works?"

"Do you want me to be yours?" he asks with a twinkle in his eye.

"I mean, I've already sampled the meat." We both laugh. "And I like the meat, so I might as well buy the steak."

"Did you just compare my dick to steak?" He shakes his head.

"Not just any steak. It's a grade A Wagyu," I praise, and he throws his head back and laughs, leaving his neck exposed. I lean in and kiss him, and he wraps his arms around me as I lay my head on his shoulder. We don't say anything as he rubs my back, and I close my eyes, taking him in. "I like you," I say softly, and I can feel his chest fill with laughter. My whole body vibrates from his laughter, and I really wish I didn't say anything.

"Really?" he says, and I push him off me.

"A little less right now." I move to get off the counter when he pushes me back and puts his finger under my chin to look at him.

"I like you, too," he says softly, his eyes staring into mine. "Like a lot." My mouth goes dry as my heart speeds up. "I've never been in love before." His voice is almost a whisper as he pushes my hair away from my face. "I don't even know what it feels like to be in love." The tears start to sting in my eyes. "Even when I was a kid, no one ever said I love you." My hand comes up to cup his cheek. "So when I started feeling these things for you, I wasn't sure what it was." I smile, but the tears fall over my eyelids anyway. "But then the video came out, and I swear to God my whole body felt like it was going to shatter thinking about you being hurt."

"I'm fine." My thumb rubs his cheek.

"I love you," he says, and my breath hitches. "I've never said that to anyone in my whole life," he admits, and my chest aches for him. "I know I don't deserve you, but now that I have you." He smiles and blinks away his own tears. "I'm not letting you go."

"Well, that's a good thing." I smile, tasting my own tears. "Because I love you, too."

THIRTY-SIX

WILSON

MY EYES FLIP open, and I look over and see the spot beside me empty. I close my eyes again and turn to stretch. I get up on my elbow. "Baby?" I call out, and when I don't hear a peep, I turn my head to check the clock beside my bed, and I see it's just after eight. Looking over toward the bedroom door, I find it closed a bit. "Frances." I call her name and nothing. I get out of bed and walk over to the door, opening it and checking to see if I can smell coffee. "Frances." I call her name, but the whole house is eerily quiet. We've been together over two months, and it's been like a dream. The worst part is when I have to travel, and I now understand why the guys bitch about leaving home. Because our last road trip was ten days, and after three days, I had to beg her to come out and see me. I almost cried when I saw her.

Walking over to the chair in the corner of the room where she tossed my shorts last night, I slip them on. I see the clothes she wore last night folded on the other chair with her pink robe draped over the side and two pairs of her shoes tucked under it. Seeing her stuff mixed with mine makes me smile as I turn to walk downstairs. I can hear a pot bang, and I walk into the kitchen and watch her move to the fridge. She's wearing an oversized white T-shirt that falls off her shoulder. I can see her bare ass in it as she grabs the milk and then walks back to the counter, pouring the milk into our coffees. I approach her, standing at her back. "Morning," I say, moving her hair away from her neck, then bending down and kissing her.

"Good morning." She smiles at me, moving her ass in front of me. My hand comes up to cup her tit while my cock wants to come out and bury itself in her.

I move her hair to the other side, baring her neck and shoulder for me to kiss. "I called out for you three times." She turns her face to me, and I kiss her forehead, then she tilts her head back as I kiss her lips. My hands go to her hips to stop her from torturing my dick. I leave her lips and kiss her shoulder, my hand moving up to slide in the front of her shirt. I cup her tit in my hand, tweaking her nipple as she lays her head on my chest. "I thought you left." I move my head to the other side of her head, my other hand going to her hip, bunching up her shirt.

"Why would you think I left?" She wraps one hand behind my neck. My hand pushes the shirt under her breast as she turns in my arms to face me.

She puts her hand on my chest. "I don't know. I just couldn't find you." She gets on her tippy-toes and kisses me. My hand pulls her other breast out as I lean down and take her nipple in my mouth. "It was so strange," I tell her as she puts her hand on the back of my neck. I stand and pull her to me. My hands go under her shirt to her bare ass, and she kisses my lips as I move us to the other side of the counter. "My heart was going nuts." I kiss her lips for a second and then cup one breast while I lean down and take the other nipple in my mouth. "I just thought you were gone." I get on my knees in front of her, attacking one nipple and then the other.

Her breaths start to come out in pants now. "I wouldn't leave without saying goodbye." She looks down at me. My hand comes up to rub along her leg to her bare ass. I look up at her. She bends her head to kiss me as my hand runs down the crack of her ass. She opens her legs, leaning back on the counter, and I can feel her wetness. I look down at the shirt covering her pussy. I look up at her and then go in to bite her nipple, then bury my hand in her hair bringing her mouth to me.

"I don't want you to leave." I spread her legs apart, seeing her pussy glistening. "I don't want you to leave," I repeat, leaning in and licking her slit. She puts one foot on the counter and the other over my shoulder. My tongue slides into her. "I hate when you aren't here, and you're at your house." One of her hands goes into my hair while the other plays with her nipple. I attack her pussy, her heavy pants filling the room. "I want you here," I say, sliding my finger into her at the same time as my tongue. One arm wraps around her and pulls her pussy to my mouth. "I want your things here." I slide two fingers in her.

"Wilson." She tries to keep her eyes open, but she can't help close them as I push her toward the edge. My fingers fuck her slow as I lean in and suck her clit in my mouth, my mouth going side to side. "Please." I slide my fingers out of her and stand, pushing my boxers down, and she scoots her ass to the edge of the counter.

She puts both feet on the counter to open for me, and I slide into her, both of us letting out a sigh. "So what do you say?" I ask her as I fuck her slower than she likes. If it was up to her, she would want me fast and hard.

"I say fuck me faster." She tries to lift her hips, and I laugh as she groans. "If you aren't going to fuck me right." She tries to light a fire up my ass. "I can do it myself."

"Is that so?" She nods. My eyes go to my cock as I watch her pussy swallow it.

"I have my toy upstairs." She lifts her ass to meet my thrust. "You liked watching me last night." She licks her lips, closing her eyes and probably thinking about last night. I walked in on her fucking herself with her vibrator. It was the sexiest thing I've ever seen in my whole life. But nothing was sexier than when she took it out and got her ass ready for me.

"I love you," I say, and her finger leaves her clit to go to her nipple, where she twists it.

"I love you more." I pull my cock out of her, grab her by her hips, and turn her around. "Yes," she says when I push back in as she arches her back. "Yes." She puts one of her knees on the counter, making herself open for me.

I slam my cock into her pussy, gripping her hips so tight. "Again," she says, and I slam into her again.

"Move in with me?" I ask her as I slam into her, licking one finger and then sliding it into her ass at the same time as my cock slams all the way into her.

"If you don't fuck me properly, I won't even sleep here tonight," she says over her shoulder. I take my cock out of her pussy and slowly slide it into her ass. "Yes." She arches her back. "More." She puts her head down on the counter as I work my cock into her. "It's so good," she says as I bury myself completely in her, then she wiggles her ass to get me to move.

"You want me to move?" I pull out just a touch and then slide back in.

"Yes," she pants out.

"Then say you'll move in with me, and I'll fuck you the way you want." I slide my hand around her to pinch her clit, and she screams. "Move in with me."

"This isn't fair." She moves her head side to side. "Wilson, please. I'm begging you."

"Say you'll move in with me, and I'll make you come all day long." I pull out, and it's killing me. Her ass is so tight my cock wants to come just as hard as she does. I slam back in her. "Say yes," I say as my thrusts start to get longer and longer.

"Yes," she cries. "I'll move in with you." That is all she has to say, and I'm pulling all the way out and slamming into her. She fucks herself with two fingers while my finger plays with her clit, and she throws her head back and screams, "I'm coming!" I close my eyes as I come in her ass at the same time.

I lean over and kiss her shoulder. "You don't play fair," she says when she finally opens her eyes, and I slide out of her. She stands up to go to the bathroom, and I follow her. "I'm not talking to you." She avoids looking at me.

"And why not?" I try to hide my smile as we clean ourselves up.

"Because it's not fair," she says, taking the hand towel and throwing it in the wash. "You used sex to get your way."

I throw my head back and laugh. "You didn't do the same thing two days ago?" I point at her.

"That was not the same thing," she huffs out. "That was to decide dinner. You wanted Chinese, and I didn't, hence the blow job until you said pizza."

"So you don't want to move in with me?" I ask to clarify, and she just glares at me.

"We already live together." She throws her hands up. "Half my clothes are upstairs."

"But I want all the clothes," I tell her. "I don't want you to have to go home."

"Would we live here?"

I shrug. "Do you want to keep your house and have me move in there?"

"You would do that?" she asks me.

"Well, I want to live with you, so I guess wherever you want to live is where I'll go." I don't give a shit where we live. Do I want her to move in here? Yes. But that's only because my place is bigger for when we have kids. But that is another subject for another time.

"Just like that?" She folds her arms over her chest, and I kiss her lips.

"Just like that," I tell her. "Now let's go celebrate."

"We just had anal on the counter." She laughs. "We can't celebrate more than that."

I throw my head back and laugh. "Oh, I'm sure we can think of ways," I say, and she wraps her arms around my waist. "I love you."

"Yeah, yeah." Her eyes go soft. "I love you, too."

EPILOGUE ONE

Frances

Six months later

"HOW MUCH LUGGAGE does one person need for a two-week vacation?" my cousin, Dylan, asks Alex as he picks up her luggage from the cart. Two more carts come with luggage as we wait next to the parked cars. I fan my face with my hand to try to get some air. "A two-week vacation on a beach. All you need is a bathing suit, six shirts, six shorts, fourteen pairs of underwear, one bra …"

"One bra?" She gasps, standing there in loose beige pants and a white tank top. "What do you think I am, a psychopath? A savage?" She shakes her head, her long brown hair moving side to side. "Unmatched bra and panties," she mumbles under her breath, and I roll my lips, trying not to laugh at the way she looks at Dylan.

"Do we have to stay the whole fourteen days?"

Wilson asks from beside me, and I look over at him. He's wearing shorts and a polo shirt with slides, and I can't help but look at him and smile. In the past six months, so much has changed for us. One, we are officially living together after Julia bought my house. He is starting the Brad Wilson Hockey School. Alex not only took it on for her job but she also set up after-school programs and a summer program, which are full with a waiting list. All it took was a little push to make him see that his name meant something. It also helped that he finished the season fourth in points in the whole league. "No one is going to notice if we dip out after a couple of days." He puts his arm around my shoulder and pulls me to him, kissing my head.

I laugh at him, wrapping my arms around his waist. "My father notices if someone isn't there after an hour." It's his first time vacationing with the whole gang. And as much as I've tried to prepare him, nothing is going to prepare him.

"But we have our own house, right?" He looks at me with big eyes when I shrug. "Frances."

"Calm down, everyone gets their own house," I assure him, kissing under his neck. "It'll be fun."

"Fun is me and you in our house with the door locked," he tells me. "And no one coming over. It was so much more simple when I was a loner."

"But what fun is it?" I ask. "Without all this commotion?" I turn around in a circle as people are walking off the big charter plane that my father had rented to make sure we all got here at the same time.

"This is much easier," Cooper points out from beside me, pushing a stroller with his sleeping son in it. "Than when we all travel solo and then meet there." Erika walks behind him, holding the girls' hands. My mother is behind her carrying Stella in her arms.

"I want to know why there isn't someone with drinks," Alex says, looking around. "Uncle Matthew," she calls my father, who looks over as he tries to get his own luggage. "You dropped the ball with the whole vacation. Where are the welcome drinks?"

"I will definitely look at that for next time," my father huffs. "What is the island drink for Turks and Caicos?"

"Rum punch," Julia says as she holds Jamison in her arms. "They make their own rum here." Jillian walks down the stairs with Bianca in her hands while Michael holds Bailey, who just turned six months.

"Remember when we did Dominican last year, and everyone was ordering MammaJuana drinks," Alex says, laughing, then smacks Dylan on the shoulder. "You even told the waitress my mamma juana you to get me a drink." Dylan laughs now, shaking his head.

"That was a good night." He puts an arm around Alex.

"You woke up with your whole face done in makeup from Emma." Alex points at him, and I hear Wilson chuckle behind us.

"Oh, there's my bag." I point at the bag placed down beside Cooper, who picks it up and throws it on our luggage cart.

"Hey, be careful with that," I say, looking at him. "My toys are in there." He just stares at me with a look of disgust. He looks like he's going to vomit. "If you rough them up, they might turn on."

"Please tell me you're joking." Cooper puts his hand over his mouth, trying not to gag.

"I want to play with toys," Emma says. "Auntie Fran, can I play with your toys?"

"No!" Cooper yells, pulling her to his side.

"You're joking, right?" Wilson says from beside me, and I look up at him.

"Maybe." I shrug. "Only one way to find out."

It takes a full two hours to load and unload the bus. The chaos is something one will never get used to. The number of times I saw Wilson with his mouth hanging open was at least fifteen. When we get to the houses, there are golf carts there to bring us to our individual homes. "How did your father find this?" Wilson asks when we pull up to the house that has four different houses in one.

"Knowing my father," Cooper says, getting out with us, "he had this built, starting last vacation." He gets out with Erika, going to the right where his house is.

"This is like a cruise ship without the water," Wilson says as we walk down the marble area toward the brown door with the number two on it.

"Tomorrow, we get the itineraries," I say, and he just stares at me. "I'm kidding."

Walking in, I dump my bag on the couch, then head out to the patio that overlooks the blue water. "Now this." I turn to look over at him. "Is what I call paradise." I look down, seeing the massive swimming pool. This is probably a resort, and knowing my father, he shut it down just for us.

He walks to me as I turn around and put my hands on the railing, looking at the blue water. I feel him at my back, putting his arms on the railing beside mine. "This." He leans down and kisses my neck. "Is what I call paradise."

I turn in his arms now. "I thought your cock in me was what you called paradise?"

I lift my hand up to touch his face. "Now that"—I wrap my arms around his neck—"is also paradise."

"Any place." His eyes go soft. "Any time." He brings his hand up to cup my face. "With you." He kisses the side of my lips. "Is paradise.

"Why don't we unpack and then change into our bathing suits and take a swim in the ocean?" he suggests with a smile.

"Oh, ocean sex." I wink at him, walking into the house and going to grab my bag. I slip into my white bikini as we head down to the beach.

"Your whole ass is out," Wilson says, looking behind me as we walk down.

"Not my whole ass," I tell him. "The middle is covered."

"I should walk behind you." He lets go of my hand and starts to walk behind me, and I laugh, turning on him. "It's just us."

I open my hands and turn around in a circle. "Just us and your five hundred family members." He exaggerates.

"If it makes you feel better." I turn back and walk toward the beach. "Our wedding can be intimate," I say, and then I close my eyes as I hear him stop in his tracks behind me. I swallow, wanting to kick myself at even mentioning marriage. And secretly blaming my father for it. "Relax, I was just kidding." I look over my shoulder, walking forward and taking off my flip-flops. I don't wait for him until I walk into the water, the warm water rushing over my feet. I slowly walk into the calm waters, dunking my head and coming up with my head back so my hair is out of my face.

His hands rest on my hips as the water rises over my stomach and then lowers again. "It's warm," he says, kissing my shoulder as we walk into the water until it's right under my boobs. He dunks under the water and comes up, and the sun glistens on his shoulders. "Come here." He pulls me to him and squats down, wrapping his arms around my waist. My legs wrap around his waist and my arms around his neck as we just lounge in the water. Neither of us are saying anything. "Are we going to discuss what you said?"

I turn my head on his shoulder and kiss his neck, tasting the salt from the sea water. "Can we not?"

I can feel his chest moving as he laughs. "Leave it to you to ruin everything."

I gasp and lean back to look at him. "How did I ruin everything?"

"Do you want to get married?" he asks, and my head screams yes.

"It's my father's fault," I start to tell him. "He was all over me yesterday at work." I really wish my mouth would listen to my head sometimes, but today isn't that day. "How do you feel about Wilson? Will you marry him?" I put my hands up. "He just put all these things in my head."

"Well, what was your answer?" he asks, and with the sun and the blue water around him, his eyes are almost a mint green.

I put my hand over my eyes to make sure I can see his eyes when we have this conversation. "What do you mean?"

"I mean …" He smirks. "How did you answer your father? Would you marry me?" My mouth gets dry, and the sun suddenly feels like it's burning my skin.

"Are you asking me to marry you?" I ask, and he looks down and then up.

"I'm asking if I asked you, what would you say?" I don't have any time to answer him because I hear our names being called and look over to see Alex, Julia, and Dylan all standing there.

"Are you guys banging in there?" Alex asks us.

"It's a public beach!" I shout back, laughing.

"I'm not going in that water," Dylan says. "Don't you guys have a bed or couch?"

"What fun is that?" Alex says. "We'll give you guys a couple of minutes to finish."

"We will not," Julia says. "Take an hour; we'll use the pool."

"An hour?" Dylan looks at the girls.

"Oh my God." Julia gasps. "He's a selfish lover."

"I am not!" Dylan shouts at her, and Wilson slowly starts walking out of the water.

"Once, I had someone go an hour," Julia says proudly.

"Impossible," Dylan says, making the girls laugh, and only when we are out of the water does he let me go.

"No one was having sex in the water," Wilson says.

"At least not now." I smirk. "Tonight is different." I walk up to the little bar that is set up on the beach. "Who wants a drink?"

"Yes." The girls both clap their hands.

The afternoon is spent with the whole gang by the beach. We laugh and lounge, and when I step into the shower that night, I can see that I've gotten a little tan. "Wilson." I call his name as he steps into the bathroom. "Look, I got color," I say, sticking out my tits so he sees the white. "Not as much as you, but still." I look over at him, and he's golden from the sun. I close the shower door and finish my shower. Getting out and drying off, I slip on my long white one-piece summer dress. The spaghetti straps on my shoulders are tied in bows, and when I open the bathroom door, I stop in my tracks when I see two roses on the bed with a note. "Wilson?" I call his name, walking up to the bed and seeing the note beside the roses.

Two roses symbolize shared and deep love.
I love you, Frances.

I smile and turn to walk out of the room, seeing that there are more roses, this time in vases. The first one has twelve roses in it with a white paper in front of it.

Will you be mine, Frances?
I love you, Frances.

Walking to the next vase, I read the note.

Twenty-one roses show my commitment to you.
I love you, Frances.

I look around to see if I spot him, and I can't see him in the room. The tears sting my eyes as I walk over to see more roses.

Twenty-five roses wish someone all the happiness in the world, and with you, I've never been happier.
I love you, Frances.

I take a couple of more steps in the living room, seeing roses on the counter in the kitchen. Three different vases with even more roses.

Thirty roses mean faithfulness. You will always be the only one I want.
I love you, Frances.

Right next to the vase lies another white paper.

Fifty roses mean unconditional love. No one will ever love you as much as I do.
I love you, Frances.

I spot the note for the next to last vase of roses on the counter.

Ninety-nine roses mean I love you until the day I die.
I love you, Frances.

I turn to look out the glass door that leads to the balcony and see him sitting there in the middle of the table. His head is looking down at his hand as he plays with something, and when I walk out, I see the biggest bouquet of roses I've ever seen in my life. "Hi," I say, standing here and not moving. The sounds of water crashing on the beach fill the air, and when I finally look around, I see little candles lit here and there, giving us some light. "What are you doing here?" I ask him, stepping forward to look at the flowers beside him. "What is going on?"

"I've been sitting here thinking," he says, his voice cracking. "Today, I asked you what you would say if I asked you to marry me, and you didn't answer me." My heart starts to speed up in my chest, and my tongue feels like it's swelling up. "There are one hundred and eight roses in this vase." He points at the flowers. "Do you know what that means?" I can't answer him because the tears are coming nonstop, and the lump in my throat feels like a baseball. He leans forward, grabbing one of my hands in his as he gets down on one knee and the gasp that comes out sounds like a sob. "One hundred and eight roses means, will you marry me?" He looks up at me. "We haven't been together long." He swallows, and I can see the tears in his eyes. "And I know that I don't exactly come from a family where I know what love and marriage is. But being with you and your family, I've seen what it is." He smiles shyly now. "I went to talk to your father three days ago and asked for your hand in marriage." My eyes widen. "The only thing he asked me is does she want to marry you." I laugh because that sounds exactly like him. "I admitted to him I had no idea. Because the truth was I didn't. I still don't know." He closes his eyes. "I don't even know what happens if you say no. Does that mean we have to break up, or is it a try again later? I have no idea about any of this. But I do know there is no one in this whole world I want to be with besides you. I want you to wear my ring forever. I want you to have my name or hyphenate it. I don't really fucking care. The only thing I care about is spending forever with you." I chuckle, my nerves making me laugh as I brush the tears off my face. "So I'm asking you, and you have to answer. Will you marry me, Frances?"

I don't know what to say, but my head nods my answer. "Yes," I whisper, and in one move, his hand is around my waist, and his lips are on mine. A clack of the box that was in his hand falling to the floor by our feet. "Is that my ring?"

"Oh, yeah, shit." He puts me down and picks up the box. "Obviously, your father came with me because who else was going to come with me? The whole time, he's asking me what if you said no." He takes the box. "It was the worst experience of my life because all I could think of is what if you did say no." He opens it now. "Thank fuck you didn't, and I can tell him he was wrong.

"Just what a girl wants to hear after she vows to marry a man. Thank you for saying yes so I can tell your father he was wrong."

He takes out the ring that is oval and huge. "Which hand?"

I hold out my left hand for him. "Right," he says, slipping the ring on me, and the smile just fills his face.

"We're engaged!" I shout, and the minute I do, I hear a bottle of champagne pop. My eyes go big when I look over the railing and see all of my family standing there cheering us on.

"Good thing you said yes." He wraps his hand around

my shoulders.

"Good thing we had sex at my cousin's wedding." I wink at him, and he closes his eyes. "You get only one love."

EPILOGUE TWO

WILSON

One Year Later

"WHAT WOULD YOUR father say if we didn't go?" I ask Frances when I walk out of the closet with my bag.

"What would happen if we had sex without an orgasm?" she asks with horror. "We don't know, and we will never find out." I shake my head and walk over to her, bending and kissing her lips as she sits in the middle of the bed watching a clip of something on her computer. "By the way, your mother called."

"Lovely," I say, looking at her. "What did she want?"

"She wanted to know how we were doing," she says, and I know she's lying to me. The first time she met Frances, she told her that she wouldn't bother remembering her name since she would be gone soon. Since then, she has decided to kill her with kindness, and at this point, I think she's just too stubborn to admit that my mother will never ever be that mother she has.

"But really?" I ask, and she rolls her eyes.

"She has a friend going on vacation." I groan.

"How much did you give her?" I put my hands on my hips.

"It's your fault. If you had let me pay you for half the house, I wouldn't have extra money lying around." I glare at her. Even if I had let her give me money for the house, she would still give my mother money.

"I forbid you to give her another penny." I can tell right away that was the wrong word to use, especially with my wife. It was two days after I proposed when she turned to me after drinking more mai tai and said, why don't we just get married here? That was all it took, and a week later, on the beach in the middle of her family, we got married. She slipped on my wedding band, and I have to say the minute she did, I felt more alive than ever, I felt so complete.

"Forbid me?" She gets up on the bed, crawling over at me. "Forbid me?" She laughs, wrapping her arms around my neck. "Is that any way to talk to the mother of your child?"

I look at her, and my eyes go big. "No," I say, shocked. "We just started trying." My eyes go to her stomach.

"Started trying is a stretch." She laughs. "I forgot my pills when we were up north for five days, and you couldn't pull out."

"It was too late." I smile at her. "The pre sperm was already all up in there," I tell her.

"Are you sure?" I ask. She goes to the side table and opens the drawer, taking out five tests.

"All these say I am, so …" I smile, holding one in my

hand. "Can you not touch them? They have my pee on them."

I sit on the bed, my eyes on the word pregnant on the screen. "A baby," I tell her, and she sits next to me. "Our baby."

"Besides our wedding and meeting your grandfather, this is the happiest moment of my life," I say, and she laughs.

"Thank God, I'm up there with Grandpa," she says, and I look at her.

"He's my hero," I reply to her. "Remember the first time I met him?"

"You called him sir," she reminds me, laughing. "And then you threw up in the garbage."

"I was nervous," I say, closing my eyes. "He's a legend."

"Well, good thing he loves you," she says, and I can't help but smile.

"He called me son," I remind her.

"I know, you got teary-eyed." She laughs.

"We had just gotten married. I was full of emotion." I get up, my phone beeping at the same time as hers.

I pick up my phone, and my eyes go big as I look over at Franny, who has her phone in her hand.

"Shit," she says. "This is not good."

Dylan Stone decides not to stay in Montreal. Our sources say he might be headed to New York, where his father just got the head coach job. Only time will tell. Where is Dylan Stone headed?